SCAVENGERS

DARREN SIMPSON

USBORNE

PART ONE

THE ROOT

ONE

CHASING COVER

The boy growled, dropped to all fours and took one end of the stick between his teeth. The dog at the stick's other end – a hefty Alsatian with long ears – bared its gums and slobbered.

Boy and dog, with eyes as locked as the stick between their jaws, circled each other on the cracked concrete. They jerked their heads in a playful tug of war, with hands and paws clawing gravel and moss.

Landfill could taste the flecks of stick on his teeth. With a snigger and a grunt, he pushed suddenly forward before pulling back. The Alsatian was taken by surprise, loosened its grip, and yelped as Landfill yanked the stick away.

"Got it, Vonnegut, I got it!" Landfill was on his naked feet, dancing and waving his prize in the air. "Two-one to me, shaggy muttler!"

Vonnegut hopped and panted in the heat, his tail wagging like the stick in the boy's hand. Landfill laughed and stooped to rub his face against the dog's. "Next round'll be yours, I bet. Now watch this."

After wiping a sweaty hand on his bare chest and shorts, he squinted at the complex of metal drums, chutes and vents several metres away, closed his eyes and hurled the stick. He opened his eyes when the stick met its target with a loud clang.

Some parakeets in the gash of a metal drum started to chirp, and a squirrel – its fur as orange as the rust below – appeared at a chute's top to investigate the noise. It sniffed the air with twitching nostrils.

Landfill's eyebrows rose in surprise. He pointed a grubby finger at the squirrel. "Joyce! Been skulking with parkits, eh? Too lily-livered to play? Get out of there and we'll see if I can catch you. I'll even give you a running start. How about that?"

He stamped his foot and the squirrel bolted, leaping across vines and onto the pipes that left the chutes. Once it had shot overhead, Landfill and Vonnegut gave chase.

"Scarper all you want, skrill!" laughed the boy. "On a winning streak today!"

Landfill followed the raised piping with gold hair flowing and his eyes on the rodent. He had no need to watch his bare feet, and hopped over the dandelions, nettles and scrap that pocked most of Hinterland's ground.

The squirrel darted through a gap between some metal flues and mounted a squat, wooden tower covered in lichen. Landfill circuited the tower until he reached its ladder. He was making quick progress upward, but faltered suddenly. Fear rippled across his features.

"Rule twelve," he muttered. He searched the sky anxiously, barely aware of the fact that he was reaching for the glass blade in his pocket. "Not fair, Joyce." He pouted at the squirrel. "You know I can't go that high."

A bark from the Alsatian waiting below sent Joyce scampering. When the squirrel hit the tubing that left the flues, Landfill's grin returned to reveal goofy yellow teeth. He dropped from the ladder and landed with fingers to the floor, the sweat on his back glistening in summer's glare. On he ran with Vonnegut, until he was following the squirrel to the Gully's edge.

While Vonnegut bounded down the Gully's sloping, concrete bank and through the sludge at its bed, Landfill wormed his way through the Hard Guts – a mossy tangle of pipes that spanned the Gully like the remnants of a bridge. He squeezed past valves bursting with flowers, and a knock of his heel against a conduit filled the air with butterflies.

Landfill giggled at the tickle of their wings, and sprang from the Guts onto a steel gangway. He followed the squirrel up some metal steps lining the base of the tall, concrete tower at Hinterland's heart, the Pale Loomer. Turning a corner, he entered the shade of the Thin Woods. Green leaves danced as Joyce leaped from tree to tree, causing a woodpecker to stop its hammering and several grey squirrels to jerk their heads. The boy continued in pursuit, running beneath the conveyor that sloped into the Pale Loomer's sooty flank.

Landfill had soon crossed the narrow strip of trees that split Hinterland's centre, and turned another corner to find Joyce scrabbling up a stout white chimney. The squirrel blinked at the boy, who was now kneeling on mossy concrete. Landfill panted for a moment, wiped his fringe from his eyes and flashed a goofy grin. "No more pipes, little skrill. So come on down. Let's see if you're as wily on the ground."

Joyce blinked and brushed his whiskers.

The boy's blue eyes sparkled. "Gutless twitcher, eh?" He cackled and thumped the ground with his palms. "Tell you what – come down and I'll give you another running start. That's more than fair."

Joyce tilted his head, scuttled groundwards and sped away. Landfill was soon back on his feet, and Vonnegut caught up to join him in pursuit. The Alsatian yapped and howled, causing other dogs to peer out from nearby toppled railway-carts. Some of them joined the chase, and the boy dropped to all fours to lope among the hounds.

They raced along the train tracks that extended from the Pale Loomer's wide concrete opening, hopping on and off the cables that flanked the rusty rails. Baying with the dogs, the boy ran and ran, following the tracks until he was forced to skid to a stop. He watched helplessly as Joyce scaled the perimeter wall.

The wall spanned far to the left and right, and Landfill took a few steps back to take in its height. He saw Joyce at the top, sat carefully between broken-bottle teeth. The dogs held off too, backing away from the nettles that smothered the wall, tangled around creepers, scraps of mirror and jutting shards of glass.

Landfill arched his neck and grimaced. He had to shout for his voice to reach the squirrel. "Okay! Game over, Joyce. Shouldn't go up there. It's not safe."

Joyce rubbed his tiny paws together. He backed away slightly, towards the other side of the wall.

"I mean it! Come down!" Landfill was pleading now. His eyes roamed the sky. "Don't go Outside. *Please.* Come down, Joyce. You're safer *in here.*"

The squirrel chattered, then was gone.

"Come back!" Landfill cupped his hands around his mouth to yell, but it was no use. The dogs wagged their tails while his gaze moved down the wall. He stood staring for some time, scratching his calf with a long toenail.

He crooked a hand and wet his wrist with his tongue,

then ran it through his hair. The dogs' ears pricked up. Landfill tensed. He could hear it too: a distant rumble.

"The Eye... It's the Eye!" He whirled around, searching for the nearest place to hide. There were shrubs and bushes, some scraps of corrugated iron, rubble and plasterboard – but nothing provided enough cover. His eyes followed the train tracks to the Pale Loomer's opening, then zoomed back to a railway cart toppled midway between the Loomer and the wall.

Landfill ran for it. Behind him the dogs barked at blue sky. The rumbling became louder and he knew this would be close. He could hear the other animals adding to the commotion, only to have their growls, hisses and howls swallowed by the drone.

It was a long stretch to run – nearly a quarter of Hinterland's breadth. Landfill's heart was pounding as he realized how heavy his legs were. He should never have tired himself out so far from cover.

The noise from above became louder and louder. He could almost feel it bearing down upon him when he sprang headfirst into the cart. He covered his ears, tucked in his legs and pushed his body as far into the cart's shelter as he could.

The boy's panting was amplified by his hands over his ears, but he could still hear the roaring from the sky. It screamed directly above, and he noticed flecks of paint vibrating along the cart's inner lining. He could see some dogs from another cart – all snarls and teeth and frothing gums – barking skywards while the shadow passed.

The noise faded, and the dogs settled down. After listening out carefully, Landfill crawled along the cart's interior and peeked up over its rim. The sky seemed to be clear. Exhaling loudly, he climbed slowly out and kneeled to stroke the dogs that gathered around him. "It's gone. We're okay." He cocked his head suddenly, struck by a thought. "Where's Woolf? Haven't seen her around."

The dogs trailed him to Woolf's fallen cart. He stooped to look inside, and when his eyes adjusted he saw the husky on her side on a musty blanket, eyes closed and ribs barely moving.

"Woolf? You alright? You don't look…too hunkadory." He moved in to stroke the grey fur on her neck, but recoiled when he saw her bulging stomach.

With a hand clamped firmly over his nostrils and mouth, Landfill backed away and turned slowly to the other dogs.

"Woolf's got the swelling. Keep your distance – don't breathe it in. I'll tell Babagoo."

He got up to go, but couldn't help pausing to scan the perimeter wall's north side. Finding no sign of Joyce, he scowled, kicked a crumbling bolt and walked away.

TWO

SHADOW TROUBLE

It took some time to reach the Nook, which was wedged into the corner where the perimeter wall's west and south sides met. Landfill plucked a leaf from the bindweed that draped the Nook's brick walls, then sat on a rotten pallet and folded it into his mouth.

He waved at a kestrel as it zipped overhead, but frowned when it went over the wall, its feathers skimming the glass spikes that stuck up through creepers and vines. The leaf became bitter in his mouth and he spat green pulp to the ground.

The boy shifted his gaze to some waste piled against the wall's west side, not far along from the Nook: mounds of mouldy carpet; a filthy metal cabinet lying aslant on its back; some upturned chairs with wheels on spindly feet; torn window blinds and tubes of cracked glass. He averted his gaze and nibbled an overgrown fingernail, but was unable to resist looking at the cabinet again.

"Babagoo?" he called. "You back?"

After peering through the Nook's windows, Landfill tiptoed up some carpet rolls and stopped before the metal cabinet. He checked over his shoulder, then slowly reached out to touch one of the its three drawers.

"*Caught in the act!*" boomed the cabinet.

Landfill sprang back like a cat and scampered on all fours across the ground. With a metallic crash, the cabinet drawers swung aside to reveal themselves as merely facades stuck to a single steel door. In the sloping doorway stood the scavenger.

"Babagoo!" cried Landfill. "I was only gandering!"

Babagoo rose while he finished mounting the staircase hidden beneath the hollowed cabinet. His eyes narrowed beneath his tattered trapper hat. "Don't give me that, boy. Your factious little finger was practically touching the door! I saw it through the crack, Landfill. I'm not the idiot you apparently suppose me to be!"

"But—"

"Save your breath! There's no excuse for going near the cabinet."

Landfill scrunched his face. "It's Woolf! She's got the swelling. And you were at the Spit Pit so long. Was worried."

Babagoo's bushy eyebrows flew up into his forehead.

His mess of a beard bristled. "Leave Woolf to me, boy. And you can wash that tripe from your jabberhole while you're at it. To worry you have to care, and if you cared you'd respect the rules. But blatantly you don't! You know very well you're not supposed to come looking for me, even if I'm Outside for a thousand cruddly days. Even if you hear me screaming while the Outsiders tear off my skin and banquet on my bowels! Rule number…?"

Landfill mumbled bitterly.

Babagoo lifted one of his hat's earflaps. "Jabber up, lad."

Landfill huffed. "Eight! I know the rules."

"You do, do you?"

"Yes."

"So what's rule seven?"

"Never touch the cabinet."

"And what were you doing?"

Landfill growled and clacked his teeth at the scavenger. The scavenger clacked back. "You're trouble, young skulk. All these years you've respected the rules – but now you've decided to start flouting them? Can't help pondering what other rules you've broken today. Hunger's Eye flew over earlier. Did you follow the rules then?"

Landfill nodded sternly. "Rule nine – hide from Hunger's Eye."

"Where'd you hide?"

"Muttbrough. One of the carts."

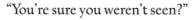

"You're sure you weren't seen?"

"Still here, aren't we?"

Babagoo tugged his beard, and glanced sideways before returning his attention to the boy. "And rule ten? Were you close to cover when the Eye came?"

"I was," muttered Landfill, eyes to his hands.

Babagoo shook his head. "Got that fibbing look, Landfill. I don't like that fibbing look. What is this? A mutiny? I thought we were on the same side."

Landfill stamped his foot. "Of course we are!"

"Enough of that lip." Babagoo wagged a flaking fingernail. "We'd better be on the same side, because if you're not on my side you're *Outside*. Got that? And for your information, my unruly worrywart, I wasn't at the Pit any longer than the usual couple of hours. Been back for some time."

"I didn't know that!" Landfill's arm shot out towards the cabinet. "You were hiding. Lurking like a troll, just to catch me out!"

Babagoo's sneer revealed a ruin of rotten teeth. "I was and I did. Thought you were due a test, and it looks like I was right. Wasn't I right, *boy*?"

Landfill paced beneath him like a trapped animal.

"I *had* to check up on you," continued Babagoo. "The Spit Pit gave me trouble today."

Landfill stopped pacing. "Trouble at the Pit?"

Babagoo lowered his voice. "Shadow trouble." He untied two of several bin bags from the rope around his waist and tossed them through the air. They landed at Landfill's feet with a fleshy thump, and Babagoo followed, scrabbling down the mound of carpet rolls and kicking up dust. A large cape made of litter slipped down the slope behind him.

"Shadow trouble…" repeated Landfill.

"Morning trip was hunkadory. Found some edible grubbins, a half-decent saw, two half-blankets that'll make one if I can forage some thread…" He shrugged and tutted. "The things the Outsiders spit out! Perfectly good things, just waiting for use." He sighed and shook his head. "Maybe all those morning treasures made me cocky. Whatever it was, the afternoon trip taught me a lesson."

"What happened?" Landfill's sour expression had all but gone.

"Was pulling a gull from a trap. Dropped my guard; didn't hear an Outsider prowling behind a heap of junk. Luckily I saw it before it saw me. Dropped down beneath my dross cape. It walked by – just a hair's breadth from my head! – and kept going. Too close for comfort, and that's when the shadow trouble started. They started creeping up close, getting sly on the scent of my fear. Gave me a bad feeling. So I scarpered.

"That's why I thought to check on you. And it's a good

job I did!" Babagoo's head tilted slowly while he studied the boy. "Don't go near the cabinet again, my lad. I'll be waiting there sometimes from now on, just in case you get more of these idiotic urges. And if I see you getting that close again, I'll jump out and make you regret it. Curiosity killed the boy, remember? Resist it."

He leaped suddenly forward and seized the boy's chin with black fingers. "You understand?"

Landfill could barely nod in the scavenger's grip. "Yes."

Babagoo's face came in close, cheeks and lips writhing as his eyes made their inspection. Suddenly his pupils darted downward. "You see that?"

"See what?"

Babagoo searched the ground. "Hm. There'll be mischief." Cautiously, he untied the knot around his neck and let his cape slide to the floor. He patted the dirt from his corduroys and plaid overcoat. "You tended to the vejble patch?"

Landfill huffed and nodded.

"Really? You said you were at Muttbrough when Hunger's Eye came. Bit far from the patch, isn't it?"

Landfill rolled his eyes. "Finished tending early. Played with the wooflers. Can you stop the intigigration now?"

Babagoo's sneer edged towards a smile. A flicker of warmth crossed his features. "I think *interrogation*'s the word you're looking for, young boyling." He chuckled abruptly, picked at what remained of a tooth and sighed. "Fine. If you think we're done, go check the wall."

"What? I've already done today's check." Landfill glanced at the bin bags by his feet. "And I'm hungry."

"That lip again, eh?" The scavenger coughed and spat some phlegm to the ground. "Dinner'll be late today – if you get any at all. I'll make a start on it. You do as I say and check the wall. Haven't you heard a word I've said?" He tapped Landfill's temple with a bandaged hand. "Shadow trouble! Can't afford to take risks today. You want the Outsiders to get in, do you? You know what'll happen if they get their claws on you."

Landfill grunted and looked away.

"So go check the wall again. We don't want a single crack to compromise Hinterland. Keep a sharp eye out for anything unusual. Be thorough, Landfill. Seems we need to keep you busy. Idle hands, eh?"

Landfill opened his mouth but didn't speak. He wrinkled his nose, backed away and plodded to the wall.

Hunger tempted Landfill to quicken his pace, but he knew that taking less than an hour to check the wall's four sides would have Babagoo sending him back to start again. As he followed the perimeter, he scrutinized the wall from bottom to top. He checked for blood or breakage on the glass visible through clumps of growth, and searched carefully for any disturbance in the nettles and creepers.

Eventually he reached the Ivy Stack – a hulking, ivy-strangled mass of corrugated steel, from which a conveyor slanted before bending to meet the Pale Loomer's side. While tugging some creepers on the patch of wall opposite the Stack, Landfill spotted a fang of glass shifting loosely in the brickwork. His shoulders tautened and he whispered Babagoo's words: *"There'll be mischief…"*

Landfill checked more thoroughly after that, his pupils flitting regularly to the sky. He soon reached the train tracks that disappeared into the wall. His eyes followed them to the carts of Muttbrough, where he saw several dogs gathered at the water trough. Realizing he was thirsty, he ran along the tracks to lap on hands and knees at the water. It hadn't rained for days, so the water was warm and faintly metallic.

He splashed some on his tanned face and chest, and turned his gaze to Woolf's cart.

"Woolf?" His voice was a raised whisper. "You alright?" He listened out for sounds, but there was nothing. He sniffed the dogs around the trough and brushed his head against their necks. "Keep your distance, wooflers. And cross your paws she'll pull through." He cleared his throat, trying to hide the quaking in his voice from the dogs. "Woolf's strong. She'll survive it."

He returned to checking the wall. By the time the Nook came into view at Hinterland's opposite corner, Landfill's feet ached almost as much as his stomach. He sat and stretched his legs by the Rippletop's rear. The vast warehouse ran alongside half the wall's eastern side, and pushing his inspection through the gloom of its shade was always a slog.

Landfill wiped the sweat from his forehead and chest, and smeared it onto his shorts. He was scanning the Rippletop's sloping, corrugated roof for lizards when he felt something furry brush his knee. He looked down and smiled. "Atwood! Bit far from the Den, aren't you?"

The lank, shabby cat purred and skimmed its side across Landfill's toes.

"Tickles," sniggered the boy. He reached out to stroke the tabby, but his hand froze when he saw a raven launching itself from the Rippletop's roof. As it passed over the south wall's top, his smile fell away.

He sniffed and rubbed his nose. "You know, Atwood, sometimes I don't like the birds." He flinched with regret at his words. "Don't mean it like that. I *do* like them. Sometimes I just feel a bit…grudging, I guess."

Atwood settled down on a warm patch of moss. She lapped at her paw and used it to brush down her ears.

Landfill mimicked her unconsciously, licking his wrist and wiping saliva through his hair. "Why grudging? I think it's because… Because they can go anywhere. They go out there and always make it back. The wall must look so small when you're up there. I bet they don't even notice it. Must be like nothing to them."

He scowled and looked towards the Nook at the other end of Hinterland. "And they don't have to put up with Babagoo and his testing and jabbering. On and on, rule this and rule that – but it can't reach them. Nothing can. They go wherever they want. *Do* whatever they want."

Landfill's belly gurgled, urging him to his feet. "Need to go, Atwood."

Leaving the Rippletop behind him, Landfill paused to pick some poppies from a vent. While threading them into his hair he spotted a large wing nut on the ground. He eyed the Hard Guts that hung above the distant Gully, snatched up the nut and lobbed it with all his strength. It landed with a satisfying clang, and Landfill grinned at the cloud of butterflies that rose from the Guts' knotted pipes. His shoulders began to loosen, then tautened again at the faint sound of rumbling.

The boy squatted abruptly, cocked an ear: just the grumbles of faraway thunder. His stomach groaned, and he continued on his way.

THREE

BLOOD AND FLOWERS

Babagoo was waiting for him at the Nook, hunched like a hawk on its rickety gutter. He puffed and scratched his cheek in greeting. Landfill returned the gesture, although not without sullenness.

"About time," muttered Babagoo. "In you go. It's getting late." He pointed at the sky, which was a darker blue now, torn here and there by streaks of pink and yellow.

Landfill went through the Nook's scuffed double door. He plodded along a dim, reeking hallway of lockers and cracked tiles, the stench of which faded when he stepped through a metal door to enter the Nook's largest room, the Den.

It was good to be back. Landfill inhaled the Den's thick, tangy, smoky scent, and his belly groaned again. Scanning the room's murky gloom – a result of the blankets that covered some of the sooty windows – he saw a bin bag puffed with feathers, then spotted some buckets of fleshy pink seagulls.

Babagoo brushed past and crouched by the stove at the Den's centre. "I've plucked them to save you some graft. You do the rest. But be quick about it. We're running late."

Landfill didn't reply. He lifted two buckets and took them to the yellowing bathtub in the corner by the door. After taking the glass blade from his shorts, he threw the first seagull into the tub and gutted it, removing its head, feet and innards with mechanical precision. His work was accompanied by slapping sounds from the entrails he tossed at the giblet sheet. Cats sauntered from an adjacent stack of boxes, and traipsed to the sheet to nibble gleaming guts.

While Landfill prepared the gulls, he heard Babagoo shuffling around the stove. The fire was soon crackling and the scavenger carried out his usual examination – ensuring the smoke was split by the pipes that branched from the stove's main vent, then heading to the windows to check for signs of smoke outside.

Landfill tilted his head. In the corner of his eye, he saw Babagoo take a bin bag to the goats, who were grazing on grass clippings next to consoles dotted with buttons.

The scavenger addressed the small herd. "Grubbins for you, my venerable lovelies." He dug his fingers into the bag and pulled out chunks of green-fuzzed bread, rotten apples and handfuls of woodchip. The goats bleated, and nudged the goods with their noses before eating.

"Dig in," said Babagoo. "Waste not, want not." He moved to a large, shaggy black goat with gnarly horns and a wispy grey beard. "And how are *you* today, Kafka!" He slapped the goat's neck. "How's it been, old bleater?"

The goat looked briefly up at him with watery, horizontal pupils, then returned to chomping woodchip.

"That bad, eh? Been an odd one for me too. Shadow trouble at the Spit Pit. And on that note…" His voice hardened when he addressed Landfill's back. "How'd your repeat inspection go? You haven't said anything, so I assume you didn't see anything…worrisome?"

Landfill was on his third bucket. "Loose glass tooth."

"Eh?"

"Just the one."

"Just the one?"

"Nothing we haven't seen before. North side. Three fifths along the Ivy Stack. Two thirds high."

"You're supposed to tell me immediately!"

Landfill kept his back to the scavenger. "Likely just weathered brickwork."

"No no no. That's what they *want* you to think. Too much of a coincidence after what happened in the Pit."

Landfill shrugged and carried on. He could feel

Babagoo glaring at his back, willing him to turn around. Then the scavenger came close, took a plastic bag of meat from the bath's side and returned to the stove. Landfill licked his lips at the thought of the skewers piercing gull meat, then heard them clatter on the stove's grill.

Babagoo cleared his throat. "What about the rest of the wall? You checked thoroughly?"

"Yes."

"Behind the bindweed?"

"Yes."

"Along the Rippletop? Gets dark back there."

"Yes."

"By the Ivy Stack? You can never resist the wooflers at Muttbrough."

"*Yes.*"

Babagoo tutted and turned the meat. "Quite the chatterbox tonight, aren't you?" He left the skewers on the grill and made a noisy fuss of fetching radishes from the top of a console. "Low on vejbles," he grumbled.

Landfill fell into the rhythm of his work, until he noticed that the Den had become very quiet. He turned from the bathtub to see what had stopped Babagoo's stomping and muttering, and found the scavenger looking at him. Landfill followed his gaze with his fingers until he touched the flowers in his hair. "Poppies," he said.

"Can see that, my boy."

"Thought they were pretty."

"You won't find a prettier petal." Babagoo closed his eyes and released a tired sigh. He headed to the water tank by the window, filled a plastic jerrycan and brought it to the bathtub. "Make sure you leave some meat for tomorrow's traps."

"I know what I'm doing."

"Finish the rest later. Can hear your belly rumbling from here. You look like you could gobble a bleater." Babagoo winked at the goats – "No offence, my lovelies." – and returned his attention to the boy. "Use the water sparingly, lad. The tank's running low."

After washing the blood from his hands and forearms, Landfill joined Babagoo at the stove. Their silence amplified the crackling of the fire, which popped and snapped over animal purrs and snuffles.

Landfill gnawed at the bitter, stringy meat and kept his eyes on his food. He could sense Babagoo watching him.

"You're sulky tonight, lad. And I don't think this is just a huff over being caught out earlier. What is it? Look like you're eating lemons, not gull."

"What's lemons?"

"Stick to the subject. What's bothering you?"

Landfill raised his eyes to meet the scavenger's. "Joyce. We were playing chase. He went over the wall."

"Ah."

"Haven't seen him since."

"That's the end of Joyce, then. The Outsiders'll have him by now."

Landfill dropped a charred seagull thigh and covered his face with his hands.

Babagoo sighed. "But you never know, my boy. Joyce is as crafty as they come. If anyone might survive Outside, it's him. Plus he's a skrill, and skrills are lightning on legs."

Landfill's hands dropped. "You think he might make it back?"

Babagoo leaned to ruffle the boy's hair. "He's got better odds than anyone else. But don't build your hopes up. Hope has no place Outside. Best to brace yourself for the worst."

Landfill nodded sombrely. "What about Woolf?"

Babagoo narrowed his eyes and pulled at his beard. "I'll have a look. If she's got the swelling she'll need time in the cabinet for healing. You just keep your distance for now, okay? Rule eleven. Don't want to be catching it from her. You're too young. Wouldn't survive it."

"Will Woolf?"

Babagoo shrugged. "Most amnals do. Until we find out, just stay well away. I know you're fond of Woolf, but there's no need to check on her. I'll handle it, as I always do."

"But—"

Babagoo's eyes widened. "Don't *but* me, boy. We've seen enough of your jip today. You need to start listening to what I say. And if you don't listen to what I say, I'll save you a lot of trouble and throw you to the Outsiders. Because that's where not listening'll get you. Would you like that?" Flecks of gull flew from his mouth. "*Would you?*"

Landfill shook his head.

"Good. Then start listening. Rule number three?"

Landfill spoke to the floor. "Babagoo's always right."

"That's the one. Always remember that. Respect the rules. They're here to keep you alive. As am I. No one else will, you know."

Babagoo threw down some bones, licked the grease from his fingers and adjusted his trapper hat. He got up and – after coughing into his hand – gave Kafka a rub behind the ears. "I'm going out to fix that loose glass and gander about. Need to be vigilant after what happened at the Pit. You finish the gulls and give the amnals their dinner. The wooflers'll be famished, and you know the birds and foxlers get surly without their meat."

He jerked suddenly and slapped himself on the side of the head. "So much for routine! All gone to pot today. Not good. Not good at all."

He eyeballed Landfill. "Leave Muttbrough 'til last; I'll deal with Woolf before you get there. And when the amnals all have their food, come *straight* back to the Den. I don't want you pottering in the Thin Woods, checking all the trees for Joyce. "

Landfill started to open his mouth, but Babagoo raised a hand.

"I *know* you, Landfill. You care too much about others and forget about yourself. Feed the amnals and get straight back here. It's not safe tonight. You understand me?"

A sullen nod.

"Say it!"

Landfill's head dropped. "I understand."

FOUR

EVERYTHING

Later that night, Landfill sat by the stove and tried in vain to stack yellowing dominoes on their ends. He was finding it difficult to focus. He'd returned from feeding the animals a long time ago, and Babagoo should have been back by now.

He hugged himself, shivering in spite of the stove. Abandoning the dominoes, he turned his attention to the dozing goats. "Room for one more, slumbery bleaters?"

Kafka looked up and belched.

Landfill soon had his head on the black goat's flank, and was beginning to drift off when a noise made him sit up. He listened carefully.

There it was again: a slow, quiet scrape against one of the windows. Landfill ducked as low behind the goats as he could, and slowly raised his head to watch the windowpanes. It was hard to tell, but something was moving out there, slipping from window to window. When Landfill couldn't see it any more, a creak echoed across the tiles in the hallway.

Keeping low, Landfill slinked across the Den, his bare belly brushing against litter and bones. He kept listening out, waiting for the sound of Babagoo's shuffling gait. But the steps in the hallway didn't sound like Babagoo's. They were too slow, too cautious. There were none of the scavenger's usual coughs and mutters.

The steps were getting louder.

Landfill kept moving until he reached the hinged side of the doorframe. As quietly as possible, he pressed his back against the wall and slid himself up until he stood at full height. By the time he had his glass blade ready, the door handle was inching downwards. The door gradually opened into the room so that Landfill was hidden behind it. He held his breath and fingered the glass.

A dark figure slipped through the doorway. As soon as it took a second step, Landfill pounced and jabbed. The figure spun quickly, and there was a spark when Landfill's blade was knocked across the room. Landfill saw the metallic flash of another blade, dodged and leaped up to bury his teeth in a slashing arm.

"Okay, Landfill, okay!"

The voice's familiarity made Landfill drop back. He recognized the scavenger's outline, and wiped his mouth with the back of his hand.

Babagoo hissed and rubbed his forearm, then cackled abruptly. "Flaming brownberries! Sit, boy. Sit."

"*What was that?*" Landfill took deep breaths in an attempt to slow his thumping heart.

"Another test, my lad. Didn't do *too* badly this time. Got into position. Attacked from behind. But you need to improve your grip on that blade."

He waved his penknife at Landfill's stunned face.

"All it took was a light parry, and you were left with nothing but tooth and nail." He rubbed his forearm again. "Not that you don't have a knack with those. Now go find your blade. It went by the mowler boxes. Let's hope you haven't killed one of the mangy things. Having said that, mowler stew'd make a nice change."

Landfill scowled and searched around the cats' boxes. By the time he found the blade in a pile of mauled carpet scraps, Babagoo had removed his hat and overcoat and got settled on the stained mattress in the corner.

He smiled at Landfill. "Don't resent it, boyling. Got to keep *you* sharp – not just your blade. Come now. It's slumbertime, so brush your gnashers."

Landfill sucked at the back of his wrist, and the tightness gradually seeped from his limbs. He plodded to the workbench and found his toothbrush among rust-pocked tools.

Babagoo watched him dip the brush in water and scrub

his teeth. "Long overdue a new toothbrush, my lad. Barely a bristle left on that thing."

Landfill pulled the brush from his mouth. "What about you? Can't remember last time you had a brush. Whenever you find one you give it to me."

Babagoo shook his head. "Better you have it than me. My teeth are beyond help. Might as well polish goat dung."

Landfill snorted a laugh and started brushing again, but stopped when Babagoo clambered from the mattress and took the brush from his hand.

"Like this, Landfill." He brushed in gentle circles along the boy's molars. "No wonder your teeth are yellowing. Need to do it properly. You want a jabberhole full of stumps, like me?"

Landfill replied through a mouthful of toothbrush. "Uh eally."

"What's that?"

"Uh *eally*."

Babagoo raised the pitch of his voice to mimic the boy. "'Uh eally'?" He lifted an eyebrow and a grin creased his face. "Uh oo eyeing oo ay?"

Landfill began to giggle, and couldn't stop the drool that spooled from the edge of his mouth. Babagoo cackled at the sight, and they both gave in to chuckles and whimpers.

After wiping the tears from his eyes, Babagoo returned

to the mattress and held his overcoat up to the boy. "You can have it. Cold's creeping in."

Landfill rubbed his own eyes and – being careful to avoid exposed springs – climbed onto the mattress. While he curled up with his back to Babagoo, he felt the scavenger drape his overcoat over him as a blanket. Landfill sniffed deeply at the coat's plaid fabric; its sour scent made him yawn and snuggle his head into his threadbare pillow.

Babagoo shifted on his side of the mattress. "No sign of trouble out there, Landfill, but that doesn't mean there isn't any. Rule six – no sign can be a sure sign. I'll be foraging carefully at the Pit tomorrow, scavenging mirrors and bottles on both trips. Need more charms and glass for the wall. No point making it easy for the shadows to slip over. You know how they work with the Outsiders. But they don't like the glinting. Puts them off."

"Off," mumbled Landfill. His eyelids were drooping.

"Need to be on our guard," continued Babagoo. "You've been dropping yours lately – getting lacksadaisy. I notice your blade's a bit on the blunt side. Got to keep it sharp. Rule number?"

Landfill droned automatically: "Seventeen."

"That's right."

"Woolf… Is she…okay?"

"She's got the swelling alright. Didn't move her to the cabinet, though. The other wooflers got all growly when I tried, and I didn't feel up to dealing with them. Not after the shadow trouble at the Pit today. I'll move her tomorrow during chores."

A groggy purr. "Butterbyes…"

"Eh?"

"Butterbyes. At the Hard Guts. So many. All the colours…"

"You've got the slumber-mumbles, lad. Used to ramble like that when you were little." The scavenger chortled quietly. "You used to ruffle my beard back then, too, every time I ruffled your hair. Tickled like madness with those little fingers of yours. But I miss it sometimes."

Landfill smiled faintly. "I remember."

"Hm. You know…" The scavenger trailed off before clearing his throat. "You know I do all this because I love you, don't you? It might seem harsh, but sometimes that's what love's like. You mean everything to me, Landfill. *Everything.* You're my wallflower – the one good thing left in this world.

"It's barbarism out there, my lad. Miles and miles of masks, fibbery and horror, as far as the eye can see. Can you imagine it, boyling?"

A vague shake of the head.

"But you can fear it?"

A firmer motion – a nod.

"That's good. Because fear is what you need. Rule five –

respect your fear. Fear is our friend. Fear you can trust. You need to embrace that fear and temper that troublesome curiosity of yours. You don't seem to fully appreciate what we've got here, what we've made – how precious Hinterland is. You're becoming too wilful lately, and it worries me. *Fear*, Landfill. Only fear will preserve you. You hear me?"

The words seemed to stretch and echo in Landfill's ears, and he gave in to sleep.

Landfill opened his eyes when the mattress began to tremble. The scavenger was grinding his teeth and gibbering while still deep in sleep. The boy sat up to hush and stroke his arm until he settled back down.

He was mopping the sweat from Babagoo's face and neck when he spotted something flashing in the gloom: a silver key had slipped out from beneath Babagoo's jumper, and was hanging from its string against his shoulder. He stooped over Babagoo for a better look, then reached into the pocket of his shorts to pull out the key he kept hidden there. Positioning himself carefully, he angled his arm and held his own key close to Babagoo's. It was too dark to compare them by sight alone so – holding his breath – he moved his free hand towards Babagoo's key, as slowly, as steadily, as he could.

His hand touched the key's tiny, jagged prongs, and in an instant was gripped in Babagoo's fist. Landfill looked at Babagoo's face. One eye was wide open, with its quaking pupil aimed right at him. But it shone with the glaze of sleep, so Landfill hushed Babagoo once more until his hand was released, then let the key drop.

The glassy eye closed and Landfill released a shaky breath. After restoring his own key carefully to his pocket, he climbed back beneath the overcoat, closed his eyes and joined the scavenger in sleep.

FIVE

FROM INSIDE

Landfill stirred in drab blue light. He wiped a drool-damp cheek against his pillow, and gradually noticed a noise that was even louder than the goats' steady snoring.

He poked his head out from Babagoo's overcoat, and gazed dozily at the torrent of rain that was hammering the windows. The sleep in his eyes gave way to a keen sparkle.

Landfill eased himself up and left the mattress. He crept past the goats, and saluted some kittens with a puff and scratch of the cheek. "Gander that, mowlings," he whispered, nodding towards the window. "Coming down heavy. The Gully'll be full."

He grinned and slipped into the tiled hallway. After urinating into the stinkbucket in the corner, he ran through the double door and hurled himself into the rain. He cackled as warm water pounded his skin and, with the gutter bubbling behind him, loped on all fours to the Gully.

Landfill stopped at the Gully's edge to marvel at the sloshing water. When he spotted two turtles bobbing there he waved an arm. "Hey! Where've you been, tuttles? Waiting for rain?"

He moved down the bank until rainwater rose up to his chest, then dived in with a whoop and glided through the water along the Gully's centre. Splashing and giggling, he ducked beneath floating petals and scum. Frogs leaped from his hands and swam to drifting chunks of debris.

"Wet weather, eh?" he laughed. "Hunkadory for gribbits!"

"For boylings too!" called another voice.

Landfill turned to see Babagoo at the Gully's rim, squatting beneath the shelter of some raised pipes. His hat and overcoat were sopping with rain, but he smiled a grim smile.

Landfill puffed and scratched a cheek, and Babagoo did the same. The boy paddled towards the bank and soon felt concrete beneath his toes. "Sorry. Sneaked out. The rain woke me, and I knew the Gully'd be full."

Babagoo shrugged. He had to raise his voice over the downpour. "Not often it gets this high."

"Jump in. The water's warm." Landfill's wonky teeth were on show while he beamed.

"Certainly not. Look how light it is. We've missed the

dawn and I've not done the Pit's morning trip. Behind schedule again!"

"But it's so good to swim." Landfill pointed at the turtles. "And Hesse and Melville are here."

The scavenger crossed his arms. "There'll be time for tuttles this afternoon. All this –" he nodded towards the scummy water – "won't be going anywhere, and neither will the tuttles. Hesse and Melville are hardly known for pace, are they?" He chuckled drily to himself.

The boy pouted. "Come in," he whined. "Come for a wash. You smell worse than the foxlers."

The scavenger huffed irritably. "More important things to do. Got to respect the routine. Rule number?"

Landfill gargled through a mouthful of water. "*Fourteen*."

"That's right. Routine, routine, routine." Babagoo jabbed his own forehead. "Got to keep the grey stuff occupied. And the devil makes work, eh?" His expression twisted into a scowl. "We saw that yesterday, didn't we, boy?"

Landfill paddled backwards, suddenly grave.

Babagoo nodded. "I'll do you a favour and empty the stinkbucket. Then I'll be straight to the Pit for gulls and mirrors. As for you, stop dawdledallying and check the wall so you're done before I'm back with breakfast. Show some respect, boy."

With that, Babagoo raised his chin, turned haughtily on

his boots and slipped on some moss. His arms windmilled while he teetered at the edge of the bank, and he submitted to gravity with a curt shriek. A few bumps on the slope were followed by a splash, and the Gully was filled as much by youthful laughter as by water.

Babagoo paddled in the scum and glared through a soggy fringe. Bubbles seethed around his lips. "Think that's funny, do you?"

Landfill's words were gasped between guffaws. "When you fell… Sounded like… You sounded…like the mowlers when you stand on their tails!" He continued to howl, and Babagoo's grimace began to weaken. Landfill could see laughter quavering in the scavenger's eyes.

Babagoo shook a theatrical fist. "Why, you little goblin! I'm coming over there to push your head in the water and be done with you! Then we'll see who's a tittering troll."

"Have to catch me first!" Landfill ducked beneath the water and resurfaced with puffed-up cheeks. With a kick of the legs he raised himself and squirted a silvery arc of water, which splashed just short of Babagoo's face.

"You little stenchpellet!" bellowed Babagoo, his voice trembling with repressed mirth. "That's it! You're done for now, boy!" He lunged forward, and they were soon splashing each other as sunbeams pierced the rain.

*   *   *

After a late breakfast, Babagoo began work on turning a bounty of cracked mirrors into charms for the wall.

Landfill, somewhat relieved that the rain had stopped, began his rounds with plastic bags of meat. The crows gorged on the gull guts left over by the cats, but the badgers in the Thin Woods weren't interested – they'd had their fill of insects and grubs, and had been good enough to stay away from the vegetable patch. Landfill tossed meat up to kestrels and sparrowhawks perched on vents and chimneys, and left food for the foxes around the cabins behind the Rippletop.

Upon reaching Muttborough, Landfill threw meat towards the dogs that came running at the sound of his rustling bags. While they tore at gull, Landfill crouched by the trough and lapped up fresh water. Once he'd quenched his thirst he looked at Woolf's cart. With the dogs quietly feeding, he thought he could hear panting from within.

"Woolf? Is that you?"

He listened out for a moment, and it took all of his self-control to get up and move backwards in the opposite direction. But then he heard shrill, tiny whines. The noises confused him, and when he recognized sounds of pain he stopped moving.

He checked his surroundings. After reassuring himself that the scavenger wasn't nearby, Landfill lowered himself to all fours and crept towards Woolf's cart. He spoke in a whisper. "Hasn't Babagoo been to move you yet?"

Covering his mouth and nostrils, Landfill drew nearer. He kept as much distance as he could while peering inside. When he saw what was in the cart, he couldn't restrain a sudden intake of breath.

The husky wasn't alone. She lay panting on her side, with four wet little creatures – not unlike large mice – biting at her red, swollen teats. Landfill's first instinct was to reach out and pull them from danger, but when his free hand got close, a growl from Woolf made him falter. After he'd withdrawn his hand, she licked and nuzzled the animals attached to her belly. Landfill stared at them, and it gradually dawned on him that they were tiny dogs, with squashed noses and grey and white fur, just like Woolf's.

"Wooflings… But where'd you…? How did you…?"

Landfill stopped whispering when he noticed Woolf's panting had become heavier. Spotting movement towards her rear, he shuffled along the cart's horizontal side and – with one hand still covering his mouth and nose – felt something sticky on his fingers. The blanket was soaked with some sort of discharge, and he could make out four small, rubbery pouches glistening in gloom, each of which sat in its own pool of fluid.

He was prodding one of them when something started to emerge from above Woolf's hind legs. At first, Landfill thought she was pushing out a stool, but the object was too glossy, too firm and wide.

The object continued to gradually protrude. After it landed on the blanket, Woolf began licking and nibbling its viscous exterior. She whined and her licking became agitated. Landfill moved to get a better view of the sac and, as some light came in from behind, he saw something moving inside – something that Woolf was trying to get out.

Holding his breath, he reached out with both hands, gripped the slippery sheath between thumbs and knuckles, and pulled it carefully open. Warm liquid oozed over his hands, and the sac slipped away to reveal another dog. Woolf moved to lick its face and nose, before washing Landfill's fingers with her tongue.

The pup tried to move along the blanket but seemed to be struggling. It was smaller than the others, and its back legs didn't look right; they were too thin, and looked oddly twisted. Landfill watched the other pups attached to Woolf's teats and knew what to do.

The little dog, with its tiny eyes unable to open, squeaked when Landfill picked it up and guided it to a teat, which it latched on to immediately. Woolf licked it while it fed, then gnawed the gore that soaked the blanket.

Landfill looked on with wide, unblinking eyes. He didn't even realize he'd started breathing again.

He started at the sound of a bark outside the cart, and some distant, phlegmy coughs from the direction of the Thin Woods made him slam his head against the cart's top.

He clutched his hair in both hands. "It's Babagoo!" he hissed. "I shouldn't be in here!"

In an instant, Landfill had backed out of the cart, grabbed his plastic bags and sprinted away. He hid well out of sight, behind the Pale Loomer's far side.

A chorus of growls rose from Muttbrough.

PART TWO

THE STEM

SIX

WASTE NOT, WANT NOT

That night, once he'd finished the animals' evening feed, Landfill returned to the Den to find Babagoo in conversation with the black goat. The Den had been tidied and Babagoo's traps and bags of litter were in the hallway, ready for the morning trip to the Pit.

The metal door thumped behind Landfill, causing the scavenger and goat to look up. Babagoo puffed and scratched his cheek. Landfill did the same.

"Dinner done?" asked Babagoo.

"Done."

"Hunkadory. The day's chores are behind us. So how about a little play?" Babagoo took a tattered wooden box from one of the consoles behind the goats. It clacked with dominoes when he shook it, and Landfill nodded curtly.

They sat by the stove to play. While Babagoo looked at

his dominoes, Landfill watched the boxes stacked not far from the bathtub. Feeble sounds of mewling came from within. "The mowlings sound unhappy."

Babagoo put a domino down. "That's because I saw to some of them earlier. They don't like getting the nick between their legs, but it's for their own good. Better to see to those poorly parts."

Landfill nodded and added a domino to the line.

Babagoo took his turn, and a cheery note entered his voice. "Got good news for you, lad. Went to Muttbrough today to move Woolf, but it turns out I didn't have to. She's hunkadory now. Swelling's practically gone! Did it all by herself! Never seen a speedier recovery."

Landfill raised an eyebrow. His lips became pale with tightness.

"Thought you'd be chirpier about it after all your fretting," said Babagoo. "And guess what I found in Spit Pit this afternoon... A tiny pack of wooflings! Impish wads of fluff, every one of them. I've given them to Woolf to look after. You can have a gander tomorrow."

Landfill stewed in silence.

"Mowler got your tongue, eh?" Babagoo sniffed. "Alright, then. If you'd prefer something more glum to jabber about, I spotted some creepers after visiting Muttbrough, eating into the Pale Loomer's lower wall. Could cause mischief over time."

He jerked his head towards the window, in the direction of the four chimneys across the Gully and Thin Woods. "You remember the damage they did to the Black Fingers, don't you? I'll tear them out tomorrow. That vegetation can eat through anything. Last thing we want is the Loomer going down in a few years' time. Best to nip these things in the bud, eh? Rule fifteen?"

Landfill only gazed at his dominoes.

Babagoo reached over and tapped his shoulder. "What's rule fifteen, my lad?"

"Look after Hinterland," muttered Landfill, "as it looks after us."

"That's the one."

After smacking his lips, the scavenger spoke again. "What's wrong? You're staring at those dominoes like they're riddles. Been in a daze since lunchtime." He touched the boy again. "Landfill?"

"Tell me where I came from."

"Eh?"

"Where I came from. Can you tell me?"

"You know where you came from, my boy. Told you many times."

"I know." Landfill looked up and spied a sliver of string against the side of Babagoo's neck. His eyes traced its course beneath the scavenger's jumper, to where Babagoo's key dangled out of sight. He realized his gaze was lingering, and quickly shifted it to Babagoo's face. "But it's been a while. Can you tell me again? Please?"

Babagoo pouted. He scratched his temples and scrutinized Landfill's face. "Okay," he finally said. "Let me see… Well, you started as a seed – a seed spat into the Spit Pit by the Outsiders. They can't have known what a precious thing they were wasting. But then again, they never do. That's why they'll always be infected by the hunger – why it eats them up and rots their insides. The hunger makes waste and wasting makes the hunger. No surprise it's such—"

"The seed," interrupted Landfill.

Babagoo ground his teeth and took a long breath. "Yes, the seed. Into the Pit it went. And that's where you started to grow, like the rarest of flowers. A wallflower from the filth." He sniffed and rubbed his nose. "A little miracle, Landfill. That's what you were – what you'll always be."

He smiled and ruffled Landfill's hair, then leaned forward and offered his beard so Landfill could reciprocate. But the boy didn't move.

Babagoo cleared his throat. "So…I happened to find you. And seeing how precious you were, I had no choice but to take you to the only place you might be safe from the Outsiders. I took you to Hinterland, and that's where we hid – where you've been safe ever since. Although, back then, Hinterland wasn't what it is now. Oh no – it was a cold, forgotten, dead place. Which was a good thing. Only a forgotten place can be such a blind spot, such a sanctuary. But back then it was all decay, steel and silence."

Babagoo sighed and stared at the flames in the stove. "It was only after you were brought in that it came alive. As you grew, Hinterland grew with you. Of course, I dealt with repairs, with the wall, boards and charms and the like. But the rest was Hinterland. I filled this Den and built the tunnel from the cabinet to the Pit, but Hinterland decked itself with flowers and vines. I locked the gates and put glass in the wall, but Hinterland hid the gates and nettled its flanks. I smuggled in seeds for vejbles, and bleaters for your milk, but all your other friends, all the other amnals… Well, Hinterland didn't so much provide them; they came in response to your little baby calls."

The scavenger chuckled to himself. "So that's where you came from. You were saved from Outside, and I for one am glad you were. Not that it was easy. We had some close calls, believe me. You suffered the fire-flush many a time. But you refused to die. Rarely even cried. You've always been such a stubborn little fighter." He laughed again and beamed at the boy.

Landfill's eyes returned to his dominoes. "A sced, then. I grew from a seed."

"Of course."

Landfill nodded stiffly and sucked in his lips. His thin

muscles tensed before he spoke again. "You didn't find those wooflings in the Pit. I saw them this morning, coming out of Woolf. From *inside* her." He looked up and saw Babagoo's smile vanish in an instant.

"What? You're not supposed to go near amnals with the swelling! I told you not to even *look* at Woolf until I'd dealt with her!"

"And you always said the small amnals come from Outside. That you rescue them, like you did me."

Babagoo's features rippled, as if unable to decide which emotion to settle on. He moved his lips, searching for words. "I said…I said…"

"And you told me to believe only Babagoo. Rule four. But how—"

Babagoo growled and clacked his teeth. "Don't throw rules at me, you little skulk!"

He was on his feet now. He had the attention of the goats, and the cats were sitting up in their boxes. "And listen closely. Never once did I say that smaller amnals *don't* come from other amnals. So if you're trying to suggest I've lied to you, you cocky little urchin, look me in the eyes and say it so I can give you a slap!"

Landfill grimaced at his dominoes. He seemed to sag, and his lips were crumpled. "But you lied about the wooflings from Woolf. And you've never said how smaller amnals come from bigger ones. I thought of seeds…

56

I thought…" He shook his head. "What about the other amnals with the swelling? Have they made smaller amnals too? Is that what happens when you take them to the cabinet?"

Babagoo didn't reply. Landfill heard coarse breaths as the scavenger's chest heaved up and down.

No one spoke, until a bleat from Kafka made Babagoo shuffle his feet. He took a deep breath, and when he spoke his voice was quieter. "Listen, Landfill…I'll admit… The smaller amnals come from bigger amnals. They come from their swollen bellies."

Landfill sniffed and wiped his nose on his forearm. His eyes were still locked on the dominoes. "So why didn't you tell me? You always said the swelling's an illness. Is it?"

Babagoo hesitated. "Not…as such." He grunted and gradually returned to sitting on the floor.

He was silent for some time, then sighed. "Landfill… I couldn't tell you the truth about where the smaller amnals come from. Had to hide it to…protect you."

"From what?"

"From the Outsiders."

"How can—"

Babagoo's finger shot up. "Don't question it, Landfill. I did this to protect you. Just like everything else I do. That's all you need to know. Don't ask questions, and take my word for it. Babagoo's always right."

"But—"

"*Trust* me, boy." Babagoo's tone was more of warning than appeal.

Landfill shrugged sullenly and flicked a domino across the floor. "Is there anything else?"

"How'd you mean?"

Landfill glanced up at Babagoo, but quickly dropped his gaze. "Anything else you haven't told me?"

"No."

"You sure?"

The reply came through clenched teeth. "Don't insult me, boy."

Landfill shrugged again. The crackling of the fire filled the long silence that followed.

Eventually, Landfill raised his head and looked Babagoo in the eye. "What about me? Did I come from inside a… a bigger me?"

Babagoo snorted. "Course you didn't."

"What about you? Did you come from a bigger you?"

Babagoo frowned at the grainy panels on the ceiling. His words were hesitant. "I…suppose I did."

Landfill's eyes flashed. "Will you ever make a smaller you?"

Babagoo's mouth hung open. A watery glaze coated his eyes. "Once…I did…I made…" He gasped suddenly, as if in pain, and slapped both hands to his face.

"Made what?"

"Nothing!"

"Is that where Outsiders come from? From inside other Outsiders?"

Slowly, Babagoo lowered his hands. "Do you have to ask so many questions?"

"Is it where they come from?"

A deep breath. "Yes."

"So you were an Outsider?"

Babagoo looked into the corner of his eye. "I was certainly Outside. You know I was. That's how I found you. And it almost killed me. Had the hunger, for a time."

Landfill's eyes were wide. "You had the hunger?"

Babagoo nodded grimly. "How else would I know how awful it is?"

Landfill was still staring at him. "What's it like?"

Phlegm rattled in the scavenger's throat, and he gave in to a sudden bout of coughs. When he was done he spat at the floor. "Hideous. Can't be described."

"Can you try?"

Babagoo clambered to his feet and started pacing. His plaid overcoat billowed behind him. "Okay. Think of the pain you get in your belly when I've not been able to get gull or grubbins from the Pit. Now multiply that pain a million times, and still you're nowhere near. The hunger infects your stomach with fear, and when your stomach's full it infects your mind with hate. It blinds you and makes you do awful, *awful* things…"

He winced and dragged a knuckle down his face before continuing. "It eats up your insides and leaves your outside as a shell to hold in your mush. Oh they wear masks to hide it, but the rot's there alright, right behind their faces – right down to the bone. Can you imagine it, boy? Can you imagine what it's like to feel your innards on the turn?"

Landfill shook his head.

"Such a cruel madness, Landfill – a madness that fills Outside with weapons and walls, screams and savagery. But something happened. I realized how sick I was – how sick *everyone* was. After that, the Outsiders chewed me up and spat me into the Pit to die. But then I found you, and Hinterland found us. And I healed, Landfill. All the rot left inside from the hunger… I got better. In some ways, I have you to thank for that."

Babagoo stopped pacing, put his face in his hands and groaned. "I'm tired. Let's discuss this another time. You look tired too, boyling. I'd say it's slumbertime." He raised a finger when Landfill opened his mouth. "*Slumber. Time.*"

After they were settled on their separate sides of the mattress, Landfill spoke from beneath Babagoo's coat. "Can I ask one last question, Babagoo?"

"No."

"Can I go to the Spit Pit with you tomorrow?"

Babagoo shook his head. "Told you a hundred times – it's too dangerous. You're not ready. Now stop asking. I'll tell you when it's time. And the time will come quicker if you stop pestering. Now goodnight. Get slumbering, Landfill."

"Goodnight, Babagoo."

SEVEN

ESCALATION

Landfill didn't go to sleep. When Babagoo started snoring, he sat up and watched the stove's fire peter out.

Darkness consumed the Den. Landfill listened to the animals, and waited for the scavenger to stir.

It didn't take long. Babagoo muttered, whined and ground his teeth. Landfill hushed and soothed, but the scavenger wouldn't settle. Veins rose on his forehead.

"Ss…" he hissed. "*Sssorry…*"

"It's okay," whispered Landfill. "It's sleep-sweats. Just sleep-sweats. Sshhh…"

"*Sshh…ame.*" Babagoo's leg twitched like a dog's.

"Shame?"

"Shadows." The scavenger's eyelids trembled. "Shadows…"

"Shush, Babagoo. No shadows. Just us. Shush now."

The veins vanished from Babagoo's forehead, and he gradually stopped trembling.

Landfill dabbed the sweat from the scavenger's face. When he seemed deep in sleep, he drew carefully away and left the mattress. After skirting the goats, he fumbled around a console's top until his fingers skimmed a pile of plastic lighters. Taking one of them caused another to drop to the floor, and Babagoo groaned at the sound. Wincing all the while, Landfill held his breath and waited for the scavenger to settle down again.

When Babagoo's snoring resumed, Landfill tiptoed to the door and – with one hand shielding the worst of the flame – quickly tested the lighter. The Den was lit momentarily, and Landfill spotted Kafka's eyes on him from across the room. The goat's slit-like pupils flashed wetly before darkness returned. Looking in Kafka's direction, Landfill raised a finger to his lips, crept from the Den and closed the door quietly behind him.

Outdoors was brighter, for the sky was star-packed and cloudless. It draped Hinterland's surfaces in pale, silvery light, so that they shone in stark contrast to the blackness of the wall, which was broken here and there where specks of glass caught the moon. Landfill jogged across gravelly concrete, hopping nimbly over heather and weeds.

He batted a hawkmoth away from his cheek; when the skull on its back flickered, he glanced at the wall and thought of Joyce, wondering whether the red squirrel might still be alive.

On the tips of his toes, Landfill crept across one of the ramshackle steel bridges that spanned the Gully. Every creak that echoed along the concrete ditch made him cringe, and as soon as he was close enough, he hopped off the bridge and into the Thin Woods. Here, the starlight was blocked by a black canopy of leaves, but Landfill dropped to all fours and loped with ease around wraithlike tree trunks. As he left the trees the starlight returned, broken only by the darkness of the conveyor overhead. He was almost at his destination.

Landfill rounded the Ivy Stack's corrugated walls. Darkness descended when he entered its murky opening, so he took the lighter from his shorts and ignited its flame. Amber light quivered against the walls, and Landfill had to duck when squeaking bats fluttered over his head and into the night. Once they'd gone, he raised his lighter and moved cautiously through cavernous spaces. The ground felt powdery beneath his soles, and disturbed piles of sediment rasped while he passed huge machines that slumbered in the shadows. He stepped over cables and fallen beams, and eventually reached the conveyor's mouth.

The conveyor had a plastic ceiling, but much of its

corrugated side-panelling had fallen away, allowing moonlight to illuminate the steps that ran alongside the conveyor's belt. Returning the lighter to his pocket, Landfill began to climb the steps.

He'd gained some height before the corridor ahead became a vacuum of pitch black. The conveyor was approaching the height of Hinterland's wall, and the panelling's gaps beyond that point had been boarded up by Babagoo – as had all windows and openings higher than the wall's crest.

Landfill stared through the final gap before Babagoo's boards began. After some time he tightened his lips, nodded to himself and climbed through. He clung like a lizard to the conveyor's exterior frame, and clambered carefully onto its top.

As he worked his way upwards he began to slow down. He could see the silhouette of Hinterland's wall dropping slowly away, and the sky's shifting shape made his stomach knot.

He fought a surge of nausea, closed his eyes and whispered to himself: "Rule twelve – never rise…above the wall." Keeping his eyes closed, he took several deep breaths and continued to climb, feeling around the plastic with his hands and naked feet. A breeze against his bare ribs made him falter, and when he opened his eyes he couldn't help crying out.

The sky had unfolded into an infinite geometry that was impossible to comprehend. Panting rapidly, Landfill clung to the conveyor, with his belly, chest and limbs pressed tightly against its top. He whimpered at the stars that spun above him, and feared that letting go would send him toppling into the sky.

With his cheek pinned against plastic, he swivelled his eyes and looked out over the wall. Darkness was all around, apart from to the west, past Hinterland's four towering chimneys. Through watering eyes, Landfill could make out a low patch bordered by luminous specks. Beyond that was an area illuminated by grids of yellow and orange light. Smaller dots of light traversed the surrounding darkness in slow curves and lines. And beyond that, a distant, fiery glow on a black horizon.

Landfill gawped and moaned, and became aware of something else. Among the sky's pricks of light, a red star seemed to be blinking. Transfixed, he watched the red star grow, and as it rose he heard a familiar rumbling. The rumbling became louder while the star drew closer, and Landfill realized that Hunger's Eye was coming for him.

An animal sound flew from his mouth. He tried to move but couldn't. It was impossible to know which way was up and which was down. His fingers refused to release the conveyor's ridges.

Hunger's Eye drew nearer; the rumbling became a roar.

But still Landfill couldn't move. The Eye was bearing down upon him, causing the conveyor to creak and rattle beneath his belly. Landfill couldn't even cover his ears when the screaming shook the panels. With his eardrums in agony, he closed his tear-filled eyes and waited for the end.

But the screaming became a roar, and the roar became a rumble.

It took some time before Landfill was able to open his eyes. When he did, he saw the red star blinking in the distance, continuing on the course from which it had come. He squinted and thought he saw the star attached to something dark – a shadow of a shadow, vaguely triangular and fading into night.

After he'd finally been able to peel himself from the conveyor's top, Landfill sprinted through the Thin Woods. He blubbered as he ran, with snot and tears streaming down his face. Upon reaching the Woods' fringe, he stooped and panted and rubbed his wrist against his lips. The scream of Hunger's Eye was still ringing in his ears – a shrill accompaniment to the hammering of his heart.

When his hearing started to return, Landfill was struck by Hinterland's silence, and wondered whether he'd gone deaf. He peered around, taking in the Gully, the Nook, the black wall and its flecks of starlight. Everything was so calm and quiet – exactly as it was before the Eye had torn up the sky.

Landfill took a deep breath. His heartbeat began to steady.

As he raised an arm to wipe the snot from his lips, something clutched his wrist from behind. His cry was muffled by a large hand that shot out to cover his nose and mouth, and he was yanked roughly back into the Woods. He tried to fight, but a strong arm had slipped down to pin his hands to his sides.

He thrashed his head and felt cracked lips against his ear. A voice growled through gritted teeth.

"Oh *now* you're done for. Now you're as good as dead."

Landfill twisted his neck to gasp through clamped fingers. "Babagoo!"

Babagoo threw him to the ground. "I saw you, *boy*. Came searching when I woke up with you gone. Saw you on the conveyor. Rule twelve – never rise above the wall!"

"But—"

"Don't *but* me! Shown your true colours now, you bony back-stabber. I've seen with my own eyes that you're a filthy little traitor!"

"Babagoo…" The boy scrabbled up, only to be pushed down again.

The scavenger was backing away with arms outstretched. "Don't come near me! Don't *touch* me! Don't you see what you've done?" Babagoo looked upwards and continued to back away. "They'll be on their way now, Landfill. They know you're here. But they don't know about me!"

The scavenger spun on his boots and ran for the nearest bridge across the Gully. Landfill got up and scampered after him, but stopped to raise his hands against the swish of Babagoo's penknife.

Babagoo jabbed the blade in Landfill's direction. "Don't come following me, boy! You got yourself into this sordid pickle, and the least you can do, after everything – *everything!* – I've done for you, is keep me out of it. Come any closer and I swear I'll put this blade into both your eyes."

Landfill could almost feel the knife slicing the air in front of his nose. "Please, Babagoo! *Please.*" He was beginning to cry. "Was just trying… I was trying—"

"You were trying to get yourself killed! Either that or you were passing a message to the Outsiders." The scavenger leaned in close to sniff air, then recoiled with his nose in the crook of his elbow. "Argh! I can smell the rot! Have you got the hunger? Is that it? Are you wearing a mask now?" He snorted, and took the boy by surprise by spitting into his eyes.

Landfill staggered on the spot. By the time he'd wiped his face, Babagoo had crossed the Gully and was running for the Nook. Landfill tried to shout Babagoo's name but choked on tears. He dropped to all fours and pursued the scavenger as quickly as he could.

When he got to the building's double door it wouldn't budge. He pounded it with his fists, then moved around the building to try the Nook's windows. Babagoo had fastened them all, and while Landfill thumped the panes he glanced regularly backwards to check the sky. "Babagoo!" he screamed. "Babagoo, I'm sorry! I blundered! I was wrong! Let me in! Please please pleeeaaase!"

He could just make out the scavenger's outline behind the panes, pacing the Den and waving its arms.

"Fat chance!" barked Babagoo. "You think I'm going to let you in here so you can knife me in the back! So you can slit my throat while I slumber! So you can spit your venom into my water!" He made a sound that was either a laugh or an agonized howl. "No no no, my little let-down. No place for you here now. You're not what I thought you were. Far from it. Easy pickings for the Outsiders, boy – that's all you are now. You're already dead."

Landfill banged the window with his forehead. "Babagoo! Pleeeeaaase…"

The outline shot towards the window. Landfill saw eyes flashing through the grime, heard clacking teeth. "GO! AWAY!"

Landfill gaped at the shadowy face, felt its horror reflected in his own. Staggering backwards, he lost his footing and fell to the ground. When he sat up, he licked his wrist and swiped it through his hair. He knew Babagoo wasn't going to change his mind, and that he needed somewhere to hide. After checking the sky again, he got to his feet and – with bleats accompanying every step – sprinted through Hinterland until he reached Muttbrough.

Some of the dogs stirred and watched Landfill dart into Woolf's toppled cart. Once under its cover, he took the glass blade from his shorts, curled up with his back against the cart's base and set his teary eyes on the opening.

The husky raised her head from her pups. She sniffed Landfill's hair and licked his cheek. But the boy felt nothing. Every ounce of his concentration was fixed on the opening. His shuddering blade was the only thing that moved as he lay listening, watching, waiting…

EIGHT

A TRICKY ONE

Landfill whimpered in his sleep. He shifted a little, and sucked some drool from his lip.

The moment something touched his hair he was up and snarling. He crouched with his back against the cart's rear, slashing with one arm, only dimly aware of the pup held in the other.

A silhouette recoiled, narrowly dodging the nip of yellow fingernails.

"*Easy*, lad. It's me. Settle down now. Easy, eh?"

Landfill gradually recognized Babagoo, who was kneeling at the cart's opening with Kafka by his side. The boy shook his head, slumped against the cart's base and trembled with tears he couldn't contain.

The scavenger nodded. "That's it, my lad. Calm down. Everything's okay. As far as I can tell, at least." He leaned back to check the sky, which blushed with dawn's fading colours. When his gaze dropped, he clocked a shadow that had settled on his boots, shuddered, and shuffled aside.

He returned his attention to the boy. "All's fine. The wall's still up. I'm still here. Kafka's still here. You're still here. We're *all* here. So you can settle down. Okay?"

The pup squeaked while Landfill held it against his chest. "But the Eye," he began. "Last night… Outsiders…"

Babagoo's lips drooped. "I know! Don't ask me." He shrugged. "A miracle, perhaps. Or, more likely, you weren't spotted in the dark. That's why I'm guessing the Eye missed you. You're a fluky gremlin, if ever I knew one." He glanced at the old goat. "Eh, Kafka? A fluky streak of bum gruel, that's what he is!"

Landfill was rubbing his forehead and looking at Woolf.

"And talking of fluky, guess what the Spit Pit offered this morning…" Babagoo moved away to reach into a bin bag, and returned with a bird in each hand. "Not one, but *two* herons! Your favourite! Quite apt for celebrating you giving Hunger's Eye the slip after –" Babagoo's lips twisted momentarily, and he released a shuddering breath before continuing – "after such an ill-advised *stunt*. Breakfast awaits. There's enough heron for lunch too! So come along, lad. Give that little woofling back to its mother. Got a routine to get back to. Routine routine routine."

"What's a mother?"

Babagoo slapped a hand over his mouth. He looked up and tutted. "A tricky one to explain, Landfill. Another time. For now, just give the muttling to Woolf."

Landfill had slipped into his thoughts, but was roused when Babagoo crouched into the cart to shake his shoulder. "These herons won't pluck and gut themselves, you know. Although what a sight that'd be." He grinned abruptly and chuckled, and watched Landfill shuffle forward with the pup still in his hand. "New friend there, eh?"

"It can't move like the others." Landfill blinked in sunlight and held the dog up to Babagoo. "Bad hind legs. Will you name it?"

Babagoo squinted at the runt. "Hmm. Sincere-looking little thing. Gangly too. Looks like an…Orwell to me. What do you think?"

Landfill tested the word in his mouth. "Orwell… Or. Well." He smiled for the first time that morning. "Yes. Orwell." He turned to place the pup gently among the rest of Woolf's litter, and paused briefly to look at the fresh scar between its hind legs. "Oh. You've seen to this one already?"

"That I have. Some other wooflings too. Orwell wasn't the only one with poorly parts."

"So Orwell's a he."

"He certainly is."

"Hmm." Landfill was watching Woolf nuzzle and lick her pups. "It's so nice."

"What is?"

"How she licks. Have you seen how she cares for them?"

"Snap out of it, lad. Take these birds and move along. But don't go forgetting your knife. Dropped it while you were slumbering. Rule sixteen." A loud tut. "Now come on. You had no dinner last night and it's way past breakfast."

The boy nodded and they started walking, followed closely by the click of Kafka's hooves. Landfill had a heron's neck in each hand, and the limp bodies slid across weeds and concrete behind him. "My stomach hurts. Can't remember the last time it hurt like this." He winced and grimaced. "And the hunger's a million times worse?"

Babagoo closed his eyes. "Even more than that. Doesn't bear thinking about. Best to be quiet now and focus on getting to the Den. The sooner we're there, the sooner you'll have meat in your belly."

Landfill continued to walk, but slowed when a large Alsatian hobbled behind them.

"Come, Landfill. Enough distraction now."

Landfill frowned. "But he's in pain." He released the herons' necks and turned around. "What's wrong, Vonnegut?" Dropping to his knees, he took the dog's huge head in both hands.

Babagoo grunted behind him. "Vonnegut's hunkadory, Landfill. Never a wilier rascal. So keep *moving*. You want to dawdledally with wooflers all day, or do you want to fill your belly?"

Landfill didn't reply. After leaning into Vonnegut and listening closely to his panting, he pulled away and lifted the dog's paw. "There it is." He angled the paw's underside in the light, and screwed up his eyes to examine the thorn stuck between two pads. After pulling the paw to his mouth and sucking, he pinched the thorn between his fingers, pulled it out and showed it to the dog. "Better now?" Vonnegut nuzzled Landfill's lap and padded away.

The boy turned around to see Babagoo watching him. The scavenger was stroking Kafka's chin, a faint smile touching his lips. "Done now?"

He reached out to ruffle Landfill's hair. Landfill ducked his head and continued walking. The scavenger kept up, chortling quietly. "Want me to take one of those herons?"

"Why?"

"You'll need a free hand for this." Babagoo rummaged in one of his coat pockets, and extracted a small chocolate bar in soiled but lively packaging.

"Sugar grubbins!"

"Your favourite. A rare and precious treat, as you very well know. Was going to save it for a special occasion, but you'd better have it now, before your stomach starts eating you from the inside."

Landfill's grin flashed in the sun. "Really?"

"Really. Now take it before I change my mind. And don't get used to such things. You know it's filth, don't you? Might as well eat a plastic bag. And you'd better brush those gnashers twice as long tonight."

Landfill had already swapped a heron for the chocolate bar, and was cramming gooey sweetness into his face while they walked. When he was done, he wiped the chocolate from his lips and licked his sticky fingers. He was beaming with ecstasy.

"Edible?" asked Babagoo.

"*Very.*" Landfill shook his head and took the heron back from Babagoo. "I don't understand, though."

"Understand what?"

"Why is the stuff that tastes so good always bad for you?"

Babagoo chuckled sourly. "Because life hates us, my boy. Then again, perhaps not you. You've been under Hunger's Eye and lived to tell the tale." His eyes flitted skywards. "By the looks of it, at least. So perhaps life likes you. You'd be the only one. But you know, it *should* like you – if it has any fairness left in its bones. As you well know, Landfill – you're the only good thing left."

The scavenger scratched beneath his hat and took a deep breath. His gaze was fixed ahead. "Landfill. I'm sorry about last night – about suspecting the worst. But I was so frightened. I was so scared of what'd happen to you."

The boy's face darkened. "Then why'd you lock me out of the Nook?"

"You know why. You broke rule twelve – went above the wall, into plain sight. Under Hunger's Eye too! You put all of Hinterland at risk. Can't you see what that looks like? Betrayal – that's what. I was so…disappointed. Heartbroken and angry."

The scavenger shook his head.

"Still am. But only because you mean so much to me, Landfill. You have to love someone very much to be able to hate so much too. Can you understand that?"

Landfill didn't answer, but tipped his head in what might have been a nod.

"So out with it. What were you doing up there? You know the rules."

Landfill sucked a finger, deep in thought.

"Jabber up, boy. Don't test me."

"Didn't realize how high I was."

"Is that right?" The scavenger huffed. "Don't think it hasn't occurred to me that you were up there after our little chat last night. You can see why I'd—"

"Skrill."

"Eh?"

"I couldn't slumber and went out. Started playing chase with a skrill. It went up the conveyor. Didn't see how high I was."

Babagoo scrunched up his lips. He was quiet for some time before he spoke. "Either way, it was mindless games or perilous neglect. You're not being wary enough, boy. You need to respect your fear. Rule five. And I saw that fear in you last night, when you were begging and crying. You were lily-livered, and rightly so!"

Landfill nodded with his eyes to the ground. They passed the complex of drums and chutes, and Landfill listened to the chirping parakeets before looking up. "Babagoo?"

"What?"

"Do I cry because I came from a seed?"

A loud snort. "How'd you mean?"

"I mean… You came from a bigger you, and I've never seen you cry. Never seen the amnals cry either."

"Ha!" Babagoo slapped Landfill's back. "I cry alright. At least, I used to. I'm done crying, lad. Was all cried out a long time ago." He began to slow a little, and gazed gloomily at the ground.

Landfill fell quiet before speaking. "So you ran out of tears."

"Guess I did." Babagoo coughed drily and thumped himself on the chest. "Nothing but dust in here now."

"Will I run out of tears one day?"

"Let's hope not. Anyway, enough jabber about tears. Today is about lessons learned, okay? No more mischief.

And no skulking out of the Den at night. That's a new rule – number twenty-two. Thought we were past making rules, but it seems not."

Babagoo checked the sky and peered over his shoulder. "We may not be in the clear. Even if the Eye missed you, you might've been seen over the wall. No sign can be a sure sign. So get your act together. Remember the very first rule – the most important rule – and stick to it."

"Rule number one – follow the rules."

"That's right. So you'll be a careful, obedient, respectful boy now, yes?"

Landfill nodded.

"*Say it.*"

"I will."

NINE

 # LONGWHITE

The next morning, Babagoo skimmed the mattress with his hands before sitting up suddenly. "Landfill!"

The boy was sitting by a window that was pink with dawn. "Here, Babagoo."

Babagoo rubbed his eyes and winced at him, then released a sharp sigh. "What are you gawking at? What's out there?"

"Nothing. Just gandering the colours."

Babagoo grunted and put on his trapper hat. "Something's up. You're looking sheepish. Or fiendish. Can't tell."

Landfill laughed. "Nothing's up. Shall we start the day? My belly wants breakfast."

Babagoo fanned a palm at him. "Okay, okay. I'll see what the Spit Pit has to offer. Just let me use the stinkbucket first, alright?"

Landfill listened while Babagoo used the bucket in the hallway. His eyebrows rose when he heard the scavenger hiss.

Upon returning to the Den, Babagoo buttoned his corduroys and addressed the boy. "Fresh squirts in the bucket for draining. There's some scats in there too. You can bag them up for the Pit before I go. Might want to pinch your nose while you're at it, though. Must have had some dodgy grubbins." He patted his stomach with one hand and wafted the air with the other.

Landfill grinned and raised a finger. "Got just the thing. Saw it the other day." He searched around the consoles until he found a dirty wooden peg, which he clipped onto his nose with a flourish. "Problem solved," he honked.

Babagoo returned the boy's grin. "Crafty goblin!"

He began to chuckle, and as Landfill's nasal giggles escalated, the scavenger pinched his nose and laughed too. The Den's animals stirred, watching with curiosity while boy and scavenger honked and spluttered.

"Okay, okay. That'll do." Babagoo wiped his eyes, took a deep breath and massaged his cheeks. "Deal with those scats 'n' squirts, boyling. We're both hungry and those gulls need getting."

Landfill nodded, whipped a plastic bag from the floor and went to the hallway. He lifted the stinkbucket and headed through the double door, on his way to the space behind the Nook where urine was drained. But when he stepped into daylight, something caught his eye. He peered closely into the bucket and frowned. There was no doubt about it: a cloud of red was blossoming in the yellow pool.

After watching it for some moments, Landfill put the bucket down carefully, re-entered the Nook and popped his head into the Den. He removed the peg from his nose. "Babagoo?"

The scavenger was chuckling to himself and donning his dross cape. "Yes, my lad?"

"There's blood in the stinkbucket. Looks fresh. I think it's from your squirts."

Babagoo's smile fell away. "Blood?"

"Too dark to see in the hallway. But it's there."

"Oh…" The colour was draining rapidly from Babagoo's face, as if the blood there had gone to the bucket too.

"Why's there blood?" asked Landfill. "Never seen that before."

Babagoo's arms fell limply to his side. He turned his head slowly and gazed abstractly at a windowpane. The boy saw his lips move, but could barely make out what he was saying: "…seasons…"

Landfill stepped into the room. "Seasons?"

"…getting shorter…"

"What do you mean?" Landfill's voice broke, and he was

startled by a sudden wetness in his eyes. "Babagoo… What do you mean?"

His anxious tone seemed to snap Babagoo from his daze. The scavenger blinked forcefully and adjusted his hat. "Nothing. It's nothing." He moved his features stiffly, attempting what Landfill assumed was supposed to be a smile.

"But the blood…"

"That's what I mean, my lad. It's nothing. Happens sometimes, when you're older."

"Oh." Landfill frowned and looked at his shorts. "So it'll happen to me when I'm older too?"

Babagoo's sham of a smile dissolved. Without warning, he swept across the Den and embraced the boy. He held him so tightly against his coat that Landfill found it difficult to speak.

"You…okay…Babagoo?"

"Hunkadory." The scavenger's voice hardened a little. He released his grip on the boy. "Now go strain those scats so I can get going."

"But the—"

"*Don't*…you worry. I said it's nothing. What's rule number three?"

"Babagoo's always right."

"Indeed he is." Babagoo pulled gradually away, took the peg and fastened it tenderly onto Landfill's nose. "So off you go."

Landfill had soon bagged up the stinkbucket's slops and given them to Babagoo, who added them to the traps and other bags hanging from his waist. Waving goodbye, the boy watched Babagoo climb into the hollowed metal cabinet and descend a little down its secret stairway. As soon as Babagoo closed the cabinet door behind him, Landfill sprinted to the wall to start the day's inspection.

He moved briskly along Hinterland's perimeter, and stopped when he reached the second set of train tracks, which started at the wall and disappeared into the Rippletop. He eyed the enormous warehouse, and spotted lizards basking on the slopes of its hot, glinting roof. After checking the sky and his surroundings, Landfill followed the tracks and entered between the huge warehouse doors.

The gloom was pierced in places by rods of light, which came down from holes in the corrugated roof. Surrounded by pallets and stacks of metal racks, Landfill continued along the tracks, passing carts and locomotives shrouded in dust. Bats dangled overhead in quiet clusters.

Landfill passed workbenches and lockers, and was soon following a corridor that became increasingly dark. After turning a corner, he reached out with a toe to touch something hard and smooth. Crouching down, he found a horizontal metal hoop and twisted it with both hands. A loud clunk resonated through the corridor, and Landfill grunted while heaving up the trapdoor to which the hoop was attached. After getting to his knees, he found some rungs and climbed through the hatch.

Descending the ladder felt like descending into blindness. Not a trace of light entered these depths. There was nothing for the eye to adjust to; just pure, uncompromising, all-consuming blackness.

Landfill finally felt the floor beneath his soles, left the ladder and searched his shorts for his lighter. He could hear sounds of scuttling, and the sudden flare of his lighter sent pale, translucent creatures scurrying into shadows. Landfill was quick enough to trap one beneath the ball of his foot. He crouched to grab it and raised it to the lighter. It was a plump white millipede, with transparent legs that writhed against his palm.

"Rule twenty-one," mumbled Landfill. "Never hurt Hinterland's animals."

Keeping hold of the millipede, he crept through the tight, musty space and found a low aperture in the far wall. He had to pocket his lighter to worm his way through the gap. When he was on the other side, the ignition of his flame caused a thin chittering to fill the stony chamber.

"It's okay, Longwhite," whispered Landfill. He squinted into the darkness at the end of the chamber, where the light failed to penetrate an intestinal mess of piping. "Just me."

The darkness chittered again.

"Yes. Got something. Wouldn't come empty-handed." Landfill held up the millipede that was curled around his wrist. "Um, Longwhite… When I told you about the rule against harming Hinterland's amnals, you said this doesn't…count. Since you'd catch them anyway. But… But what if some might have scarpered? This millipede might've given you the slip and escaped."

For the briefest moment, two ruby eyes caught the lighter's glare. Landfill nodded.

"Okay. They'd never slip your fangs." He raised the millipede to his face and – after mouthing a silent sorry – threw it at the tangled pipes. In the light of one flicker from his lighter, the millipede was suspended in the air; with the next it was gone.

Landfill had to look at his feet while quiet sounds of crunching came from the darkness. When the noises stopped he looked up, sniffed and wiped his nose. "Talking of rules, I've broken a few."

Those flashing red eyes.

"I don't know why." Landfill grimaced and scratched his head. "I saw something. It was Woolf. She had the swelling. I should've stayed away, but I was worried. You know how I like Woolf. But I saw… I saw wooflings come from inside her. From *inside* her body."

Darkness chattered.

"I know!" Landfill's eyes were wide in the trembling light. "Babagoo always said the small amnals come from Outside. Said the swelling's an illness. But now he's said it's not true. The smaller amnals come from inside bigger amnals! The swelling's *not* an illness. It's how smaller amnals fit in the big ones!"

The light rose as Landfill put both hands to his head. "I'd pondered before. Small amnals usually came in while bigger ones healed from the swelling. Like a pattern. It made me wonder…"

He lowered his hands and shook his head. "Longwhite… It was such a thing to see. And other amnals have been doing it too! But Babagoo didn't tell me. He's been lying about it. It makes you…think."

Something moved behind the pipes. Something pale and slinking.

"I asked him why. He said it was to protect me. From the Outsiders. But how's that right? How can knowing make danger?"

Landfill's eyes narrowed. "Rule eleven – stay away from amnals with the swelling. Babagoo said that rule's to keep me safe. Like the other rules. But it wasn't keeping me safe from the swelling. It was keeping me from…from something Babagoo doesn't want me to know.

"I couldn't stop thinking. About Babagoo and the rules. One rule kept bubbling in my head – rule twelve. Never rise above the wall. It wouldn't leave me be, and while Babagoo slumbered I climbed the conveyor. Was thinking of the birds, Longwhite – of how high they go. Of what it *feels* like up there. Always wanted to know. Wanted to see what they see. Never would have gone up before. But after what happened..."

A curt squeal.

"What'd I see? I don't know. Can't understand it. But Longwhite..." Landfill covered his mouth and forced a loud breath through his fingers. "I saw Outside. *I saw it.* Over the wall there's for ever. The stars don't stop. They go on and on and they're *everywhere*. There's light and there's dark. There's something so...*big* it swallows you up."

The boy started hopping gently from foot to foot.

"And that's not all! While I was up there, Hunger's Eye came! I looked right at it! Was like... Like a bird made of night, pulling a red star. And it came right for me! But look!" He gestured from his head to his toes with shaking hands. "I'm here! Nothing happened. Except Babagoo caught me out. Went into one of his fits. Said I only gave it the slip because it was dark. But he's said before that it sees just as well at night."

Two glints of crimson. A flash of fur.

Landfill breathed deeply at the cool, musky air, then sat cross-legged on the stone floor. "It gets the grey stuff mulling. About Babagoo. He always said the little amnals come from Outside; but when I gander something else he says they come from bigger amnals. He always said a look from Hunger's Eye would have me snatched by the Outsiders; but then he says it can miss you. So why not say these things from the start?"

He sucked in his top lip. "What else isn't he telling me, Longwhite? He keeps things from me. Like... Just this morning I saw blood in his squirts. He tried to tell me it was 'nothing to worry about–'" Landfill coarsened his voice in imitation of the scavenger – "but I could see it was. He looked all worrisome, and he was trying to hide it.

"There's another thing he won't tell me, too. Do you know about the thing around his neck? Never takes it off, and won't let me near it. When I ask about it he gets cranky. Insists it's a pendant. But I know it's a key."

The boy took his own key from his shorts and held it up. "Just like this one. Found it ages ago, in a locker in the Rippletop. Locks and unlocks the door. But what does Babagoo's key unlock?"

Landfill shook his fringe. "Rule four," he muttered. "Believe only Babagoo."

He grabbed some rubble and lobbed it through musty air. A shrill hiss filled the chamber.

"Sorry, Longwhite. But do you see what I mean? There's fibbery and secrets. Babagoo even *said* there's something he doesn't want me to know. And when I think about it...

there are secrets I have too. Like you. He doesn't know about you, Longwhite. You're the only amnal he hasn't named. He doesn't even know about this place. Haven't told him, because I like it here. I like having it…just for me. And I want to keep you to myself. Is that wrong?"

The pipes scuffled and rang.

"But it *feels* wrong." Landfill shrugged. "Babagoo always jabbers about trust. But…" He licked the top of his wrist and rubbed it against his cheek. "He says the hunger makes the Outsiders cheat each other. Says they're full of rot and lies. But me and Babagoo are keeping secrets from each other!"

Landfill sighed glumly. "Maybe we're like the Outsiders. Maybe the hunger's got into Hinterland and infected us. Maybe you don't know when you've got it. Babagoo says it's agony but…I'm not so sure about what he says." He groaned and rubbed his eyes.

Movement behind the pipes. The darkness chattered quietly.

Landfill rubbed his ear. "Course I want to know more. But how?"

It chattered again.

"A secret?"

Darkness replied, and Landfill listened.

TEN

THE SECRET

Every dawn during his daily inspection, Landfill thought of Longwhite's advice. He studied the wall not only for signs of tampering, but for the best place to begin work on a secret he wasn't sure he wanted: his own tunnel to Outside.

It didn't take long to find it: a small section of wall parallel to the Rippletop's side. It was tucked into a blind spot between two of the rickety, vine-choked cabins that skirted the warehouse's wall, and had slightly sparer foliage around its base. Whenever Landfill reached that stretch he'd stop, look the wall up and down and check how far left and right he could move before seeing around the surrounding cabins.

One day, after Babagoo had entered the cabinet for his afternoon trip to the Pit, Landfill took a detour before attending to his chores at the vegetable patch. He crossed the Gully and whipped through the Woods, and was soon loping through the Ivy Stack's entrance.

After a few moments, he popped his head back out, checked for Babagoo, and sprinted – with head bent low and shovel in hand – for the Rippletop. He hid the shovel behind some rusted, sloping shelves in one of the cabins, clapped the soot from his hands and raced to the vegetable patch.

During the next few days' inspections, Landfill paused by the cabins to retrieve the shovel and work on his secret. He'd soon cut through the nettles at the base of his chosen patch of wall, and carefully moulded a blanket of vegetation that could be propped on some chair legs from the cabin. His hands and wrists were red and itchy from the task – something he blamed on a tumble near some nettles when Babagoo asked – but it was a small price to pay for hiding his secret.

Each day, with foxes occasionally looking on, Landfill would prop up this dense, prickly blanket, then dig up a few shovelfuls of dirt before distributing them evenly around the cabins. Then he'd drop the blanket, arrange its foliage, restore the shovel and chair legs to their hiding place and continue on his journey around Hinterland's perimeter.

*   *   *

One morning, Landfill was working on his secret in heavy rain. The hole was getting fairly deep now – so deep that he had to dig on his knees – but the wall's foundations seemed to go on for ever. He dug for longer than usual, wondering whether the wall would ever actually end.

Suddenly, his nostrils twitched.

There was a new scent in the air. It was fainter than the must of freshly churned mud, and partially hidden behind the rain's fresh, metallic fragrance.

Landfill turned to two foxes who'd been watching him dig. "You smell it, foxlers?" He sniffed again. The scent was stronger now – a fetid, sour tang…

Landfill jolted when he realized Kafka was nearby. There was another scent too. Kafka wasn't alone.

Sensing his rising panic, the foxes exchanged glances and scarpered into their cabins. The scent intensified.

Landfill was scooping mud back into the hole when he heard Babagoo's voice from the south side of the Rippletop.

"Landfill! Where are you, my boy? Quick meat at the Pit today. Thought we could have an early breakfast and squeeze in some dominoes before chores."

Panting quickly, Landfill got the remaining dirt back into the hole as quickly as he could. He kicked the chair legs away so the blanket fell over them and covered his secret.

Babagoo was close now – he must have been walking

between the wall and the cabins. It was only a matter of seconds before Landfill would be in his sight.

Landfill looked in the direction of Babagoo's footsteps, then looked down to find the shovel still in his hands. When he clocked Babagoo's boot extending from the corner of a cabin he spun from the wall and tossed the shovel into the air. It landed with a loud thump on the cabin's roof, and slid down the felted slope before stopping with a clang against some guttering.

"There you are," grunted Babagoo. While Kafka's horizontal pupils were fixed on Landfill, Babagoo's eyes darted around. "Only at the cabins? Should be on the south side by now. And what was that noise? All that banging…" His lips tightened when his gaze settled on the boy. "And why's that look on your face? I know that look. What've you done?"

Landfill put his hands in his hair and looked at the ground.

"Spit it out, Landfill. What were you up to? What was that noise?"

Landfill raised his eyes to Babagoo. His expression wavered when he spotted something in his peripheral vision: the tip of the shovel protruding over the gutter's edge. Landfill caught himself before looking at it outright, and bowed his head again.

Babagoo moved towards him. "So this is how you regain

my trust, is it? By getting up to no good?" He swivelled his head in search of clues, causing the ears on his hat to flap up and down.

When Babagoo started to search above face-level, Landfill shouted: "I was kicking the cabin, okay? Seeing if I could break it."

Babagoo stared at him, his mouth agape and trembling. He glanced back towards Kafka, who was watching the scene with his usual dull expression. Babagoo clenched his fists and turned back to the boy. "I beg your pardon? I hope I misheard, Landfill. It sounded like you said you were kicking the cabin and trying to break things."

Landfill sniffed in the rain. His pout began to loosen. "Sorry, Babagoo. I'm really sorry."

"Rule fifteen…"

"I *know*, Babagoo. I know."

"Number fifteen. What is it?"

"Look after Hinterland as it looks after us."

"That's right. And is that what you were doing there, lad, when you were kicking cabins and doing who knows what damage? That's you looking after Hinterland, is it?"

Landfill clasped his hands together and gave his most repentant look. "I'm really sorry, Babagoo. Don't know why I did it. Wasn't thinking. It—"

"No!" snapped Babagoo. "You never *do* seem to think these days, do you!" How can you be so stupid, Landfill?

How can you be so disrespectful? And I don't mean just to me. I mean to Hinterland! This place is the only thing that separates us from Outside. It's practically…sacred! Do you know how hard I work to maintain this place? Do you have any idea how hard it is to fight the rot and the rust and the weeds? And what are you doing? You're trying to…to smash the place up!"

"Baba—"

"Shut up. Shut that puny, ungrateful jabberhole. I don't want to hear your ugly little voice. In fact, I don't want to even look at you. Go to the Den and think about what you've done. I'll finish checking the wall. At least someone around here gives a scat."

Landfill sagged, nodded and turned away. As soon as he'd gained enough distance from the scavenger and goat, he allowed a sigh of relief to pass his lips.

After that, Landfill made sure his digging stints were brief. One morning, while digging so deep that he had to stand inside the hole, Landfill was surprised by one of the foxes, who came in close to sniff at the cavity's edge.

"What is it, Rushdie? You smell something?" The fox was joined by another. "You too? What is it?"

Landfill crouched to inspect the hole, but nothing looked any different. It was the same old hole, with the same hard, vertical edge of the wall's foundation at its far side.

Landfill nudged the foxes away, checked about him and crouched within the hollow. He poked and rummaged with his shovel and, after digging up more dirt, noticed that something felt different. When he jabbed beneath the bottom of the lowest brick, the shovel met very little resistance. He jabbed again and scraped mud away with the shovel's tip, and froze when he comprehended that the hole was moving horizontally. It was creeping towards Outside.

The shovel dropped from the boy's hand, and the foxes watched him climb quickly out from the hole. Once out, he got to his feet and backed slowly away, with his eyes fixed all the while on the opening. He barely seemed to breathe, and his face was unusually pale.

After licking his wrist and wiping it through his hair, Landfill blinked and moved abruptly back to the hole. There was something mechanical in the way he pushed mud back in, in the way he tidied the foliage and returned the shovel and chair legs to the cabin. When he was finished he threw a look at the foxes, then sprinted to the Gully to wash the dirt away before resuming his inspection of the perimeter wall.

ELEVEN

TRACKS TO NOWHERE

Several days later, Landfill was teasing cats in the Den while waiting for Babagoo to return from the Spit Pit. The boy no longer worked on his secret. Every time he passed the cabins during inspections, he'd slow to stare at the foliage covering the hole, but that was all. Sometimes the foxes left their cabins to look expectantly at him with bright, amber eyes. But Landfill always shook his head and moved on.

When Babagoo arrived at the Den with his bags, they exchanged silent greetings, and Landfill noticed the key glinting between the folds of Babagoo's overcoat.

Shortly after that, while preparing gulls in the bathtub, he stopped gutting dinner and stared at the blood crusting beneath his fingernails. "Babagoo?" He didn't turn to address him.

"Hmm?" Babagoo's voice came from the stove.

"Your pendant's out."

The scavenger grunted, and Landfill heard a quiet rustle as he put the key away.

Landfill tossed some gore to the cats and sliced into another gull. He cleared his throat before speaking again. "You use it in the Spit Pit?"

"Eh?"

"The…pendant. Sometimes it's out when you leave the cabinet. Is it something you use at the Pit?"

Landfill turned his head, just a little. He could just make out Babagoo frowning and exploring his nostril with a blackened fingernail.

"We've talked about the pendant, boy. It's not used for anything."

Blood flashed on Landfill's forearms while he hacked at the bird. "Nothing at all? It's got little prongs. Look like they do something."

"No no no." Babagoo shook his head. "The only purpose that pendant serves is…" He looked at the ceiling and scratched his beard with spidery fingers. "Making me look pretty." Putting his bandaged hands to his cheeks, he smiled coyly and fluttered his eyelashes at Kafka, who responded by bleating and breaking wind. Babagoo hooted, and his laughter became a fit of coughing that didn't seem to stop.

Landfill didn't turn around. He didn't leave the bathtub

to check on Babagoo or thump his back. He narrowed his eyes, cut a bloody necklace around a gull's neck and pulled off its head.

The next morning, Landfill returned to toiling over his secret. He continued to keep his bouts in the hole brief – just a few shovels of dirt before hiding his work and washing in the Gully. But with time he found himself digging upwards, with the wall's buried bricks behind his shoulders.

There finally came a day when a knock of the shovel brought down not only dirt, but also a thin beam of light. Landfill inhaled sharply. Holding his breath, he used the shovel to probe the darkness above his head. After making the beam of light a little wider, he tilted his ear in its direction. No sounds came from above.

He started jabbing gently. Mud continued to fall, and the tunnel became illuminated by a green glow. Dirt was tumbling down to reveal a ceiling of barbed vegetation even denser than that lining the inner wall. After clearing enough mud, Landfill took his glass knife from his shorts and cut cautiously at stalks and creepers. Then he reversed back into the tunnel to pull the chair legs from the inner foliage.

Landfill crouched down, shuffled forward again and looked up at the newly exposed greenery. He had to take a long, deep breath before he could straighten himself and use the shovel's handle to push the foliage up, just a little. Then, clutching the tunnel's lip with his free hand, he stretched on the tips of his toes and gradually raised his eyes above ground level. He blinked in the dawn's golden light, and his mouth hung open as Outside flooded his senses.

There was no need to duck or run. There were no Outsiders. There was only a rippling, rolling vastness of purples, greens, greys and browns – of heather and grass, rocks and shrubbery. The vastness rolled on and on, spilling outwards without walls or borders or anything at all to hold it back. Landfill's eyes watered at the sight of tall slopes on the horizon – an end of things more distant than he'd imagined was possible.

While gaping at the slopes, Landfill was startled by a shrill cry from above. He stretched and leaned as far as he could, and saw a kestrel soaring away from Hinterland, its wings and feathers dark against a backdrop of pink and orange clouds.

"Winterson…" he whispered.

The sight seemed to rouse him. He cut through more stalks and used the chair legs to prop up the foliage around the hole. After digging his toes into the tunnel's wall, he pulled himself up, just enough to ease his head from under the nettles and check to the left and right. In both directions he saw the wall stretching away, its darkness glassless and cold against this bewildering, vivid and impossible endlessness.

When Landfill strained his ears, he heard only moaning wind and the rustle of heather. The air smelled strangely alien to him. There was none of the rusty mustiness he was used to; just a smell he could only think of as blue-grey, dappled with scents that brought Hinterland's moss and flowers to mind. And something else. A trace of something similar to...to the tang of treasures from the Pit.

Seeing no sign of Outsiders, Landfill clambered out from beneath the vegetation.

He tried to stand up, but swayed when vastness engulfed him from all directions but behind. In all of his life, Landfill had never experienced such boundless immensities of space. He was struck by a rush of horizontal vertigo; the ground tilted beneath his feet, and he crouched quickly to clutch at grass and bracken.

After some moments the ground stabilized, but the boy could barely stand without making it slant and spin. An unseen force – a queasy collision of giddiness and fear – pulled him groundwards and held him close to Hinterland's wall.

Landfill kept his eyes to the ground, and clung to handfuls of grass to drag himself along the perimeter. Sometimes the wind would ruffle his hair and he'd peek up and away from the wall; but the purples and greens undulated as if they were alive, and caught him in their swaying so that he stumbled.

It took some time to reach the crook where the wall's east and north sides met. Landfill slowed down before peeking gingerly around the corner, and shrank back when he saw the ground stop abruptly in the distance, just beyond Hinterland's west face. Beyond the brink there was only sky.

Landfill crouched and took some deep breaths. He caught a whiff of that tang again, and realized that Babagoo may soon return from his morning trip to the Pit. Upon retreating, he told himself that it was this and not cowardice that was sending him back the way he'd come.

He continued to back away, until an airborne cry stopped him in his tracks. He looked up and saw the kestrel, Winterson, wheeling in the sky, and followed her arc with his gaze until she disappeared around the wall's corner. Landfill crept forward, and his nostrils flared when he peered around the corner and again saw ground give way to sky.

Something orange moved. The boy stiffened, then exhaled with relief when he recognized the squirrel in the heather. "Joyce? You're...*alive*."

Still clutching grass between his fingers, Landfill edged around the corner and followed the wall on all fours.

He stopped when he reached some train tracks, and stared at the base of the wall from which they came, visualizing how the rails led to the Rippletop on the wall's other side. He looked further along the perimeter and saw the other pair of tracks, which passed through the wall and led to Muttbrough.

Some chattering from Joyce made him turn around. The squirrel was sitting on the tracks. Landfill stretched out a hand. "Come on, Joyce. Come here. Can't do this alone."

Joyce didn't respond.

Landfill smiled. "Come on. Need you with me."

The squirrel sniffed the air and hopped backwards. Landfill's mouth dropped, but its edges began to curl. He clucked his tongue and chuckled. "Still playing chase, little twitcher? Think you have the upper paw, eh?"

Joyce hopped back again. Landfill looked over his shoulder at the wall, and checked to the left and right before fixing his gaze on the squirrel. "Okay. Here I come. Ready…or not…"

He reached out and grasped the nearest rail with both hands. The smile on his lips faltered as – with all toes and fingers on the rail's rusting surface – he heaved himself away from the wall in Joyce's direction. After three more heaves, the grim smile returned to his face and he began to gather momentum. He glanced up now and then, and saw the squirrel watching him. He could see that the tracks ended just beyond Joyce – that they faded into purple and green, apparently without destination.

Landfill drew closer and closer. He was just one heave away from Joyce when the squirrel sprinted forward and scuttled over his head. Landfill spun and fell onto the rotten sleepers that carried the rails. With eyes agape, he watched Joyce scarper along the tracks and shoot up Hinterland's wall, which was now so far away that Landfill winced with the pain of his knotting stomach. "No! Joyce!"

The wind picked up. That blue-grey scent overcame Landfill, and he felt distance crashing into him from every side.

"Joyce! Don't leave me here! Don't leave me!" He threw both hands over his mouth when the squirrel disappeared behind the wall, and the wind against his exposed back and ribs felt cruel enough to bruise. It changed direction, and a gust racing along the north wall carried what sounded like faint screams.

Landfill was suddenly adrift in this merciless rolling of greens, purples, pinks and oranges. He could feel the edge of Outside – with its sudden brink and infinite sky – pulling him away from the wall, sucking with its endless emptiness. The ground began to tilt downwards from his feet. When he saw Hinterland receding down the slope he gritted his teeth, grabbed the rail and pulled himself back along the tracks. His pace quickened when he caught sight of something in the undergrowth: the leathery corpse of a dog, glistening with flies.

Landfill whimpered and carried on. He soon reached the wall, and moaned like a wounded animal while he clawed his way around the corner and finally back to his hole.

TWELVE

A CRACK

Landfill studied the pale cockroach clasped in his hand. Its pearly legs twitched and kicked, and when Landfill held his lighter close, he saw innards throbbing beneath a translucent shell.

"Don't be scared," he whispered. "It'll be quick." He stroked the cockroach's belly with a fingertip, closed his eyes and tossed it at the tangled pipes. Darkness devoured the boy's offering, and chittered gleefully when it was done.

Landfill took a seat on the cold stone ground. "I did it, Longwhite. Yesterday. I saw Outside. I *went* Outside."

Pipes chattered and chimed.

"Almost didn't. When I reached the bottom of the wall I got scared. Wasn't sure how much I wanted to see Outside. Thought what Babagoo's told me about it would do. But he carried on with his fibbery. I asked again about the pendant and he kept on with his secret. So I kept on with mine."

Landfill's sigh sent dust swaying through the chamber. "Longwhite… You ever been Outside?" He shook his head. "The way it is out there… The *space*. There's so much of it. Enough distance to make you…fade. You don't feel there, when you leave the wall. You're like smoke from the stove. Can't know what's where or where's what."

Landfill fell silent. He gnawed his fingernails before carrying on. "I saw something beyond the wall's west side. It's like Outside stops. Turns into sky – into clouds at your feet. Clouds you could fall into and never come back. There's a pull out there, Longwhite. Or a push – I don't know. Whatever it is, it's stronger than falling from up high. Sucks the breath from your mouth. Makes your heart stop."

Landfill heard the brush of coarse fur against metal. He smiled and held out a hand when Longwhite slipped from the pipes.

"It lilies your liver out there," he continued. "But scary as it was…"

With long back arching, Longwhite darted across the ground and sniffed the boy's fingers. Landfill giggled at the twitch of a tiny, pointed snout against his knuckles.

"Scary as it was," he repeated, "there was also…beauty. So much beauty it gooses your bumps. And too much space for anything to stop it. Too much space even for…for rules. And all of it was colour. Like the butterbyes.

"That's something Babagoo's never said about Outside. He jabbers about the hunger and madness. He jabbers about fear and hatred, about monsters, masks and puppets. About all the rot and pain. Maybe I heard some of that, on the wind… But he's never mentioned beauty."

Longwhite squeaked, mounted an ankle and curled up in the niche between the boy's crossed legs.

Landfill nodded. "Been mulling about that. Much as it feels like I saw *everything* out there, there must be more! I didn't see the Spit Pit. Don't think I did, at least. Didn't see gulls or treasures."

He gnawed again at a fingernail, lost in his thoughts. "When Babagoo goes through the cabinet, he heads past the wall's west side. He'd be heading for where the ground becomes sky. There must be more after that edge. The Spit Pit must hide behind it, but out of sight with the distance. Just like the Gully – the way you can't see into it from the Nook."

Another squeak.

Landfill stroked Longwhite's slender body, felt a bony warmth beneath that pale, coarse fur. "My secret's still there. Did my best to hide it on both sides of the wall. Some of me wants to go out again. To see more. Maybe I can find out what Babagoo doesn't want me to know.

"But it's a sticky pickle. Staying out too long could get me caught out. Babagoo might even gander me while he's Outside."

Landfill winced and shuddered. "I heard screams, too. There was a dead woofler, covered in flies. The Outsiders must've got it. Maybe they were closer than I knew. Rule six – no sign can be a sure sign." He frowned and bit his lip. "And you're so bare out there. So…alone."

He felt the tingle of whiskers against his belly.

A shake of the head. "I'd *have* to go alone. Can't put any amnals at risk. And I can't get Babagoo involved, can I."

Longwhite chittered and hissed.

"Babagoo won't take me to the Pit. I've asked so many times, but it's always the same. He says I'm not ready. Says it's too dangerous."

Longwhite squeaked. His red eyes glittered in the light from Landfill's flame.

"Find a crack in Babagoo?" The boy tilted his head. "You mean…like a way to change his mind?"

Longwhite uncurled his long, lithe body before slinking back into the pipes.

Landfill sat in silence and pondered.

Later that day, Landfill and Babagoo were spending lull-time in the Gully. Landfill splashed through the shallow water, which was losing its depth to the summer heat. He scattered rainbows while kicking spray into sunlight, and Babagoo trod carefully behind him with his trousers rolled up.

"Babagoo! Watch this." Landfill showed Babagoo a smooth chip of rubble he'd found among foxgloves on the bank. He surveyed the long course of water that led to the knotted, suspended pipes of the Hard Guts at the Gully's end. After tilting his head he whipped his arm.

Babagoo watched the sparkling chip skim the water. It bounced several times, then sank next to some ducts that hung like huge taps over the concrete bank.

He raised an eyebrow. "Not bad, my lad. Not bad at all. But sit back and learn. I'll show you how it's done."

Landfill smirked and headed for a patch of burdock by the edge of the water to pluck and nibble some leaves.

Babagoo searched the sticks and rubble on the bank. "Aha!" He held a rusty washer out to the boy and wriggled his bushy eyebrows. "This'll do nicely, if I say so myself. Very nicely indeed."

The scavenger smiled smugly and turned to face the Hard Guts. Rubbing his hands together, he tilted his head and judged the water. He rubbed the washer between thumb and finger, and winked at Landfill before carefully assuming the correct stance. Then he crouched a little, closed one eye and narrowed the other. Slowly, his arm pulled back. Babagoo muttered silently to himself, apparently calculating under his breath. He nodded gently, then flicked his hand and released the washer.

His throwing arm remained stretched out, and he held his pose as the washer flew in a skewed line above the Gully, bounced off the concrete slope, rose with a chime into the air and plopped gracelessly into the water.

Hinterland was filled with boyish laughter. Landfill clutched his belly and shrieked with joy. Babagoo remained in his throwing position, but gradually swivelled his head to show the boy an exaggerated scowl. The scowl didn't last, and the scavenger was soon hooting too.

When the laughter finally died down, Babagoo grinned at the sun and fingered his beard. "Made a woofler's turdhole of that, didn't I, boyling?"

Landfill's smile was crammed with goofiness. "A woofler's turdhole is prettier. Look!" He pointed up at the Gully's ledge, where Kafka was munching honeysuckles and looking blankly on. "Even Kafka's shamed to know you." He held his skinny belly and howled again.

Babagoo wagged a finger at the gnarly goat. "Be kind, old bleater. There's hair clippings from the Spit Pit in my bag. Your favourite. Think about your loyalties if you want them with your dinner."

Kafka bleated and tore up another mouthful of flowers.

Babagoo nodded, and slapped his hands together.

"Right. Another go. That was just a warm-up. A demonstration of how *not* to do it."

"I'm sure, Babagoo, I'm sure." Landfill took a seat on the bank and watched Babagoo rummage through shrubs and scrap metal. Slowly, his smile disappeared. "Um. Babagoo?"

"Yes, my boy?"

Landfill licked his lips. "Talking of the Spit Pit…"

"Mm-hm."

"Can I go there with you soon?"

Babagoo kept his back to the boy. "You know the answer to that. No point in asking."

"I know, I know. But I've been mulling."

"A dangerous pastime, Landfill. Maybe we need a rule for that." Babagoo picked up and inspected a small stone. "Go on, then. What've you been mulling about?"

Landfill was watching a frog that was half-submerged at the edge of the water. He held his palm out and croaked quietly: "Come along, gribbit. Hop on." The frog croaked and hopped towards him.

"What were you mulling about?" repeated Babagoo.

"You always say you live for me."

"Yes."

"And I'm the only thing left to live for."

"Yes." The scavenger was getting into position again, eyeing up the water.

The frog was on Landfill's palm now. He stroked its

back, felt the cool slime against his fingertips. "Who'll go to the Pit for gull and scavenging when you're not alive?"

There was a quiet plop. The stone had fallen from Babagoo's hand. He turned to face the boy. "Where'd that come from?"

Landfill shrugged. "When I saw blood in your squirts, you said something about...about the seasons getting shorter. Didn't know what you meant. But then I remembered you once said you're in autumn and I'm in spring. So I started mulling about what happens when you reach winter."

The boy swallowed sorely, his throat suddenly dry and swollen. "Started pondering how to get gull and grubbins after that."

Babagoo stood in the water for some moments. Water dripped from the ends of his rolled-up corduroys. Only his eyebrows moved.

Eventually he sniffed and screwed up his face. "Don't you worry about that, Landfill. I'll think of something."

Landfill nodded earnestly. "I know. You always do."

They both fell silent, until a faraway rumble had them looking up as one. Babagoo's face paled. "Hunger's Eye."

Landfill nodded and eased the frog to the ground. Then they dashed together through the water, up the Gully's far side and under cover of the Woods.

THIRTEEN

A STUBBORN MIRACLE

Three days later, Landfill finished the animals' morning feed and returned to the Nook with Orwell in his arms. When he pushed through the hallway's metal door, he found Babagoo grinning in the Den.

The scavenger was sat on the three-legged stool by his workbench, with all his brown teeth – and all the blackness between – on show. He nodded towards the young husky.

"Orwell joining us for lunch?"

"Had his fill. The wooflers went to the Gully after their meat but Orwell can't swim. Felt sorry for him, all alone." Eyeing Babagoo closely, Landfill buried his nose in the fluff between Orwell's ears. "What's that look for?"

The scavenger's lips rippled around a rotten grin. His eyebrows danced while he crossed his arms and leaned back on the stool. "Been busy."

"You're always busy."

"The devil makes work. But I've been working on something special. Something for you."

Landfill looked towards Kafka, but the goat was absorbed in chewing some rope and didn't return his gaze.

The boy licked his lips. "What is it?"

Babagoo just grinned.

"What is it? Tell me, Babagoo." Landfill was starting to hop on the spot, ever so slightly. Orwell panted happily, with his head bobbing up and down.

Babagoo cackled. "The joy of a boy."

"What's that grin for? Never seen a sillier smirk."

Babagoo's smile widened and he tapped his teeth with a black fingernail. "There's always a grin beneath the skin, my lad."

"Tell me! Please-please-pleeeease…"

Babagoo hooted and leaned back again. "Okay, my boy. Okay. Just step back and give me some room. And take some deep breaths. If you're not careful you'll explode and line our Den with guts."

Landfill backed away and watched with bright, blue eyes as Babagoo moved the stool aside, crawled beneath the workbench and came out again with a large bin bag in his arms. He got up and grunted. "Close your eyes."

"But—"

"Close those peepers. Or you'll get nothing."

Landfill scrunched his eyes shut. He strained his ears at sounds of rustling plastic and clunking cans.

Babagoo's voice was a raspy whisper. "Right. You can open them."

Landfill opened his eyes and saw what Babagoo was holding. It was a large rectangular patchwork of soiled cloth and plastic, covered on one side by a grimy tapestry of cans, packaging, bones and filth.

Landfill had to blink several times. "Is that…?"

"Yes. Your very own dross cape. You're old enough now, Landfill. I'd say it's time." Babagoo chuckled. "Come on. Let's see how it fits."

Landfill seemed in a daze when Babagoo took Orwell from his arms and eased the pup onto the workbench. The scavenger moved behind the boy, draped the cape over his shoulders and tied the string around his neck. After lifting its hood, he walked back around Landfill and looked him up and down. "Suits you."

Landfill stared at Babagoo with wide eyes, and Babagoo studied his face. He shook his head. "Just look at you. You're becoming a man now, Landfill. Once upon a time you were less than a boyling – a bungling little amnal, waddling around the rubble and wrestling with wooflings. But now you're nearly a man."

Landfill's brow creased. He thought he could see water at the rims of Babagoo's eyes. "Are you—" His words were cut short when Babagoo lurched forward and took him in his arms.

"You've come so far," croaked the scavenger. "Such a miracle. Such a stubborn, wilful, *obstinate* little miracle! It's my blessing that they threw you away, Landfill. Their loss and my dearest gain."

Landfill winced at the jab of Babagoo's chin into his shoulder. He wriggled in his grip and dropped the hood of his cape. "Does this mean…I can go with you to the Spit Pit?"

Babagoo was silent. After wiping his face on Landfill's shoulder, he stepped back. His expression became stern. "It does. Time you learned to forage and trap. And besides, going to the Pit might do you some good. You're obviously getting restless. Any idiot can see that. You're getting itchy feet. So let's go Outside. Maybe it'll help you appreciate how precious this place –" he circled the air with his finger – "is. I'm not sure Hinterland's been getting the respect it deserves of late. I seem to recall a young brute kicking some cabins, just to see if he could break them."

Landfill nodded eagerly. "Can we go today? Can we go now?"

The scavenger shook his head and his finger rose again. "Don't be overkeen, my lad. This is a serious thing, and it can't be rushed. There's mischief and danger out there. More than you'll ever appreciate. We'll go tomorrow. Today

we need to go over some new rules. The Spit Pit has a set of
its own, and breaking any of them could see you snatched
up and wrung out by Outsiders. You hear me, boy?"

Landfill nodded.

"Say it."

"I hear you."

"Good. We'll go over the rules at lull-time, then again
at dinner, and once more after evening chores. You got
that?"

"Yes."

"Also good." He slapped his hands together. "Right!
My belly's squirming. I believe it's time for lunch. Get the
vejbles and what's left of the meat together. I need to visit
the stinkbucket."

Landfill headed for the consoles after Babagoo left the
room, but paused when he passed Kafka. He grinned at the
gnarly old goat and flapped his cape. "Hunkadory, eh?"
The boy's eyes sparkled, and he glanced at the metal door
before winking at the goats. "Hey, who's this?" He threw
the cape's hood over his head, stooped a little and hobbled
about, all the while gibbering under his breath and fobbing
the odd gob of spit to the floor. "*Afternoon, bleaters,*" he
grumbled. "*How're my venerable lovelies today, eh?*"

The goats stared blankly on. Landfill jiggled his
eyebrows at them, but jumped and spun when the door
slammed behind him.

Babagoo looked him up and down. His brow furrowed, but lost its creases as a smirk crept onto his face. "Being Babagoo, are you? Well, two can play, young stinkpellet. If you're me, I'll have to be you. Which means this little scamp here is mine-all-mine."

He dropped to all fours and – with his rump raised and wriggling – shuffled across the floor before hopping up to pluck Orwell from the workbench. He cradled the pup against his shoulder, and grinned at Landfill when the husky licked his hands.

Landfill scoffed. "Best leave being me to me."

"Good, because you're doing a dismal job of being me. Nowhere *near* dashing enough."

"Dashing? You're slower than the tuttles!"

Babagoo guffawed. "Different sort of dashing, young goblin!" He ruffled the top of Orwell's head, and beamed when the pup reached up to paw his beard. "And gander this! The woofling does a better impression of you than you do. Look! When I ruffle his hair he strokes my beard. Just like a little Landfill I used to know." He chuckled at Orwell's yapping and panting, and continued to ruffle the fur between the husky's pert, furry ears.

Landfill rolled his eyes.

The scavenger cackled. "Jealousy doesn't suit you, my lad."

"Going to the stinkbucket. When I get back, I think we should all be ourselves again."

"Can't get as good as you give, eh?"

Landfill passed the chortling scavenger and entered the hallway. After closing the door behind him, he sniggered quietly and touched the shoulders of his dross cape, as if to make sure it was real. Then he inhaled deeply, crouched on cracked tiles, took the lighter from his pocket and sparked its flame. When he held it to the bucket, his smile became a grimace.

There it was again: the red blossom in the yellow pool.

FOURTEEN

THE BURROW

The sky was honey-yellow with dawn, and giving off a warmth that had Landfill itching beneath his cape. He was standing with Babagoo by the junk stacked against the perimeter wall. A bag of stinkbucket slops hung from the rope tied at his waist, along with some bin bags yet to be filled.

With one squinting eye, Babagoo looked Landfill up and down.

"This is usually wall inspection time. You can start your check later while you give the amnals their morning feed. Finishing the job will cut into your lull-time. We'll need to think about the routine if you're coming with me regularly."

Landfill nodded. His eyes flitted towards the metal cabinet sat upon rolls of rotting carpet.

Babagoo's mouth twitched. "Don't be impatient, boy.

Impatience is folly out there." He checked the rope and bags hanging from his own waist, then raised an eyebrow at the boy. "Okay. Let's see what the Pit has to offer."

Landfill followed Babagoo up some carpet rolls, and watched him stoop at the slanting cabinet to pull its door open.

"Into the Burrow we go." Without looking back, he raised a hand and beckoned with a grotty finger.

Landfill reached the cabinet and watched Babagoo descend into darkness. He turned suddenly and took in Hinterland, as if for the last time. Some cats and dogs lounged at the Gully's edge. Crows cawed from the Black Fingers' tips. Blue poppies nodded in a warm, perfumed breeze.

"You coming or not?"

Landfill jolted, and slipped through the cabinet's doorway.

He'd started to descend some brick steps when another gruff bark stopped him: "And close the door behind you!"

After doing so, Landfill followed the steps until he felt a cool, clay-like floor beneath his soles.

"Babagoo?" He squinted into the gloom, unable to make out more than ghostly outlines. He heard a cough up ahead, which was followed by the rasp of a lighter's wheel.

The darkness was lost to shivering amber light, which

revealed a dank, muddy hovel with a ceiling propped by planks and old pipes. Landfill gaped at the pale, hairy roots hanging just above his head. When Babagoo turned to face him the light raced along the walls, illuminating cardboard boxes stacked against the wall up ahead, and what appeared to be a pile of crusty, gore-stained blankets to Landfill's left.

Landfill stared at the blankets. "Babagoo? The swelling… Is that where the amnals—"

"No time now, Landfill. Can't afford to dawdledally." Babagoo moved towards a short ladder propped directly opposite the stairs they'd descended.

As the scavenger mounted the ladder, his flame bathed the boxes to his left in fiery light. Landfill spotted something familiar next to them: something long, metallic and rectangular – not unlike the lockers in the Rippletop, but alone and on its back in the dirt.

He frowned at the locker and stroked the contours of the key in his pocket, but was distracted by a grunt from Babagoo. "Come along, boy." The scavenger was scuffling beneath a round, black cavity in the wall. The flickering light dimmed when he clambered into its mouth.

Landfill climbed the wooden rungs, felt around the cavity's edge and peered inside. It was the opening of a narrow tunnel that sloped downwards from the Burrow. He could see Babagoo on his hands and knees ahead, his flame illuminating the ribs of twisted metal that buttressed the tunnel's sides.

"You in yet, lad?"

Landfill clambered into the tunnel. "Yes."

"Good. I'm going to turn the lighter off. Got to save fuel. It'll be dark, Landfill. Darker than having no eyes. But there's only one way to go, so you can't get lost. Just keep heading down. Keep your breaths slow and steady, you hear?"

"I hear."

The darkness was as instant as it was complete. Everything disappeared, and there was only the smell of damp earth and slops, the rustle of bags, a sucking moistness against palms and knees.

Landfill had no idea how long he'd been crawling before Babagoo spoke.

"All okay back there?"

"Yes."

"Fit for some revision, then. Let's make sure those Pit rules haven't slipped that little skull of yours. Rule twenty-three. What is it?"

"Never remove your dross cape."

"That's right. Wear it as if it's your skin. Twenty-four?"

"Stay low."

"Correct. A variant of rule twelve. Don't go any higher than you have to. The higher you go, the more chance you

have of being spotted by Outsiders. Which reminds me…
rule twenty-eight. Tell me."

Landfill scrunched his eyes and concentrated. "If…if
seen by an Outsider, move away from Hinterland and hide
until it's safe to return."

"Why?"

"To lead them away from Hinterland."

"That's right. Heading for Hinterland would draw gazes
in its direction. Want our blind spot to remain a blind spot,
don't we, boy? And what do you do if you're captured by an
Outsider? Which rule number?"

"Twenty-nine. If you're captured by an Outsider, cut its
throat, cover it in rubbish and return to Hinterland as
quickly and carefully as you can."

"Mm-hm. And you think you can do it?"

"Which bit?"

"Slit an Outsider's throat."

"Of course."

"It may not be as easy as you think. Remember, they're
monsters and they're rotting inside, but they have masks.
They don't look very different to you and me. Don't let
that slow you down. A moment's hesitation could snatch
away your blade and have you torn to shreds – if you're
lucky. If you're unlucky, they'll have their way before
putting their mouths to your eyes and sucking you up
through your sockets."

Landfill swallowed drily in the darkness.

"But it's okay," muttered the scavenger. "Shouldn't come to that. Stick to the other rules and you'll be safe. They're there to stop you needing rule twenty-nine. Understand?"

"Yes."

"Good."

The tunnel seemed to level off. Landfill felt the weight shift from his shoulders and wrists, and no longer had to pull back against the slope. After some time, he spoke again. "Babagoo?"

"Mm."

"Are there always Outsiders at the Pit?"

"Usually. More in the daytime, though. Most go away at night."

"Oh." Landfill sniffed. "Why not forage at night, when there's less around?"

"Too dark at night for foraging, my boy. We'd need to use light, and that'd stick out like the biggest, sorest thumb you've ever seen. Might as well douse ourselves in fuel, set ourselves alight and wave our arms at them." He snickered quietly.

"Oh."

"Much easier to blend in with the rubbish in the day. Darkness can be as much foe as friend. The shadows are mischievous in the Pit, lad. And they hide all the better at night. Ruthless, relentless, sticky things."

The scavenger's shuffling noises stopped. Landfill stopped too. "What is it?" he whispered.

"Tunnel's end."

A thin, right-angled white line appeared just ahead, and broadened into a rectangular glare. Faint shrieking noises entered the tunnel, and Landfill shuffled backwards, remembering the sounds he'd heard when Joyce abandoned him outside the wall.

Shielding his eyes, he saw the scavenger's silhouette crawling into the light.

"Move along, Landfill. Don't have all day."

Landfill could just make out Babagoo sitting on the ground by the tunnel's exit. Still squinting, he dragged himself out and crouched with his palms on the scavenger's shoulders. His head darted to and fro while his eyes adjusted to the light. He gradually took in the crooked band of sky above his head, bordered by leaves and the occasional tips of mattresses, wardrobes and slabs of plasterboard. It soon became clear that the tunnel led to a small, uneven glade of trees and precariously stacked flotsam.

Babagoo patted the boy's hand and pulled gently away. Landfill heard something creak behind him, and spun around to catch the scavenger slamming an off-white, aluminium door mottled by mould. The door seemed to protrude from a large mound of rubbish, with rusting bicycles, car tyres, planks and even a blackened sofa at its top.

Landfill nodded towards the jutting doorway. "The tunnel's mouth… Some sort of locker?"

Babagoo shook his head. "Used to be a fridge. I hollowed it out like I did the cabinet. To hide the tunnel."

"What's a fridge?"

"Winter in a box."

"Really?"

Babagoo smirked. "Really. And there's a rule for that too – *always* close the fridge door behind you. Same goes for the cabinet at the other end. That's rule thirty. Got it?"

"Got it."

"Then let's keep moving."

As Landfill followed the scavenger, he peeped between tree trunks at the mattresses, fridges and furniture piled on rocks and thickets.

"By the way," began Babagoo. "If you ever hear Hunger's Eye coming while you're here, run to the fridge or to that tunnel." He gestured towards some bushes to which the glade led, and Landfill spotted an opening at their base.

Landfill nodded. "What's that noise?"

"What noise?"

"Sounds like…screams. Screams and cries. Like injured amnals."

Babagoo lifted an earflap to listen. "That'll be the gulls. You won't notice their racket with time. Handy at the Pit, though. Covers our noises."

When they reached the bushes, Babagoo got to his knees and squeezed through the gap. Landfill dropped down, followed him through the opening and began to move along a dark, thorny crawlway.

The rustling of twigs stopped just ahead. Babagoo's voice became a hoarse whisper: "We're here."

Landfill leaned to look past Babagoo's rear. The crawlway's exit was blocked by some chain-link fencing. Beyond the fencing he saw only rubbish, piled in dunes so huge they blotted the sky and knotted his stomach.

The scavenger was feeling along the fence's base. He found what he was looking for and rolled up the wire, so that not even chain-link separated Landfill from the vastness ahead.

Babagoo threw up his dross cape's hood. "Look alive, my lad, and cover your head. We're going into the Pit."

FIFTEEN

THE SPIT PIT

They were soon trekking through a ravine that wound its way between bluffs of reeking waste. The stench had Landfill breathing through his mouth, but was so strong he could taste it. It was like the scent in Babagoo's overcoat, which usually brought comfort, but at this intensity it made him gag. He held Babagoo's hand, kept his gaze low and treaded carefully. Sometimes he'd look skywards and wobble on his feet, until the scavenger grabbed his arm and pulled him along.

Babagoo sighed and wafted the flies from his eyes. Dark, buzzing clouds of them hovered everywhere, gathering around the pulp that oozed from torn bin bags.

"Suppose this is a bit much for you, isn't it?" Babagoo had to raise his voice over the screaming of gulls. "You've never seen how big Outside is. But its size should be the least of your worries, my boy. There's much worse out here than open air. Much worse."

Landfill didn't reply. His eyes were skimming the dreck at his feet, and he had to hop carefully over tin cans and shards of metal and plastic. Sometimes he looked briefly at the gulls that blanketed the landscape.

Babagoo looked at the boy's feet. "Remember to keep an eye out for shoes in your size. I know you're not fond of covering your feet, but you'll need to here. And not just because of all the sharpness and hazard. There are rats out here as big as your head. Give them half a chance and they'll gobble your toes for breakfast. Before you know it, you'll be hopping on stumps."

As if to emphasize the point, Babagoo knocked aside a rotten fruit crate to expose a huge black rat. He kicked it with his boot, and its slick, oily fur flashed as it scampered into a nearby cardboard box.

"So yes," continued the scavenger. "Look out for shoes. What other treasures are we scavenging?"

Landfill frowned and sucked his top lip. "Packaged grubbins. Lighters. Jerrycans. Oil. Fuel. Clothing. Blankets. Nails and screws. Tools. Bo—"

"Yes, yes, yes." Babagoo flapped a bandaged hand. "All standard treasures. What are we looking for specifically at the moment? Other than shoes for you, I mean."

Landfill looked upwards in thought, but quickly

dropped his gaze. "Piping. Metal piping."

"Correct. For the stove. Some of the old vents are going to pot." Babagoo grimaced and tugged Landfill's arm. "Now pick up the pace. You'll have to get used to this quickly. I can't do much while I'm holding your hand. You'll be as useful as a broken arm like this."

Landfill nodded, and the scavenger glanced at him before stopping. He smiled, causing black teeth to glitter within his beard. "You look so pale, my lad. Don't worry. You'll get there. You always do. Chin up, eh? This is a big day for you."

He held out a hand, which Landfill took in his own. "Now let's keep going. Those traps aren't going to empty themselves. And watch your step. Stay away from that stuff." He pointed at a thin stream of dark orange liquid, which trickled slowly along the ravine's lowest fissure.

"Dirty water?"

"Worse. It's poison. Poison from the Pit – from the Outsiders. Never go near it. Don't even smell it. It's very, *very* bad for you. Trust me, I know. And never pick up grubbins that've been anywhere near it."

Babagoo tugged his arm and they were moving again. After turning a corner in the ravine, Landfill paused.

Babagoo gnashed his teeth. "What?"

Landfill didn't speak. He pointed at the slope to their left, where what was left of a cat was draped across an old vacuum cleaner. Its exposed ribs were crawling with maggots.

Landfill's finger remained suspended while his stare moved to Babagoo. His mouth hung open in distress.

Babagoo frowned and fingered his beard. He cleared his throat before speaking. "Outsiders. You see now? Some of the small amnals do actually come from Outside. But it looks like the Outsiders got to this one before I did."

He cleared his throat again and sniffed loudly. "You'll see more of that. No doubt about it."

The boy's eyes began to water.

"Come, Landfill. Nothing to be done here." He tugged with his hand, but Landfill didn't move. "We're almost there now. In fact, this could be a good time to drop those scats."

Babagoo fumbled at Landfill's rope and untied the slops bag. Try as he might, the boy couldn't tear his eyes from the squirming mess.

"We'll leave this here," said the scavenger. "But don't leave any scats near here in future. Rule twenty-seven: scatter your scats. Don't go making piles. They'll stand out."

When Babagoo threw the bag down, Landfill started and glared at him. "No." He shook his head. "Not here. Not near the dead mowler."

Babagoo raised an eyebrow, then shrugged, picked up

the bag and handed it over. "Move along, then. Take it somewhere else."

They soon rounded a bend where the ravine opened up a little, its steep slopes dipping to the left and right.

Babagoo stopped. "Right. Drop those scats now, Landfill. We're here, and with some luck you'll need room on your rope." The bag landed with a wet thump, and the scavenger waved an arm across the area ahead. "I set up my last traps around here because it's a relatively safe area. These slopes offer good cover, and the Outsiders shouldn't be troubling this patch for a while."

Landfill looked up at Babagoo. "How'd you know?"

"Oh I know. After a while you'll get a knack for how they move around. And when you do, make the most of it." He narrowed his eyes, and his fingers scuttled like spiders through his beard. "Now, boy. Look ahead. See anything unusual? Anything I might've left here on a previous jaunt?"

Landfill scanned the ground and saw only flies, filth, seagulls and scrap. "What am I looking for?"

Babagoo pointed at a gull just ahead from where they stood. It was squawking and flapping, but seemed unable to leave the ground. "There. Gander that gull. The one that's not going anywhere."

"One of your traps?"

Babagoo slapped his back. "That's right. Can't see it though, can you? What's rule twenty-six?"

"Make sure **traps** are invisible."

"That's the **one**. And there's an example of how to do it. Building them from scrap helps, but you've got to bury them a little. Not so deep that they won't get a gull, but deep enough to be discreet. Got to be sly with your trapping. Come on. Let's get some meat."

Babagoo pulled his hand from Landfill's and headed over to the seagull. Landfill followed, but kept his distance from the thrashing bird. He inhaled sharply at the sight of its foot, which had been caught and mangled by the trap's wire jaw.

"Watch and learn, boy. Got to do this quickly. Short and sweet." Gritting his teeth, Babagoo forced his hands through flapping wings, and cursed when the seagull's beak jabbed the bandage on his hand. The pain seemed to spur him on; Landfill could barely follow the scavenger's hands as they clutched the bird's neck and ended the thrashing with a pull and twist.

Exhaling noisily, Babagoo kneeled to loosen the trap and tossed the gull into one of the bags on his rope. He was muttering to himself, but his lips froze when he saw the boy's expression. "What? What is it?"

Landfill's voice was muffled by the fingers clasped over his mouth. "Always knew you killed the gulls. Just never…" He stared at the bag, then looked at the seagulls squawking all around them. "Never seen them alive before. They're always dead when you bring them to Hinterland. They're just…meat. But now…" His brow furrowed. "Never really mulled about it. There's a rule against hurting amnals in Hinterland. Why's it okay to hurt them Outside?"

One of Babagoo's eyebrows fluttered. He scratched his temple and moved his lips, but nothing came from his mouth.

When Landfill tried to speak again, Babagoo raised a hand. "It's different with gulls, my lad. They're Pit vermin and better off dead. They'll be dead soon anyway. The poison'll get them – if the Outsiders don't get them first. You saw that mowler, didn't you? Who knows what they put it through before they left it for the maggots." His hairy nostrils flared. "So no, we're not hurting the gulls. We're putting them out of their misery."

Landfill was frowning at a dirty breeze block next to his foot.

"You don't look convinced."

Landfill didn't move his gaze or reply.

Babagoo grunted. "Listen. These gulls give you your meat. They've allowed me to give you meat since you were as tall as my knee. They've kept you alive and they've kept you strong. So don't go getting squeamish on me now, boy." His voice was rising and he had to catch himself. "Don't you realize how ungrateful that is?" he hissed. "Don't you see that? Didn't you always like the meat?"

Landfill raised his eyes momentarily, but Babagoo's scowl forced him to drop his gaze again. "Used to."

The scavenger eyed him silently, then pushed a finger to his nostril and huffed snot to the ground. "*Fine*. We'll talk about this later. This isn't the place for debate." He tipped his head towards some other gulls that were trying in vain to leave the ground. "There are other birds to bag up. I'm assuming you don't want to be involved today. We'll talk about that too. For now, make yourself useful."

He nodded in the direction past Landfill's shoulder. "There, around the bend we just came from. It's due a foraging. See if you can find anything useful. And be thorough."

Landfill's eyes met Babagoo's. The stiffness in his lips softened, and he nodded with a sigh.

He turned and stepped carefully over some glass bottles. Babagoo called after him. "Things are different Outside, Landfill. Always told you they were. Maybe now you'll appreciate what we've got in Hinterland."

SIXTEEN

PERSPECTIVE

A short while later, Landfill returned from around the corner. Babagoo had made some progress along the ravine, and was stuffing another gull into one of his bags.

Upon seeing the boy, he held up a palm. "Watch your step! I've put some fresh traps down." He narrowed his eyes. "What's that smile all about?"

Landfill's grin gleamed in the sun. He held a bin bag up high as he approached Babagoo.

"Found good treasures." He beamed goofily at Babagoo, who slowly smiled too.

"The goblin can scavenge, eh? Okay, then. Let's have a gander. What've you found?"

Landfill reached into the bag and pulled out something thick and dark, sealed in transparent film. "I think it's grubbins. Had to fight a crow for it." He brandished a gashed finger with pride. "It is food, isn't it?"

Babagoo nodded. "That it is, my lad. Black pudding."

"*Pudding?*" The boy's eyes widened.

Babagoo snorted. "Nothing sugary, though. Don't get all excited about it."

A glum pout. "So what is it?"

The scavenger scratched a shaggy cheek. "Hmm. It's essentially a large scab."

Landfill screwed up his face. "What? A scab?"

"Yes, a scab. But it's not as bad as it sounds, and it looks like some of it might still be edible."

Landfill cringed and dodged when Babagoo reached across to ruffle his hair. "A good find, young scavenger," he chuckled. "Not a bad start at all. Maybe you'll be good at this. What else have you got in there?"

Landfill returned the black pudding to the bag and rummaged around. "This is for you." He extracted a dirty toothbrush and held it out to Babagoo.

The scavenger's eyebrows rose. "Impressive! But you have it. It'll be wasted on me."

Landfill shook his head. "It's for you. You always give me the toothbrushes, but I found this one, so I decide who gets it."

Babagoo cocked his head, sniffed and nodded. "Suit yourself." He took the toothbrush, jammed it into his mouth and spoke: "*Ank oo ery uch.*"

Landfill answered in kind – "*Ur elcum*" – and they giggled together while the boy reached once more into the bag. "Don't know what this is but it looks nifty. Full of the patterns we've got around Hinterland. On doors and consoles, places like that. And there's pictures!"

The scavenger's smile was fading. He bit his lip and leaned to look into the bag.

"Pictures of Outsiders!" continued the boy. "And you're right – they *do* look a bit like us. Do you think the smaller ones are like me? But they've got queer teeth and hair in… in shapes. They look so…smiley. Is that the masks, how they trick you? There's—"

Babagoo snatched the object Landfill was removing from the bag. Landfill gasped when it flew into a pile of bin bags. "But—"

Babagoo spat, and clacked his teeth. "Don't ever touch those! There's plenty more about, and if you ever see one, you need to look away and keep your distance."

"What are they?"

"They're called magazines, and they're as toxic as the poison that runs through the Pit. It's one of the ways the Outsiders poison each other. Sneaky, treacherous things. Stay well away. Those things are packed with the hunger." He shuddered and wiped his hands on the sides of his plaid overcoat. "Same goes for books."

"Books?"

Babagoo pointed at the magazine. "Like that, but shaped in blocks. Plenty of danger there too. Just avoid them, Landfill. Same goes for anything with pictures of Outsiders. You'll see a lot of that in the Pit, especially on packaging. Big white smiles. Shiny hair. But they're nothing like you, boy. Nothing is! Masks. Trickery and poison. That's all it is. Keep well away. You hear me?"

The colour had left Landfill's face. "I hear you."

"For your sake, I hope you do." Babagoo winced and pinched the bridge of his nose. "Any more *surprises* in your bag?"

"Just this." Landfill reached solemnly into his bag and extracted a thin, rectangular sheet of metal. "There're more if you think they'll be handy. Found them behind some bits of wood."

Babagoo squinted with one eye at the sheet in Landfill's hand. "Hmm. Could be useful, I suppose. In fact…"

"Thought you could use them for fixing the stove. Maybe you can bend them—"

"Into pipes!" Babagoo grinned. "Well goose my bumps. That's good thinking, my boy. That's the right spirit! Everything's got a use. Waste not, want not, eh?" He cackled and smacked his scabby lips. "You say there's more of these?"

Landfill nodded. "A whole pile. I can spread them across my bags so they don't get too heavy."

Babagoo nodded approvingly. "A clever little imp. Off you go, then. I'll finish here while you get those sheets, and then we'll head back." He looked at the sky, which had changed from yellow to a pale, cloudless blue. "Should be cooking breakfast by now. Routine-routine-routine. So off you go. Get to it."

Still smiling, Landfill nodded, spun around and headed for the bend. Some of the timidity had left his feet, and he hopped squirrel-like across the rubbish.

After collecting more sheets and distributing them across his bags, Landfill paused to look around. He studied the birds that seemed to cover every surface, then frowned when he noticed two gulls brawling some way up the slope. It wasn't until he squinted that he saw a tiny starling caught between them. The starling was opening and closing its beak, its pellet-like eyes sparkling with terror while it flapped and flailed. The sheet in Landfill's hand fell to the ground, and as soon as one of the gulls jabbed the starling, he started to climb.

With his fingers and toes seeking crevices and footholds, Landfill kept his eyes on the starling and moved nimbly upwards. The bank was steep, but soon levelled a little and became easier to climb. Protruding edges caught Landfill's belly, palms and knees, occasionally scratching deep enough to draw blood, but he didn't notice. He moved up the slope like a lizard, and tapped one of the gulls just as it sent its rival into the air and hopped around to face the starling.

"Why're you fighting?" croaked Landfill. "Why hurt each other?"

The seagull went for his hand, but Landfill dodged the jab, put his palm to its side and pushed with all his strength. The gull left the slope and stayed in the air, its wings a white blur. It squawked and stabbed again at the boy. Landfill threw fistfuls of rubbish until it finally retreated and took to the sky.

Landfill turned his attention to the starling, which was still agitated and flailing. "There there," he hushed. "It's okay. It's alright." He dipped his head to check beneath the starling's speckled breast, and saw one of its feet snagged in some netting. Landfill reached for the netting with both hands, and bit his lip when the starling screamed and pecked his knuckles. "Ow! Now *you're* hurting *me*? I'm trying to help!"

His hands were speckled with blood by the time he'd torn the plastic webbing. "Go," he grunted. "Go on, you can go!"

The starling trilled and hopped into the air, then shot across the ravine. Landfill shifted his torso to watch it go, but his head stopped turning when he spotted the Black Fingers' tips, thinned by distance and emerging over the crest of the opposite slope. He continued to climb higher, glancing back regularly to watch the Loomer's top rise similarly into view, followed by the wall's west side.

Landfill could soon see the hill that lifted Hinterland to that endless plateau of purples and browns. He spent a moment trying to comprehend what he saw, then twisted suddenly into the bank, pushing his body against its slope and gripping so hard that it hurt. His eyes were clenched shut, and it took a while for the dizziness to pass.

When he opened his eyes again he looked up and gasped. His own slope's summit was just above his head.

After checking the bend below, Landfill closed his eyes and took some deep breaths. Making his decision, he opened his eyes and moved cautiously upwards. While approaching the summit, he adjusted the hood of his dross cape. Then, as gradually as he could, he raised his head until his nose was just above the crest.

His eyes widened, his mouth hung open and his knuckles turned white. After that, only his golden hair moved, flicked by a rancid breeze that sent wrappers whistling past his head. He struggled to take it all in – the Outsiders made small by vast distance; the motley hues of the landscape and faraway buildings; the rolling, grinding machines with their huge spiked wheels…

"*Landfill.*" A gruff but restrained call from below. Landfill twisted his neck and puffed with relief to see that Babagoo hadn't turned the ravine's bend.

But it wouldn't be long before he did.

Doing his best to ignore the junk that scraped his skin, Landfill whirled around and scrabbled down the slope. His eye caught a dull flash to the right. When he recognized it as a metal tray, he leaped sideways onto it and, speeding down the hill, released a frightened cry that was almost a giddy laugh. With his cape flapping behind him, he leaned back and held tight, and caught sight of Babagoo as the tray soared over the edge where the bluff suddenly steepened.

A howl escaped Landfill's throat just before he crashed into a heap of broken chairs. The tray protected him from spikes of rotten wood, but made a metallic clatter that had Babagoo searching the slopes with eyes as full of terror as of rage.

"*What…*" he began. "*What…?*"

Landfill rolled and cried out when flames of agony exploded in his wrist and shot up his arm. Babagoo was stomping towards him, glaring back and forth between the boy and the slope from which he'd come.

"How high did you go?" He spat the words through gritted teeth. "How *high* did you go?"

Landfill could barely hear him over the roaring in his ears. The pain from his wrist seemed to spread to his stomach, and he could taste bile rising beneath his tongue.

Babagoo raised his voice. His cheeks bristled and writhed with a life of their own. "*How. High. Did. You—*"

"To the top!"

Babagoo stopped abruptly. His arms shot out, dirty fingers pinching frantically at the air. "Have to move."

Landfill cradled his arm and licked his wrist, and bleated in agony when Babagoo hauled him to his feet.

"Move or die," quaked Babagoo. "You went too high. They'll have seen you. They'll be coming."

Landfill did his best to stay upright while the scavenger dragged him along. They were soon scrambling through a network of grooves in the rubbish – a winding labyrinth with close, reeking walls lined by shrieking gulls.

Babagoo stopped and cursed. His foot had sunk into some loose rubbish, and something was making him wince with pain.

Landfill clutched the scavenger's arm. "What is it?"

Babagoo was trying to pull his leg up with both hands. "Stuck! It's stuck!"

Landfill crouched and reached for Babagoo's ankle, but was sent recling by a violent shove.

"Don't meddle with it," gasped Babagoo. "Something heavy on my foot. You'll make things worse. Been in this fix before."

Landfill's pupils darted in every direction, frantically checking crests and corners for any sign of pursuers. "What did you do?"

"Leverage. Used a curtain rail to lift the weight away."

The scavenger's head swivelled back and forth. "But there's nothing like that here. You'll need to find something – anything long and strong. We can use that crate over there as a fulcrum."

Landfill's hand rose to his mouth. "Can't leave you. The Outsiders…"

"Exactly! They'll have us if you keep pottering. So get searching! Go, boy, *go!*"

While Babagoo wrestled with his bags, Landfill turned away and – doing his best to ignore the pain from his wrist and the cuts on his feet – ran as quickly as he could. He scanned the ground and walls as he moved, but after turning several corners still hadn't found anything of use. He glanced over his shoulder and – realizing he wasn't sure of the way back to Babagoo – wheeled on himself and dropped to all fours. He tried to retrace his route, but the rubbish surrounding him looked unnervingly unfamiliar.

He couldn't help calling out for Babagoo, but his voice was snatched by the breeze and lost to the gulls. He got back to his feet and tried moving more carefully through the maze, scrutinizing the waste for anything he'd seen before. Upon approaching a bend he stopped. Something had appeared at the bottom of the corner ahead…

It was a thick black boot, attached to a leg covered in coarse, flapping trousers.

Landfill's head twitched to and fro in search of somewhere to hide. There was nothing. He was surrounded by tight, looming walls, and the corridor of crud extended far behind him, with the cover of its nearest bend painfully beyond reach.

Taking the blade from his pocket, Landfill crouched into a pouncing stance, and watched the Outsider step into view.

SEVENTEEN

SKIN-DEEP

The Outsider stopped when it saw Landfill crouched in the filth. It rubbed its gloved fingers together and stayed where it was.

Landfill couldn't tell how the Outsider was reacting. Its eyes were hidden behind thick, plastic goggles, which were darkened beneath the cap of a white hard-hat. A wide bandage, stained with dirt and blood, was tucked into its grimy shirt and coiled scarf-like around its lower face, covering the tip of its nose, its mouth, chin and neck.

After eyeing Landfill for some time, it reached slowly into its grubby yellow vest. Landfill remained poised with his blade aimed high, and watched the Outsider extract a chocolate bar from beneath the vest. The Outsider shook the bar at the boy, causing its wrapper to glitter and flash. Then it held the bar out and beckoned with a finger.

Landfill glowered and jabbed the air. "Go away." His voice broke, and he had to shout against the cacophony of gulls. "Go away or I'll kill you!"

The Outsider tipped its head, jiggled its chocolate treat.

"Go away!"

The Outsider shrugged and took a step backwards. Landfill nodded sternly, but was thrown when the Outsider hurled the bar into the air. Landfill followed its trajectory, saw seagulls screech and flap as it flew into their midst.

When his eyes returned to the ground he saw the Outsider sprinting forward; by the time he managed to spin away, the Outsider was on top of him. It grabbed his wrists and rolled him roughly onto his back, and Landfill howled at the agony that shot once more up his arm. When he kicked with his knees, the Outsider released his wrists and wrestled his legs to pin them beneath its own.

With his hands free, Landfill took aim and swiped at the Outsider's throat. But the Outsider saw it coming, and caught Landfill's hand just before it reached the bandaging beneath its chin. Landfill's legs were trapped, and his injured wrist was once more in the Outsider's grip and crushed against the ground. The boy grunted and spluttered, trying to force his attacking hand against the Outsider's fist – to slowly push the blade towards the Outsider's face.

To his surprise, the Outsider's arm seemed to give, just a little. The shaking blade was moving slowly away from

Landfill, edging closer and closer to the Outsider's cheek. With his blade inching through the air, Landfill glared into the Outsider's face. He could almost see eyes boiling behind those lenses, and noticed something wrong with the skin exposed between the goggles and crusty bandaging. The pink-grey flesh was blemished by black and green pocks, and bulged lewdly while the Outsider pushed back against Landfill's hand.

Landfill roared and jerked his torso upwards, and the Outsider shuddered when the blade entered rippling grey flesh. Taking advantage of the Outsider's surprise, Landfill dragged the blade down its cheek. The Outsider pushed back enough to stop the glass from going deep, but as the blade moved downwards the flesh swelled and parted.

"Wha—" Landfill gaped in horror when something moved within the wound. The Outsider growled and shook its head, and Landfill saw a small beetle emerge from the now-flapping skin. It scuttled out from the gash and across the Outsider's goggles, causing the Outsider to jerk its head back in an attempt to cast it off.

With the Outsider distracted, Landfill twisted to one side, put his teeth to its grounded wrist and bit as hard as he could.

The Outsider's scream was muffled by bandaging. When it pulled its hand away, Landfill slammed his freed palm against its face. The flaring pain in his wrist made his eyes water, but he pushed with all his might so that the Outsider began to topple. Landfill continued to push until he could wriggle away and clamber to his hands and feet.

Panting and grunting, he loped away without even a glance back. He flew from one corridor of dross to the next, dashing in random zigzags in an attempt to shake off his pursuer. Something caught his eye in the ramparts of rubbish: a blue plastic barrel nestled horizontally in refuse, just above ground level. It was empty and looked like it might just be big enough.

After checking behind him, Landfill sprinted to the barrel, crouched, pivoted and backed into its hollow. He covered his mouth with his good hand and, trying to control his trembling sobs, watched through the barrel's opening for any sign of feet.

Landfill had no idea how long he'd been hiding when he heard the crunch of soles against rubbish. He tried to squirm deeper into the barrel, but could get no further from its opening. As the crunching continued to draw nearer, he realized he'd cornered himself. If the Outsider found him, he'd have nowhere to run.

Landfill scrunched up his eyes. He could feel snot and tears streaming hotly down his face. Doing his best to hold

his breath, he watched through the opening and willed the Outsider to continue past the barrel, to not notice something so low down.

That crunching reverberated through the barrel, and Landfill saw a boot come down close to his face. A whimper escaped his lips, and became a throaty cry when he saw corduroy above the boot. "Babagoo!"

"Landfill?"

The boy popped his head through the opening, and looked up to see a bewildered Babagoo jerking his head every way but down. "Babagoo, I'm here."

The scavenger looked down. His grisly expression dissolved when he saw the boy clambering at his feet. "Landfill! You're… You're okay!" The words caught in his throat and came out almost as a question. Reaching down, he pulled Landfill up and held him tightly against his chest. "You're okay," he croaked. "I feared the worst."

Landfill sobbed into Babagoo's shoulder. "Outsider… It came…"

"I know, my boy, I know. I heard it coming. Had to force my foot free so I could hide around a corner." He winced at the memory and gasped. "May have done myself some harm, but harm's a small price to pay. I stayed low and hoped against hope the Outsider wouldn't cross your path. Where's it now? What happened?"

"It tried to give me sugar grubbins. Didn't work, so it

went for me. Had me down but I cut its face and gave it the slip. Never been so scared." The boy struggled to talk between sobs. "So much hate there, Babagoo. There was rot and hate and…"

He gave in to a fit of tears, and felt Babagoo tense suddenly against him.

"What happened after that, lad? Where'd the Outsider go?"

"Don't know. I ran and hid in the barrel."

Babagoo's grip was loosening. He looked around with bulging eyeballs. "Then we have to keep moving. We have to get back to Hinterland. Come, Landfill, come!"

After lowering the boy, Babagoo took his good hand and they ran together. With their dross capes flapping behind them and bin bags knocking their knees, they hissed and hobbled, but kept up a brisk pace.

It wasn't long before they'd reached the Pit's edge, shuffled through the prickly crawlway and entered the glade. Babagoo sent Landfill through the fridge first, slipped in and slammed its door behind him, then followed the boy up the steep tunnel. Landfill moved blindly but swiftly, with a feeling of crawling into black sky.

Babagoo coughed behind him, and paused to catch his breath before carrying on. "It used sugar grubbins, eh? That'll be bait – something sweet but rotten inside. That's the Outsiders, alright. There's always masks. Always deceit."

His voice hardened. "Now tell me, boy – did you follow rule twenty-eight?"

Landfill screwed up his eyes. "Twenty-eight… Is that… Is it—"

"Not good enough, Landfill! Rule twenty-eight – if you're seen by an Outsider, move in a direction away from Hinterland and hide until it's safe to return. Did you do it?"

Landfill spluttered. "I don't know! Was too frightened."

"Again, boy – not good enough. When you're frightened is when you need the rules the most. Fear should be your friend, not your foe." He was silent for a moment. "It's a worrisome thing. That Outsider got to us far too quickly. Shouldn't have been so close. I only hope this doesn't mean they're on to our scent – that they've turned their eyes to Hinterland. Can't help pondering whether that's something to do with your mischief on the conveyor a while back."

"It can't be! That was so long ago."

"Don't be so *stupid*, boy! It's just like the Outsiders to take their time. Rule six. What is it?"

"No sign—"

"Can be a sure sign!" Babagoo's tone became increasingly bitter. "The Outsiders are sly like that. The hunger breeds cunning. We can only hope I'm wrong – that this is all coincidence."

He wheezed and growled in the gloom. "This would never have happened if you'd followed the rules, young skulk. You won't be leaving Hinterland again any time soon, mark my words. No more Spit Pit for you. You're scared of taking gulls, you're a terrible sneak and you've got no respect for the rules. As useful as a lump of boy dung. In fact, *boy*, I'm sorely tempted to drag you back down there and leave you for the Outsiders. I thought there was a use for everything, but in your case I'm obviously… obviously—"

A loud bout of coughing rang through the tunnel. Landfill scuffled backwards in the darkness to find Babagoo slumped and shuddering.

EIGHTEEN

COWARDICE

Landfill squatted in the Rippletop's black belly. The chamber was lit by his lighter, but he stared glumly at the ground, trying his best to ignore the crunch of cockroach. When the sounds finished, he raised his face to the dark pipes.

"It worked, Longwhite. Got Babagoo to take me Outside. A couple of days ago. I know now. I know."

A pale scuffling.

"Babagoo's not hiding anything about Outside. It's horrorific. It's madness, and it doesn't make sense. I saw a dead mowler, Longwhite. Just like the woofler outside the wall. Dead, and left to stink in the sun. They get buried in Hinterland, but Outside it's rot and maggots – that's all they get."

His eyes shimmered in the lighter's flame. "There's a

sickness out there. I saw amnals turning against each other. Saw gulls fighting. Fighting so they could hurt a starling! Must be the hunger. Even the amnals are infected."

Longwhite slipped out from between pipes. He squeaked and ran his length across the boy's ankles.

"The edge?" Landfill nodded. "It's like I thought. Saw it from below – from the other side. The ground doesn't become sky beyond the wall's west side. It falls away in a slope. Hinterland's on a hill, with the Spit Pit at the bottom."

A muted squeak. Landfill sat down so Longwhite could curl up between his crossed legs.

He ran his fingers through warm, coarse fur. "Yes, there's lots of Spit Pit down there. I climbed up high. Looked over a crest and saw…saw how *big* the Pit is. A lot bigger than Hinterland. So much waste. Big piles of it, rising to the sky. I saw Outsiders. A few in the distance, moving around the Pit, and one up close. *Too* close. They wear white, round hats and yellow vests. I saw a few cabins at the Pit's edge, like the ones in Hinterland. And there were things… Yellow machines with spikes on their wheels and huge…shovels.

"But beyond the Pit… I saw ground like the ground around the wall – grass, heather and rocks. And there was something else, quite close to the Pit. A grey and red area with buildings – most of them in rows with sloping roofs. Things were moving between them. Shiny rolling machines and…more Outsiders. I think that's where I saw that grid of lights, when I was on the conveyor that night. Must have come from there.

"There were grey lines leaving the area, with rolling machines on them. They moved along the grass and heather, sometimes past patches like the Thin Woods, but not so thin. Some of the lines joined a thicker line that headed west – a strip that shone with more machines. It went right to where the ground stops again and becomes sky. It goes *so* far, Longwhite, and it falls away! Is it another edge?"

A long chitter.

Landfill nodded. "I've got more questions too. But they won't be answered."

Longwhite uncurled and left Landfill's lap with a hiss.

Landfill grimaced. "I'm not going Outside again, Longwhite! Not even if Babagoo lets me. Have you seen this?"

He moved his lighter to illuminate the cuts and bruises all over his body, then licked the back of his arm. "Nearly broke my wrist! And I told you about the amnals – the way they are out there. Dead or mad! And that's not the worst.

"The Outsider I saw up close – it attacked me. And I deserved it, because I broke the rules. The rules are there for a reason, Longwhite. They keep me safe. They keep us *all* safe."

Longwhite was upright on his hind legs. His jaws parted to reveal needle-like teeth.

Landfill raised a finger. "Don't want to hear it. All breaking rules does is cause trouble. I nearly died out there. Nearly got Babagoo killed too – he barely made it back. The strain had him off his feet all day yesterday. His legs are all swollen and the mattress is soaked with sweat. The little strength he had was spent on curses for me. And him being stuck there meant no meat from the Spit Pit, which meant no feeding for the amnals!

"They had to go hungry, Longwhite. They were unhappy. Something was in the air. Something…awful. And it was all my fault, Longwhite. All my fault."

Landfill stared at the floor. He was silent for a while, until a squeak from Longwhite made him lift his head. "What? What else is out there?"

Chattering quietly, Longwhite dropped back onto all fours.

Landfill raised his eyebrows. "Beauty?" He frowned and rubbed his lips. "Yes, there's beauty." A sudden shake of the head. "But not enough. And I don't care. Hinterland has beauty. Hinterland *is* beauty. I don't care about Outside any more. The only thing I care about is keeping it out. It's just too big. And it keeps getting bigger! Every time I think I'm used to it, I look again…and see it still moving away, in every direction."

An abrupt hiss.

Landfill glared. "What?" His voice began to rise. "Cowardice before curiosity? That's what you think?"

He waved his flame when Longwhite drew nearer, fangs flashing in firelight. "What do you know anyway?" He snarled and clacked his teeth. "You don't know anything! You just hide here and make mischief for everyone else. Why can't you leave me alone? I've had enough, Longwhite – enough of sneaking and games!"

Longwhite's pale fur bristled. His back began to arch, and a musky stench filled the chamber.

"I don't care if Babagoo's got secrets! I don't care what they are. He can keep them. It's for my own good – all for my own good!"

Landfill shuffled back on his haunches, and kept the flame raised to Longwhite as he followed. "Cowardice before curiosity," he spat. "Don't you know, Longwhite? Curiosity killed the boy!"

Landfill saw a bony back hunching, and leaped aside when Longwhite lunged forward.

The lighter lost its flame and Landfill rolled in a darkness as thick and black as tar. He heard the chittering draw upon him, and scampered on all fours to the wall, where he searched blindly with his hands, found the aperture and squeezed through to the outer chamber. A quick spark from the lighter gave him just enough light to take aim and pounce at the metal ladder.

As he shot up its rungs he heard angry noises below, filling the darkness with hiss upon hiss upon hiss.

Landfill blinked in sunlight when he exited the Rippletop. After checking to his left and right, he bounded around the warehouse's corner to the cabins.

Landfill stopped a few paces before reaching his secret, kept his distance and grimaced at its blanket of greenery. He was wiping his wrist through his hair when he heard a spry chirp from above. Looking up, he saw a red-beaked parakeet at the top of the wall, perched between teeth of sparkling glass.

"Swift!"

He puffed and scratched his cheek. The bird blinked in sunlight, twitching its head on a plump green neck.

Landfill looked back and forth between the parakeet and the foliage. He scrunched his nose and scratched his head. "Swift… You parkits have sharp eyes. You see anything here?" He pointed in the direction of the hidden hole. "Anything unusual?"

The parakeet blinked at the cabins.

"No," said Landfill. "That's…good. What about the other side? In the same area. Anything out of place?"

With a ruffle of feathers the parakeet took to the air.

The boy nodded slowly. "Okay… Nothing visible there." He put a hand to his chin and started backing away. "Then I'll leave it be. Just for a while. Just…in case."

He nodded to himself again, then tensed when he heard a remote rumbling. With just six leaps he was around the nearest cabin's corner, through its door and under a table. Wincing and covering his ears, he watched while several foxes snarled and circled the debris on the floor. The ceiling panels shook when the rumbling rose to a roar, and the foxes leaped and snapped at windowpanes, barking in reply to the screaming Eye.

PART THREE

THE BUD

NINETEEN

RED SWELL

Summer waned and withdrew, and autumn found Landfill in the Gully. He held Orwell against the baggy, threadbare jumper he'd put on to curb the cold, and was wearing tattered jeans rolled up to the knees. With the water cool against his calves, he waded down the concrete bank, and stopped momentarily to watch red leaves floating around his legs. A mild breeze sent them fluttering from the Thin Woods, which had changed from green to crimson and gold. Chrysanthemums and crocuses splashed the earth there with colour.

Orwell, who was now large enough to cover Landfill's chest, yapped and licked the boy's face. Landfill laughed and yapped back, burying his face deep in the pup's fur. "Want to know why we're here?"

Orwell yapped again, his sapphire eyes sparkling in

the light. Landfill adjusted his hold so he could support Orwell's belly and let his legs hang down. "A little treat. I know how you watch the wooflers in the water – how you watch but can't go in. And I've never seen a sorrier muttling. So I'm lending a hand."

He crouched and lowered Orwell into the water. With a huge canine grin, Orwell began to splash excitedly with his front legs. Landfill smiled in the spray, but sighed at the sight of the pup's rear legs, which hung limply beneath the water's surface. A cheery bark brought his smile back, and he rocked Orwell from side to side in the water.

"How's that for a bath? Better than a wash from Woolf's tongue, eh?" The water rose to the hem of his jumper as he moved deeper into the Gully. Orwell splashed and paddled, and Landfill joined in with his sprightly yipping.

Suddenly the boy fell silent. He cocked his ear. He could hear noises from further down the Gully: barking from Muttbrough. The dogs were agitated. Something was wrong.

Pulling Orwell to his chest, Landfill splashed through the water towards the nearest bridge, then ran up the bank so he could crouch in the nook where the bridge's end met the slope. He listened out for Hunger's Eye, but there was nothing; only the dogs. When the barking continued without any hint of a rumble, he left the Gully and moved quickly, under cover of the Woods. He longed to drop to all fours and lope between the trees, but didn't want to leave Orwell behind, so he continued on his feet.

The towering concrete wall of the Pale Loomer began to appear between the tree trunks ahead, and Landfill could see dogs running. Something else caught his eye: a shadow slipping along the gangway that bordered the Loomer. Before he could get a better look, it vanished with a slam of the Loomer's side door. Landfill jumped behind a tree and leaned cautiously out to look again. The shadow was gone, leaving the dogs to bark and scratch at the door's flaking paint.

With a steady eye on the door, Landfill hid behind tree trunks and continued towards the Loomer. When he reached the dogs, he crouched next to Woolf and handed Orwell over.

He unrolled his wet jeans from his knees while whispering, "What was it, Woolf? What went through the door?"

Woolf lapped silently at Orwell's wet fur, so Landfill crawled to the other dogs. His glass blade flashed when he took it from his pocket. He kept his voice low and patted the dogs' heads. "Easy, wooflers. *Easy.* Settle down and stay here. Might not be safe."

Landfill crept to the door, but hesitated when he touched its handle. Returning the blade to his trousers, he bit his lip, lowered himself to all fours and followed the wall around its corner.

He stopped at the edge of the Loomer's main opening. Putting his hands against the wall, he tilted his body and peered inside. Sunlight entered through windows and holes, falling upon mildewed pallets, scuffed train tracks and a floor green with mould. Machines were covered in powdery crusts of turquoise and emerald, and stalactites hung dripping from stained arches and gangways.

Seeing no sign of intruders, Landfill crouched and – keeping to the cover of machines and concrete pillars – crept through the cavernous chamber. After treading through a pool of stagnant water, he climbed some metal steps and prowled the raised gangway that lined the inner wall.

The boy's nose twitched. A new scent was in the air – something that pierced the must and mould. Something faint and flowery, but with a sweetness that tickled his nostrils. A noise came from a doorway he'd just passed – an echoing scrape – and he dived into a shadowy alcove. When he heard footsteps on the gangway, he covered his mouth to catch his shuddering breaths.

The footsteps were moving away from him, towards the stairway. At one point they stopped, and all became so quiet that the drip-drop of stalactites rang like a downpour in Landfill's ears. A brief flash filled the chamber, obliterating shadows and forcing Landfill to shrink even further into the alcove. Then the footsteps continued.

As they descended the steps, Landfill held his breath and leaned a little from the alcove. Skin prickled at the nape of his neck. A dark, hooded figure was leaving the stairway and stopping at the edge of the stagnant puddle. It seemed to look around, scrutinizing machines and dials. Its head stopped moving, so that its face was aimed at the rusty fire extinguisher propped against a wall.

Landfill's spine turned to ice; the intruder must have seen the mice that lived in a crevice by the extinguisher. He whimpered and pushed his hands into his belly, trying to fight the nausea. When the Outsider took a step towards the extinguisher, he left the alcove and squatted by the railing.

The Outsider drew in on the mice, and the boy found himself sneaking, on toes and fingertips, along the gangway. While the Outsider tampered with a black device in its hands, Landfill descended the stairs with his belly almost brushing every step. The hairs on his arms felt as brittle as glass, and the steps seemed to slip and sway beneath his clammy palms.

The intruder was on its haunches now, leaning in over the extinguisher. Slowly, soundlessly, but with his heart racing so hard he feared it would give him away, Landfill crept across concrete and inched his way to the Outsider's rear. He held his breath and stopped just behind the crouching figure, realizing with a painful twist of the gut that he had no idea what to do next.

Fretting silently, Landfill noticed long hair – as slick as silk and impossibly clean – tumbling down from the side of the intruder's hood. He couldn't resist tilting himself, just a little, trying to get a glimpse of its face.

His nostrils flared. He could only see hints of some features – the protruding nub of a nose, a shadowy cheek – but they were enough to keep him tilting, twisting, leaning just that little bit further.

Brown eyes and soft lips – *smiling* lips – came into view. Landfill was trying to comprehend that the face wasn't like that of the Outsider in the Pit – that if anything it was more like his own – when those brown eyes flitted towards him. He realized with a whimper that he'd gone too far.

He straightened up to twist and run, but the Outsider shot to its feet and clipped his chin with the side of its head. Landfill yelped and reeled, with pain sending white flickers through his vision. He saw the intruder flinch and rub its head. The knock to his chin had sent his hand to his pocket, and as soon as he pulled out his blade the Outsider gasped. With lips twisting, it lunged and butted its black device against Landfill's nose. A small glass rectangle glimmered before his eyes, and with a click and a flash, everything disappeared.

Blinded by whiteness, Landfill heard a gravelly scrape and took a thump to the chest. The air seemed to hurtle behind him, and he felt hard ground fly up to wallop his back. He lashed out wildly with his blade, felt it catch and heard a cry. The blade was knocked away, and Landfill wailed when something heavy crushed his outspread arms.

When his vision returned, he saw the Outsider straddling his torso and arms and holding something above its head. Its chest rose and fell in brisk jerks, and its eyes were wide and white with terror. Landfill struggled to tear his pupils from the red swell on the Outsider's temple, and when he finally did he clocked the fire extinguisher gripped between its raised, trembling palms. He turned his head aside and winced, waiting for the impact of metal against skull.

TWENTY

TRICKS AND GIBBERISH

But the extinguisher didn't fall. It remained in the air, and Landfill saw the Outsider's grimace quake and falter. A tear ran down its cheek and – after tossing the extinguisher aside – it shuffled from his body and retreated towards a pallet, where it sat and put its head in its hands.

Landfill scrabbled onto his haunches. With his eyes brimming, he found his blade and backed himself quickly against the wall, where he snivelled quietly and tried to control his breathing. When he finally found his voice it was quivering and weak. "Could have hurt me." He sniffed and rubbed the tears from his cheeks. "But you…you…"

The Outsider lifted its head slowly from its palms, and looked at the fire extinguisher on the ground before returning Landfill's stare. "Didn't? Course I didn't. How… Why…" Something seemed to catch in its throat.

Landfill gawped at the intruder's mouth. It took him a moment to process what he'd heard – to grasp that he'd understood the Outsider's words.

The Outsider wiped a sleeve across its eyes and tried again. "Why would I? You looked even more terrified than me."

Its voice was thick with phlegm, but Landfill heard delicacy beneath the clog of tears. There was no rawness to the intruder's tone – none of the gruffness or bile he was used to from Babagoo. He became aware of a stickiness on his hands, and glanced down to see the blood on his blade and fingers. He swayed on his haunches, lost for a moment in that red, lurid sheen.

A small sniff had him raising his eyes. He stared at the intruder, eyeing the black device that hung from its neck, and noticing the stark cleanness of its grey hooded top and tight blue jeans. The Outsider had long, auburn hair that shone like foxes when they left the Gully. And its face… There was a softness to it that confused the boy – a softness as intriguing as it was alien. A plump roundness in its cheeks. Small lips. Brown, heavy-lidded eyes beneath thin, tidy eyebrows. It looked young – perhaps not much older than Landfill himself.

The intruder spoke again. "And look at you. You're just a kid." It touched the cut on its temple and hissed, and its voice hardened. "What's *wrong* with you? Why'd you sneak up on me like that?"

Landfill glanced at the crevice in the wall. "You were going to hurt the mice."

"*Hurt* them? I was taking pictures." The Outsider pulled at its hood to dab the wound. "Why would I want to hurt mice?"

Landfill didn't reply. He was grappling with the words lodged in his throat, and finally managed to force them out. "How'd you get in?" He grimaced and braced himself for the answer, his stomach cold with dread.

The Outsider studied him while it replied. "A tunnel under the wall. Beneath some nettles. I've been looking for a way in for ages. Is that how you got in?" Its eyebrows rose. "What? What is it?"

Landfill's entire body had become pale. He fought the fresh tears that threatened to spill from his eyes, and battled an urge to vomit on the spot. He belched roughly, and had to take a deep breath before he could speak again. "Why'd you come here? Was it Hunger's Eye? Did it see me?"

The Outsider's face was blank. "I…I don't know what you mean. I came here for photos."

Landfill shook his fringe. "You *do* know." He pointed up with his blade. "The Eye. Flying above all the time. Looking for…for me."

The Outsider furrowed its brow and blew some air through its cheeks. Then it looked at the sky through the chamber's opening. Its eyes widened. "You mean the jets? From the base?" It tilted its head. Something that was almost amusement crept into its expression. "They're not looking for you. It's just military exercises. They wouldn't even notice you."

Landfill was scrunching his face and shaking his head. He had his free hand pressed against his ear.

The Outsider's voice softened, just a little. "Hey, why don't you put that glass down. I'm not going to hurt you. Not if you don't hurt me." It got slowly up from the pallet, took a step forward.

Landfill stopped shaking his head and hacked the air. Some colour had returned to his face. "Stay back! Stay back and shut up!" The hairs stood erect on his arms. "You won't trick me! You're jabbering nonsense. Fibbery and mischief!"

The Outsider stopped moving and held up its palms. "Look. Calm down. I—"

The glass flashed again. "Stay back!"

The Outsider stayed put. With those soft lips drooping, it rubbed its chin. "Where are you from? You're not from town, are you? I've never seen you there. Are your parents with you?"

Landfill only glared in reply.

"Where's your mum and dad? Do they know you're running around barefoot and assaulting people?"

Landfill grimaced. "Nonsense words. Tricks and gibberish."

The Outsider frowned. Its tone hardened again. "Your mother and father. Are they here?"

Landfill's blade dipped. His gaze dropped as he repeated the word beneath his breath. "*Mother…*" He spoke more to himself than to the intruder. "Heard that…somewhere…"

The Outsider nodded. "Yeah, your mother. Where is she?"

Slowly, Landfill raised his eyes. The Outsider studied his straining features, and its face darkened. "Something's wrong here."

Landfill stepped towards the Outsider and raised his blade – still wet with blood – to its face. "*You're* wrong here."

The Outsider took a step back, its eyes shimmering. "No. Something's very…off here. Why—"

A distant shout, cracked and harsh: "*Landfill! Where are you, boy?*"

Landfill flinched, and they glanced as one through the Loomer's opening. The boy's face crumpled, his breaths bursting and shallow.

"Who's that?" The intruder's forehead furrowed. "Hang on. They don't have security here, do they?"

Landfill was wincing and pressing a hand to the back of his head. He opened his eyes and jumped towards the Outsider, slashing with his blade. "Leave," he hissed.

"Go the way you came and don't come back."

The Outsider looked him in the eye, nodded and started to sprint. Landfill sprinted too, following the Outsider into daylight and across asphalt. Babagoo's voice also seemed to follow, narrowing its distance from the pair: "Landfill! Where are you? You should be at the vejble patch!"

The Outsider dashed past the Rippletop's front and around its corner, followed closely by Landfill and his flashing blade. When they got to the cabins, they found some dogs sniffing around the tunnel's mouth. Vonnegut was among them. The huge Alsation tensed before twisting to bare his fangs at the Outsider.

Landfill grunted and waved his hands, and the hounds backed away. He turned to the Outsider. "Get out."

The Outsider climbed into the hole, but paused to look at Landfill. "You coming too? You don't want to get caught in here. Your parents could get fined."

Landfill clutched his blade in both hands. "*Please* get out." He aimed the blade at the Outsider, but a note of pleading rang in his voice. "Please go away and never come back. Never come back or tell the other Outsiders. *Please.*"

"Outsiders?" The intruder gawped at him from the hole, and its brow began to crumple. "Listen. I'm going to be back tomorrow. Meet me, okay? Here, in this spot."

Landfill blinked and stuttered, unable to work out what he wanted to say. Meanwhile, the Outsider had wriggled into the tunnel and vanished from sight.

Another call from Babagoo: "Landfill!"

Landfill dropped to the ground to scrabble frantically with his hands, grabbing at foliage and doing his best to cover the hole. Vonnegut barked and nuzzled his hair, and Landfill kept working while he replied. "I know! I'll fill it in later. The Outsider won't… It won't get back in. I'll block it soon. No time now."

When the tunnel was hidden, Landfill sprinted from the cabins with the dogs bounding beside him. He turned a corner and saw Babagoo crossing the Rippletop's tracks.

Landfill puffed and scratched his cheek in greeting, but the scavenger just raised an eyebrow. "What're you playing at? I heard noises."

"I… It was the dogs. They…got worked up."

"You're hurt."

The boy followed the scavenger's gaze, and saw the Outsider's blood on his fingers. "Cut myself playing. That's why the dogs got worked up. Nothing worrisome. Just a nick."

Babagoo searched his expression, then took a deep breath. "You should be tending vejbles, and I need to get to the Pit. Respect the routine, Landfill. Rule—"

"Fourteen."

Babagoo's eyes narrowed. "Yes, fourteen." He nodded slowly and tapped his trapper hat. "So stop dawdledallying and hop to it."

Landfill took his opportunity and scarpered. He lapped at his wrist as he ran, and nearly fell over when his tongue crossed a sticky trickle of red.

He gaped again at the Outsider's blood. It tasted exactly like his own.

Later on, Landfill wolfed down dinner and got an early start on the animals' evening feed. He loped around Hinterland with his plastic bag of gull, with eyes that moved constantly towards the Rippletop.

He was sweating when he reached Muttbrough. The dogs gathered around him, tongues flapping against spittle-soaked jaws.

"Can't stay, wooflers," he panted. His voice dropped to a whisper. "Something needs doing. Got a hole to—"

He fell silent when he saw Woolf at Muttbrough's trough. She was lifting Orwell by the nape of his neck and propping him at the trough's edge. The boy's eyes widened when he remembered where he'd first heard that word – the one Babagoo had used for Woolf that time. He whispered it – "*Mother…*" – and took a slow step back.

Landfill threw down some meat and ran. He completed the evening feed in good time, stopping by the hole only to tidy its foliage.

TWENTY-ONE

LANVILLE

The following day, Landfill ate his lunch as quickly as he could.

Babagoo watched him from the other side of the stove. He picked some meat from his beard and plopped it into his mouth. "I take it you don't fancy some gull with those vejbles."

Without taking his mouth from his food, Landfill shook his head.

"Didn't think so." The scavenger rolled his eyes. "Then at least take your time with those taytoes, lad. You'll choke if you don't slow down."

Landfill gulped down a wad of potato so big it made his eyes water. "Hungry," he coughed.

"Hungry and quiet. Can't help noticing you've barely spoken a word today. Weren't exactly chatty last night either. What is it? Something on your mind?"

"No."

"Hmm." Babagoo chewed some more gull, spat a bone to the floor. "No sign can be a sure sign."

Landfill ignored him.

"How's your cut?"

The boy looked at the nick he'd cut into his finger the day before. "Fine." He polished off the last of his beetroot and got up.

"Where you off too?"

"Lull-time, isn't it?"

"Well, yes. That it is. You just seem in a rush. Going to give yourself belly pains. Where're you heading?"

"Nowhere. Just want a wander. Feeling restless."

"Restless, eh?" Babagoo wriggled his bushy eyebrows at Kafka, who was grazing on the remains of a mouldy straw basket. He returned his attention to the boy. "If you're that restless, you can come help me mend panels in the Ivy Stack."

Landfill was already exiting through the metal door. "Not *that* restless."

He heard the scavenger grunt, just before the door slammed. "Didn't think so."

Upon nearing the Rippletop, Landfill checked over his shoulder. No sign of Babagoo. He looked up and searched the sky's deep blue. Hunger's Eye hadn't passed over since he'd encountered the Outsider. He wondered miserably whether that meant anything.

There had been no trace of the intruder during his dawn inspection. He'd checked around the hole during the animals' morning feed too, but there was nothing. He half-expected to find nothing again when he passed the northernmost cabin, and inhaled sharply at the sight of the Outsider sat cross-legged next to the hole, plucking petals from a purple crocus. Its grey hood was down, and it wore a plastic band around its neck, with two cups at its ends, the padded rims of which rested beneath the Outsider's jaw.

Landfill whipped out his blade. He aimed it at the cabin nearest to the hole. "In there. *Now*."

The Outsider raised an eyebrow. "How about you put that glass away first? Hasn't it done enough harm already?"

Landfill shook his head and the Outsider shrugged.

"Okay," it sighed. "We'll do things your way. But if you come near me with that thing, I'm going to shout and make all the noise I can. Maybe that man'll come check it out. You didn't seem keen on him finding us yesterday."

It got up and brushed dirt from its hands. Before following it into the cabin, Landfill glanced over his shoulder again and tidied the hole's foliage with a shaking foot.

When he entered the cabin, he saw foxes bristling beneath a wonky table. The Outsider was standing by the window, watching them with a white, tidy smile as curious as it was unsettling.

"God," said the Outsider. "I *love* foxes. They're gorgeous, aren't they? You see them around town at night sometimes, but I've never been this close." It clucked its tongue at the foxes. "Hey. Hey there…"

"Get down," hissed Landfill, his eyes on the window. "Low."

"Alright, alright." The Outsider crouched, but its attention was still on the foxes. "Hey, don't be scared." Its brown eyes twinkled. "Ah, just realized… Got something you might like."

Landfill crouched too. His eyes flitted between the Outsider and the window, and he raised his blade when the Outsider reached into its top.

"Fancy some of this, little guys?" It took out a small packet of biscuits and held one out to the foxes. "Don't be shy," it said, then peered at Landfill. "You want one?"

Landfill shook his head, and held up a palm when two foxes edged out from under the table, their dark nostrils twitching. "*No.* Rushdie. Carter. Stay away. Get back."

"They've got names? Cute. And what about you?" The Outsider turned its eyes to Landfill. "You might not have shoes, but I'm guessing you at least have a name."

Landfill shook his head. His lips were pressed firmly together.

"That man, the voice we heard… He called for Lanville. You responded to that. Is that your name? Lanville?"

Landfill's lips were rigid.

"I'm Dawn, by the way. If you're not going to answer, I'll assume you're Lanville. Is that right, Lanville? Strange name, though. *Lanville.* Sounds a bit posh. You certainly don't look posh. You hiding a silver spoon somewhere, Lanville?"

"*Landfill,*" blurted the boy.

The Outsider tilted its head. "Your name's Landfill? As in rubbish?"

"As in *precious.*"

The Outsider's laugh was buoyant and bright. It fluttered around the cabin like an exotic bird. "Suit yourself, *Landfill.* Hey!" The last word was addressed to the foxes, who were finishing the biscuit still in its hand. Two further foxes had left the table to sniff its fingers, and it took more biscuits from the packet.

Landfill adjusted himself so that his knees were on the floor. The Outsider's laughter had weakened his legs somehow. His stomach tingled in an unfamiliar way, and he struggled to steady the blade in his hand. "Don't even *try* to hurt the foxlers."

The Outsider glared at him abruptly. Its cheeks and small lips tautened with something close to disgust. "Can you *stop* with this hurting animals stuff? And what's with the 'foxler' talk? They're *foxes.*" It shook its head, pouting

189

slightly. "And talking of hurt, you cut me pretty badly yesterday." It tapped a brownish patch that hid the wound on its temple. "That bit of glass you're messing about with isn't a toy, you know. I'd throw it away if I were you, before someone gets *seriously* hurt."

Landfill didn't respond. He had to blink the sweat from his eyes, even though the cabin was musty and cool.

The Outsider adopted Landfill's posture by resting its knees on the frayed carpet. Its pout gradually disappeared, shifting into something more resigned. "Listen. I'm not sure what happened yesterday. I think we both got a bit of a scare – freaked each other out. But you know, that's what happens when you go sneaking up on people. Accidents happen, yeah?" It tapped the patch on its temple again and sighed. "Anyway, for what it's worth, I'm sorry."

Landfill had been braced for anything but an apology. It struck him like the parry of a second blade, and the glass began to slip between his thumb and fingers. His mouth fell open. "Sss…sorry?"

"Yeah." The Outsider nodded glumly. "For knocking you over like that. For nearly…you know…with the extinguisher…" It puffed its cheeks and shrugged. "You scared the life out of me, and when you got that glass out I thought it was a knife. You can imagine what went through my head, right? I lost my senses for a second. It was a close call."

It forced a laugh and puffed out its cheeks again. "Anyway, I wanted to clear the air and check you're alright. *I* was scared, but *you* looked terrified. Like, ready to soil those tatty jeans of yours. But you're okay, right?" The Outsider frowned. "You don't look okay, if I'm honest. Are you still a bit rattled? I know it took me a while to stop shaking. Adrenaline, huh?"

The words sounded strangely faint to Landfill. They trailed behind the movements of the Outsider's lips, as if they came from far away. He felt like he wasn't really there – like he was watching the scene from outside the cabin. He gazed abstractly at the Outsider's face, contemplating the smoothness of its skin, its strange softness. There was something in the Outsider's shape too – in the curves of its chest and waist…

His mouth became suddenly dry. The Outsider must have noticed him licking his lips. "You thirsty?"

He shook his head.

The biscuits were gone, and the foxes had moved on to licking the Outsider's fingers. "Tickles," it giggled. It watched the foxes lapping away and chuckled lightly, and Landfill felt that tingle in his stomach again.

The Outsider's smile disappeared when it returned its attention to Landfill. "So what's the deal? Do you hang out here?"

Landfill didn't reply. He was unable to follow or connect

his thoughts. A detached numbness was spreading through his head and body.

The Outsider shifted awkwardly on its knees. "Actually, there's another reason I came back. Your face, when that man called… First I thought we were running from a security guard or something, but this place has been shut off for years. And he called out for you. Mentioned a vegetable patch, which seems sort of odd. Who was he?"

Landfill was thrown back into his senses. He gasped suddenly, as if surfacing from the Gully for air. "He…he's… gone. You won't find him, so don't even try."

The Outsider shrugged. "But who is he? Why were we running from him?"

"He's *gone.*"

The Outsider raised its eyebrows and whistled quietly. "Touchy subject, I guess." It sat on the carpet and crossed its legs. "Are there any other kids here? It's not the safest place to play, you know."

Two foxes had their heads against the Outsider's thigh. Landfill watched the Outsider's hands while it stroked them. Its fingers were so smooth – so clean and nimble. They moved in such a gentle way, circling Carter's dark ears and brushing Rushdie's chin.

All moisture seemed to have left the boy's mouth. He swallowed with some difficulty before speaking. "You're different."

"How'd you mean?"

Landfill gestured towards the Outsider's hips with his blade, then pointed at its chest.

The Outsider's back straightened. Those heavy-lidded eyes sharpened. "You *what?* You think you're funny?"

"The other Outsider… In the Pit. It didn't have that shape. Me and…" The boy bit his lip. "I don't have it either. You're…different."

"Outsider? In a pit? You called me an outsider before. Is this a game? Is that what you play here?"

Landfill didn't respond. The Outsider rolled its eyes. "Okay. I'll play along, *Landfill.* I have this…*shape* because I'm female." It tilted its head and turned its palms to the ceiling.

"*Feemail?*"

"Yup. You're a he and I'm a she. Are we done now?"

Landfill's eyes widened. "You're…you're a she?"

"Wow." Dawn huffed through her nose. "Now you're being plain rude. I've got to say, your manners are nearly as bad as your BO."

"BO?"

"You know exactly what I mean. You don't smell too great."

Landfill's nostrils flared. "I smell hunkadory." He leaned forward and sniffed. "It's you who smells queer. You don't even have a smell. Not one that's…yours, anyway."

193

"I'll take that as a compliment." Dawn matched Landfill's glowering look. "Shall we drop this now? I didn't actually come here to play games." She got back to her knees, shuffled forward and started when Landfill moved away, his blade raised and quaking.

"Don't come closer!" he said. "Stop jabbering and stay back! Stay back or I'll…I'll…"

The foxes began to bristle. Dawn shushed and stroked them until they settled down, all the while with a close eye on the boy.

"Nonsense and trickery," continued Landfill. "It won't work! Don't want to talk to you."

"Really? Then why'd you come to meet me? And can you *please* stop waving that glass about? I can see you're too scared to do anything with it. I'm not stupid. You can barely hold it straight. You're trembling like a leaf."

Landfill didn't respond. They scrutinized each other in silence.

Finally, Landfill released a deep breath. He ran his tongue across dry, cracked lips. "You said something. Yesterday. You asked about my…mother. What did you mean?"

"Oh god, here we go again…"

"What's my mother?"

Another roll of the eyes. "Em-Oh-Tee-Haich-Ee-Arr. The person who made you. The person you came from."

Landfill's eyes grew larger. His blade dipped. "From… from inside the mother?"

"Yessss," droned Dawn. "The woman who cares for you. Who probably shouldn't be letting you—"

"Lies!" Landfill's blade snapped back into place. His voice was harsh. "I wasn't made by a mother. I don't have one."

Dawn forced a laugh. "Of course you do. Everyone has a mother. Even I have one." She paused and shrugged. "Had one, at least."

"Well I'm not like you! I didn't come from a mother and I don't have one! I don't have…*anything!*" Landfill's chest was heaving, and the breaths shuddered from his nostrils as he tried to control his voice.

Dawn's mouth hung limply open. The boy gulped at air and became dizzy when her scent – that ticklish, flowery aura – filled his lungs. The way she looked at him made his face prickle with heat. Her expression was almost too soft – too wounded – to bear.

"You're getting all worked up," she said. "Maybe you should put that glass down and try to relax."

The blade felt heavy in the boy's grip – so heavy he needed both hands to keep it up. He tried to speak harshly, but couldn't contain the quaking in his throat. "If I put this glass anywhere, it'll be in you."

Dawn shook her head. "You don't mean that."

Landfill snarled. "I do."

"Then why are you crying?"

The boy squeezed his eyes shut and whined when he felt the tears run down his cheeks. He was barely aware of the fact that Dawn had eased down his blade and put a hand on his shoulder. She spoke quietly, her breath warm against his ear.

"Hey. It's okay."

She reached into the neck of her top, and Landfill saw something gleaming through the blur of his tears.

"See this necklace?" said Dawn. "My mother gave it to me. It's the only thing I have left of her. I was really young when she died. Never actually knew her. And my dad went AWOL before I was even born. I'm fostered." She touched Landfill's shoulder. "So I know what you're saying. Sometimes it really does feel like you never had a mother. Like you came from nowhere. I know how it is. I've cried and got angry, just like you. Sometimes I still cry, even now. And that's okay, you know? It's good to cry."

The foxes were gathering at Landfill's ankles, brushing their whiskers against his jeans. He smelled that honey-flower scent again. It seemed to come from Dawn's hair, which hung so softly, so silkily, like a balm against his cheek.

She rested a hand on his back, right between his shoulder blades. "It's funny, isn't it? To miss something you never had. You surround yourself with friends and keep yourself distracted, but it's always there, every time you think about it. A big empty hole. The feeling that…you're alone."

Landfill's chin had sunk into his jumper. He croaked at the floor: "Alone…"

"Yeah."

The cabin became quiet, until Dawn broke the silence with a long sigh. The golden gleam disappeared beneath her top. "Tell you what – how about we head to town for an ice cream or something? It's never too cold for ice cream. I think we could both do with a bit of perking up."

"Don't understand. I don't understand…anything…"

"Come on. Let's get out of here."

"Out. Of here…?"

"Yeah. We'll fetch your shoes from wherever you've put them and head back through the—"

She stopped when Landfill tensed and pulled away. He wiped his face with a woolly sleeve and muttered bitterly. "Traps."

"What do you mean?"

"Won't work. Not going Outside."

"Come on, Landfill. We'll—"

"Mischief. Get out. Go back." Landfill shuffled further away. He kept his eyes to the ground, unable to raise his face to Dawn.

"But—"

"Leave me alone. Won't fall for it."

"Fall for what?"

"Just go!"

Landfill couldn't see Dawn, but he heard her tone hardening. "Listen, Landfill. I'll be honest. When I got into this place, I just wanted to fill up some camera film. I thought I'd get some good photos. But what I got instead was a boy in rags who's scared of me and scared of some guy looking for him. A boy who's wielding glass and playing weird games one minute, then crying in cabins the next. I don't know what's going on here, but whatever it is, it can't be good."

Landfill finally managed to raise his eyes. "Please," he begged. "Please go back."

Dawn raised her chin and considered him silently, then nodded with reluctance. "Okay. You really want me to go. I can see that. And I'm sorry. I never meant to upset you or make you uncomfortable. And I don't want you to feel pressured. I know what it's like when people try to force you to talk about things. But I'm only leaving if you promise you're safe and that you'll meet me here tomorrow. Deal?"

Landfill put his palms to his eyes.

"*Deal?*" repeated Dawn.

The boy nodded. There was a pang in his chest when Dawn got up and brushed past him. Her voice came from the doorway. "Tomorrow. Promise you'll be here."

Landfill lowered his hands, moved to the window and looked outside. He saw Dawn stopping by the hole to peer closely at the creepers on the wall. She reached out timidly, touched a protruding shard of glass and looked suddenly back towards the cabin. Landfill ducked out of sight, then raised his head to watch her disappear into the ground.

TWENTY-TWO

WALLFLOWER

That evening, Landfill and Babagoo ate in silence. The stove glowed as the Den's windows darkened, its crackles blending with the sounds of cats stirring in their boxes. After tearing the flesh from a gull's thigh with his teeth, Babagoo threw the bone to Kafka, who guzzled it down with a grateful grunt.

"You're very welcome, old bleater," slurped Babagoo, speaking through his food. He took some bones from his lap and tossed them one by one to the other goats. "Dig in, my lovelies. Only the best, only the best."

He chortled and grinned at Landfill. Meaty lumps glistened from gaps between rotten teeth. "Come on now, boyling. Surely it's time you got back to gobbling gull. I almost see where you're come from with them – I honestly do. And it's laudable, in its own sweet, demented way. But you can't live on carrots and shrooms for ever. You need proper belly fuel."

Landfill shook his head, and Babagoo did the same.

"I don't know how often I have to explain it, Landfill. Gulls are an exception. They're Pit vermin. Doomed to die, and if we don't eat them we waste them. And we don't like waste, do we, boy?

"And don't go thinking I'll be gutting these for you much longer. That's your work and you need to get back to it, whether you're eating gull or not. I've got enough to do around here."

He looked at Landfill, who began gazing glumly at his lap, then shrugged.

They ate in silence again, until Landfill cleared his throat and looked up. "Babagoo?"

"Mm-hm."

"The Outsiders…"

Babagoo stopped chewing. His face contorted as if he'd tasted something bitter.

Landfill continued. "Do they have hes and shes?"

"I beg your pardon?"

"Do they have hes and shes? Like the amnals."

The scavenger scratched a bushy eyebrow. "They do, my boy. Although sometimes they're like two separate species. Why'd you ask?"

Landfill shrugged. "No reason." He coughed quietly

and looked away, trying to dodge Babagoo's eyes. He gazed at the bathtub in the Den's corner, still slick from gutted gulls. "What about the rot? Can you smell it?"

"Usually. Unless they cover up the stench. All about disguise, are the Outsiders."

"Cover the stench…" Landfill rubbed his nose. "What about blood?"

"Blood?"

The boy glanced at the pocket that held his blade. He swore he could still taste Dawn's blood. That coppery tang seemed to linger, faint but familiar.

Swiftly, he shifted his gaze from his jeans to Babagoo. "Do they have blood? Like us and the amnals?"

Babagoo frowned and rubbed his lips. He looked up at the ceiling panels. "Guess they do."

"And they bleed if you cut them?"

"Should hope so."

Landfill gnawed at a fingernail. "But the Outsider in the Pit… It didn't bleed. There was just the rot there."

Babagoo's back straightened. "Hmm." He clucked his tongue. "All depends on how the rot has spread. Some have lost all their blood to it. Just filth left, my lad."

The boy's eyes glimmered. "So some have less rot than others?"

Babagoo began to squirm. "I—"

"Does that mean some aren't as bad as others?"

Landfill's voice was rising. "That some—"

Babagoo raised a hand and glared at the boy. "Now hold it there, Landfill. I'm not sure I like where this conversation is going. Where's all this coming from? I knew it. You've been far too quiet lately. You've been pondering, and not in a healthy way." A tilt of the head. "Now tell me – why might some Outsiders be…'not as bad'?" He choked a little, and gobbed a web of mucus to the floor.

Landfill closed his eyes, then looked again at Babagoo. "Well…I was mulling… You said the Outsiders have small Outsiders come from inside them. Just like the small amnals come from big amnals – from the swelling. And I was mulling about Woolf – about how she cares for her little wooflings. I pondered whether the Outsiders look after their little Outsiders like that. If they do, are they all so bad?"

Babagoo gawped at Landfill with his greasy mouth open. He began to shake his head, his features tightening. "You're jabbering gibberish, boy. Dangerous, misguided drivel. Certainly, the big Outsiders create the…the small ones."

He stalled, then scowled and wiped his lips roughly. "But they don't raise them so much as warp them. They pass on the hunger and the suffering – fill their tiny heads with hate, fear and fibbery so the rot sets in. You could almost pity the little creatures, if they weren't responsible for sustaining the disease."

Landfill returned his gaze to his lap. He licked his wrist and ran it across his hair. After a pause he spoke again, so quietly that Babagoo had to lean in to hear. "What if the Outsiders can change? Do you think they can get better?"

Babagoo's laugh was as bitter as it was shrill. "Course not! They can only get worse."

Gradually, the boy raised his eyes. "But you got better. Didn't you?"

Babagoo opened his mouth to speak, but nothing came. His lips and eyelids spasmed. "Now… Ah… You'd…" The grubby skin above the hair on his cheeks reddened. "Now watch your jabberhole, Landfill. Be careful what you say. Words can be dangerous things. Sharper than any knife."

"But you did get better. Lost the hunger. You said so."

"I only got better after…after…" The scavenger scratched his forehead so fiercely that skin gathered beneath his fingernails. "There are always…*exceptions*. I'm an exception. You're an exception."

Landfill maintained eye contact. "Sometimes it feels like…there's a lot of exceptions. Like—"

"Watch that brattish little mouth!" Babagoo was on his feet, glaring down from above. "I warned you about words, Landfill. Boys can be cut by what they say. Boys can be too young to understand, and should respect what they're told and what they're supposed to do."

He kicked away some bones and shot a look at the black

windows. "And talking of what you're supposed to do, isn't it time you went out and got some meat to the amnals? Get out. I can't look at you."

His shaking finger was aimed at the door. Landfill looked at it with welling eyes. Then he sagged his shoulders and got up to go.

After the evening feed, Babagoo and Landfill were sitting on either side of a short line of dominoes. They stared at their piles, but neither of them moved. The goats had already settled down to sleep.

Landfill looked at the scavenger. He sighed quietly. "Babagoo?"

Babagoo grunted, his eyes locked on black spots against yellowing white.

"Babagoo, I'm sorry about before."

The scavenger's eyes remained on his dominoes. "You should be."

Landfill wiped his nose with the back of his wrist. "You know how you say there's nothing like me? That I'm special?"

"A special pain in the neck."

Landfill carried on. "It used to feel good. But now... it doesn't."

Babagoo shifted uncomfortably while Landfill went on.

"Sometimes I ponder why there aren't more like me. When I watch Woolf with her wooflings, I feel…alone. It makes me sad that I came from a seed. I ponder why I didn't get to have a…a…" He trailed off and brushed a tear from his cheek.

Babagoo looked up. He pursed his lips, rubbed the bridge of his nose and groaned. "Listen, my lad. There's nothing wrong with being what you are. You're my wallflower. A rare, precious bud, purer than anything in this filthy world.

"And you shouldn't feel alone. That's nonsense. You have me. You have the amnals. You have Hinterland. Out there, Outside" – he nodded towards the windows – "out there, there's nothing for you. Everything you need is here. You just need to learn to *appreciate* it again. Like you used to. You need to stop all this mulling and deal with *facts* – with fear and all I've done for you."

Landfill nodded. He sniffed and wiped away another tear.

Babagoo sighed. "Okay. I think we're both very tired. Maybe we should get some slumber."

After brushing his teeth with Landfill, the scavenger stretched out on the mattress and offered his overcoat to the boy. "Come on, goblin. You need to rest."

Landfill curled up on his side of the mattress. He inhaled the coat's sour scent and pulled it close. They lay there soundlessly for some time, until Landfill yawned and croaked: "Will I ever get the swelling? So I can make something like me?"

Babagoo only snored in reply.

The boy's eyes were red and stinging, but he knew sleep wouldn't come easily. He fidgeted beneath the overcoat, and rolled over to notice a dull glimmer just ahead of his nose. The top of Babagoo's key was peeking out from the neck of his jumper.

He eyed the key, then slowly reached out. As soon as his finger touched it, the scavenger snorted. His eyelids flickered, and Landfill jerked his hand back as if scorched by the metal. Babagoo mumbled through a mouth sticky with sleep. "Wha... Lan..."

"Babagoo?"

The scavenger stirred on the mattress. "Mmyy boy..."

"Can..." Landfill's eyes were misty with tears. "Can we slumber closer?"

Babagoo murmured and grunted, and the mattress shuddered as he shifted to enfold the boy in his arms. Landfill sniffed and gave himself to that woolly, acrid hug.

Later, as the glow from the stove's embers faded, Landfill began to wriggle in Babagoo's embrace. He needed it, just as thirst made him need water, but those arms felt too tight to bear.

TWENTY-THREE

INSIDE OUT

Landfill checked the cabins during his morning inspection of the perimeter wall, but there was no sign of Dawn. A light queasiness fizzled in the boy's belly; he couldn't tell whether it was relief or disappointment.

After lunch, Landfill left Babagoo to thin out some bindweed that was eating into the Nook's exterior. He attempted to saunter casually along the Gully towards the Rippletop, and as soon as the scavenger was out of sight, he leaped to all fours and dashed across Hinterland. Yapping dogs tried to join him at Muttbrough, and he shooed them away as he passed the Rippletop's entrance.

He slowed down upon rounding the warehouse's corner, and peered through a cabin window to find Dawn sitting with Rushdie's muzzle on her thigh. The black device that had blinded him in the Pale Loomer hung against her chest, and she wore the plastic band with cupped ends around her neck.

She smiled when he stepped cautiously into the cabin. "I see you've got rid of that glass. That's progress, right?"

Landfill tapped his pocket. "Still here. I'll get it if you try using that lightning box on me again." With his stomach cramping, he checked behind him and closed the door.

"Lightning box?"

Landfill nodded towards the black device, and Dawn followed his gaze. "That? It's my camera." Confusion skewed her laugh. "I still don't know how to take you, Landfill."

"*Take me?*" Landfill shuffled back towards the door, his hand reaching for his blade.

"Hey, calm down." Dawn raised her palms. "I mean *understand* you. I still haven't got the hang of what you're playing at. Just take it easy, yeah? You're so tense."

Landfill swallowed painfully. His fingers lingered by his pocket.

Dawn stroked the fur on Rushdie's neck. "So are you feeling a bit better today? You're here again, so I take it you're ready to talk about it."

"About what?"

"About what's going on. About this place. Like, why there's all that glass in the walls." She looked through the window towards the glinting shards. "I'm no expert on coke works but—"

"Coke works?"

"That's what this place is. They used to process coal here. But I doubt they put that glass in the walls. Any idea how it got there?"

Landfill's gaze flitted to the window and returned to Dawn, who was watching him closely. She tapped her lips and carried on.

"I'm guessing it's supposed to stop something climbing up – something in here, since the glass points inwards. But what? And maybe those dogs dug their way in, in which case maybe it got out?"

She looked expectantly at the boy, then returned her gaze to the window. "But why would the dogs have come in in the first place? And why are they hanging around? None of it makes sense. And it seems like so much trouble, putting all that glass in the wall. Do you know anything about it?"

She gestured again at Landfill, who frowned at his hands to avoid her gaze.

"No? Then maybe we could try asking that man. The one who—"

"The man's *gone!*"

Dawn cocked her head. Landfill could feel her scrutinizing his face. "How do you know?" she asked. "Who was he?"

Landfill shifted the subject. "The glass keeps...keeps

the shadows…" He stared through the window while he spoke, his words rising in pitch as if to form a question. Then he pressed both hands to his ears and grimaced. "It keeps Outside out. It keeps the *danger* out." He nodded pointedly towards her.

Dawn gave him a quizzical look. "But that makes no sense. If it keeps danger out, why is it on the *inside*? That suggests the danger's in here rather than out there, doesn't it? Besides, there's no danger beyond that wall."

"Lies!"

Rushdie bristled in Dawn's lap. She shushed and stroked him. "Lies?"

"I've *been* Outside. I was attacked!"

Dawn's hand froze in the fox's fur. "You…you've been attacked?"

"By an Outsider," spat Landfill. "In the Pit. Tried to give me grubbins. Just like you."

Dawn held up a palm. "Hang on. Slow down. I'm not following. When was this? Who attacked you?"

Landfill recognized an anxious sadness in Dawn's eyes. He felt the tension leaving his cheeks, and his reply was hoarse. "An Outsider. It was filthy and full of hate and rot. It wasn't…like you. Wasn't like you at all."

Rushdie scampered beneath the table when Dawn got up. "I've heard enough now. Something's iffy here and I won't pretend I'm not worried about you. I hoped I'd figure this out, but the more I find out the worse it looks." She took a deep breath and held out a hand. "Will you come with me, Landfill?"

The boy shrank back against the door. "Come where?"

"To town. You just said you were attacked, and from what I've gathered you don't have parents and you're all alone. I think we need to find you some help. So let's get out of here."

"You mean…Outside?" Landfill's hand moved once more to his pocket.

"I'll take you to the authorities."

"Othritees…"

"People who can help."

"What's peepul?"

Dawn's chin dropped. "People! The ones like me – like you! – out there. The authorities can find out what's happened. They can look after you. God knows they're not perfect, but they've got to be better than whatever's going on here."

"Tricks and traps!" barked Landfill. "They'll hurt me. And then they'll get in to hurt…to hurt…"

"No." Dawn's voice was gentle but persistent. "No one out there's going to hurt anyone. Trust me on this."

Landfill sneered. "I *told* you. I've been Outside. It was all rot and madness. Was horrorific."

Dawn pursed her lips. "I don't know where you were,

Landfill, but it's not like that out there. When was the last time you went outside? Hang on a second…" Her hand rose slowly to her mouth. "A vegetable patch. That's what the man said…" Her eyes widened as her fingers fell away. "How long have you been in here? Where else exactly have you been?" She put a palm to her forehead. "Did someone *tell* you it's dangerous out there?"

Landfill's tongue felt thick in his mouth. "I… It…"

"I'll take that as a yes." Dawn stepped towards the window and stared at the glass in the wall. Slowly, she turned her head to Landfill. Her lips churned, but it took some moments for words to leave them. "Landfill…I think someone's been confusing you. And I think we need to get you out of here."

"I won't go Outside!"

"It's safer there. Please trust me."

Landfill buried his hand in his hair. "Can't trust you!"

"Why not?"

Tears gathered in the boy's eyes. "You're an Outsider!"

"But I'm not an outsider! If anything…if anything *you* are."

Landfill wrinkled his nose. "Watch your jabberhole."

"There are people out there in towns and cities, Landfill. People living together. And if you insist on staying here away from all that, *you're* the outsider. You've got it all the wrong way round. Or inside out." She tapped the

windowpane. "Out there over the wall, you're inside. If you stay here, you're out."

"Gibberish. Makes no sense."

Dawn sucked in her upper lip. "Well maybe inside and outside aren't as simple as they sound." She put out her hand again. "Now will you come with me, Landfill? Please?"

Landfill crossed his arms.

"If you won't come for me, how about you do it for yourself?"

"Myself?"

"Yeah. Someone's told you it's dangerous out there, and I'm telling you it's safe. Why believe one person and not the other? How do you choose? Surely if two people tell you different things, you should find out for yourself. Make your own choice."

"I *did* find out. I was attacked, remember."

"Whatever happened out there, it was an exception." She released a sharp sigh. "I mean, yes, sometimes people get attacked. Sometimes people do bad things to each other. But whoever attacked you – that was *one person*. You can't judge everyone else based on that. Most people are nice, if you give them half a chance. Believe me, I'm well aware of how crappy people can be. But even I know that for every horrible thing someone does, someone else does something good."

Landfill's tone was mocking. "Good? What good?"

Dawn shook her head in exasperation. "Things like… Like… Charity! Human rights! Firemen and nurses, people inventing med—"

"Gibberish!"

Dawn persisted. "Even the little things. Like a hug you didn't ask for, when you really need it. Or a joke about the boy who dumped you – a joke so funny it nearly makes you pee. Really *little* things. And guess what… Those things, no matter how small – they're worth a lot more than the bad things. They're *big* little things. *Huge* things!"

Landfill was shaking his head. "Don't know what any of that means!"

Dawn closed her eyes and pushed her thumb and forefinger into her eyelids. "Well, maybe that's your problem, right there. Maybe that's why you need to come with me."

Landfill didn't budge. His arms were still crossed, and he glared sternly at the carpet.

Dawn groaned. "So that's that, is it? You'd honestly rather stay here?"

Landfill didn't respond. Something was kicked across the cabin, and he heard Dawn pace back and forth before settling back down on the floor.

"Okay," she grunted. "Stalemate it is."

The air seemed to thicken with each minute that trickled by. Landfill wiped his wrist through his hair and wondered what to do. He threw a glance at Dawn, who was fidgeting sulkily with something that glimmered against her neck. "Is that…" he began.

Dawn looked up. "Hm?"

"Your mother. The mother you…came from. You said she gave you that."

"She did." The creases left Dawn's brow. She moved her hands to the back of her head. "You want to see it again?"

Landfill rubbed his calf with his toe while considering the question, then moved slowly towards Dawn and stooped to look at what she'd removed from around her neck. His eyebrows rose, and Dawn angled her hand so that the thin, delicate chain glittered in her palm. Landfill pointed at the small golden shape at its centre. "Looks like…"

"A bird? Yeah. See its wings there? And that's the beak."

Landfill lowered himself for a closer look. "I like birds. Sometimes I don't, but mostly I do." He sighed, and saw the bird mist with his breath.

Dawn took the chain's ends between her fingers, and as she clasped them behind her head, Landfill's eyes moved to the plastic band around her neck.

Dawn tapped it with her finger. "You like my headphones?"

"Hedfoans?"

"What sort of music do you like?"

The word felt strange in the boy's mouth. "Me…
Meeyoo…"

Dawn narrowed her eyes. "Wait there. Are you…?
You're not honestly telling me you don't know what music
is, are you?"

Landfill's expression seemed to answer her question.
She stared at him with her mouth falling open, then pulled
the band from her neck and raised it towards his face.

He flinched and pulled away.

"It's okay," said Dawn. "Put them on. They won't hurt.
Trust me."

He studied the padded cups and gnawed his lips.

"God, Landfill. If I wanted to hurt you I'd have done it
already. I nearly smashed your head with a fire extinguisher,
remember?"

Landfill gave this some thought, then nodded slowly.
He winced at the brush of plastic across his hair, and felt
the pads close in against his ears. Everything became quiet,
until Dawn reached into her pocket and pressed
something.

Landfill shrieked, clawed at the band and threw it
forward, so that it jerked on the end of a thin cable and fell
to the floor.

"Hey!" Dawn leaned forward to recover the band.
"Those weren't cheap, you know."

Landfill was panting on his haunches. Every little hair

stood up on his arms and neck. "Head!" he gasped. "Sounds in my head!"

"Sshhh, Landfill." Dawn touched his arm. "It's okay. They weren't in your head. They come from here." She pointed at the foam in one of the band's cups. "You see?" She held the cup in the air, and Landfill heard faint, tinny noises. "You want to try it again?"

Landfill eyed the pads warily, but curiosity soon had him nodding.

"I've turned it down a bit, okay?" Dawn raised the band again, and Landfill clenched his eyes shut when the pads enveloped his ears.

Slowly, gradually, his eyes reopened. His lower lip began to descend, little by little, until his mouth hung wide open. His heart pumped so hard that his fingertips throbbed and tickled, and his pupils circled and roved, trying to process, trying to follow.

He was only dimly aware of Dawn tapping his elbow. She leaned into view, smiled and soundlessly moved her lips. Then she lifted one of the cups from his ear and tried again. "You like it?"

Landfill felt his lips moving too. "Starlings. Like starlings."

Dawn looked confused. "You mean…like birdsong?"

"Like when they fly together. Flowing. One way then another. Like sky ripples. That's what it's like. But how…"

He touched the cup still pressed against his ear. "How's it happen?"

"What? The music?" Dawn rubbed her forehead. "Well, the stuff that's been played and recorded goes through those headphones into your ear."

"Play?"

"*Played*. On instruments."

"Insrumens."

"Oh god… Let me guess. You don't know what instruments are?" Dawn closed her eyes momentarily and put a palm against her forehead. "*Instruments*. Things that…that are made to…" She looked at the ceiling. "It's complicated, I guess. People make instruments – out of wood, string and metal and stuff – and other people learn to play them. That's how the music's made. People play their instruments together – sometimes loads of them, like whole orchestras and stuff. And then there's all this technology to record and play it, so people can listen to it." She lifted an eyebrow. "Actually, it's pretty mad, when you think about it…"

Her eyes lit up and she grasped the boy's wrist. Landfill – lost somewhere between the sounds in his head and Dawn's growing giddiness – couldn't resist her hold.

"But that's what I mean, Landfill! You have no idea what you're missing! Those people out there… That music you're hearing is by them! They've worked together for years, from one generation to the next, imagining instruments, mastering their craft, practising and practising and making technology to catch it all – centuries of passion and graft to put that in your ears!"

She tapped her lips, her eyes as full of wonder as the boy's. "I've never really thought about it like that. You take it for granted, you know? It doesn't feel like a big deal, but it is! Again, Landfill – the *big* little things! That's what's out there. That's what your *outsiders* are capable of. And there's so much more… So many good things they can do for each other – for you!"

Landfill could barely follow. The hairs on his arms and neck were prickling again, but this time the sensation was pleasant. Dawn lowered the cup back onto his ear and – being careful not to nudge the plastic band – Landfill sat down and crossed his legs. He swayed without realizing, and at some point Dawn grinned and eased a cup up with her fingers.

"Well look at that! Turns out you have a smile, Landfill." She laughed, and Landfill found himself laughing too, but not without a rush of wet heat to his eyes.

The boy swayed and listened, listened and swayed. He shook his head in amazement, then noticed, with a shiver, that the colour had left Dawn's face. Her lips moved quickly, but he couldn't hear what she said. She was gaping at the cabin's window, and Landfill turned his head to follow her gaze.

Babagoo's face was pressed so hard against the windowpane that it looked set to crack. His shoulders were heaving up and down, and the breath that misted the glass did nothing to hide the fury of those wide, quaking eyes.

TWENTY-FOUR

TIME FOR TEARS

Dawn's eyes moved from the window to the door, but she faltered on the spot. Landfill's lips twisted, searching for words, until he yanked off the headphones and sprinted from the cabin.

"Babagoo!" He held up his palms. "It's not… She's—"

"Getting away, that's what!" Babagoo hurled him aside so that he flew with a crack into the cabin wall. Dawn ran through the cabin door and the scavenger met her course, shouldering her neck and knocking her to the ground. She screamed when he stooped to grab her wrist and a fistful of hair, and before Landfill knew it, he found himself clutching plaid and pulling the scavenger away.

Babagoo was taken by surprise and fell back against the boy.

"Argh! *Like that, is it?*" He shot back up to his feet, and pulled Landfill round to his front so he could grip him tightly with an arm across his chest. His penknife jutted from his free hand, and slashed crosses into the air while Dawn climbed to her feet.

"Stay back!" snarled Babagoo. "Stay back and don't even *try* your trickery! Your mischief may work on the boy, but it's wasted on me."

Dawn stood with legs apart and knees bent, her hands held out as if for balance. Her fingers trembled, but her paleness had given way to a red flush of anger. She pointed at Landfill. "He needs to come with me. He—"

"Shut up! Shut that mouth and keep your poison from his ears!"

Landfill sobbed and winced, and struggled to breathe beneath the squeeze of Babagoo's arm.

"It won't work!" Babagoo spat in Dawn's direction. "I won't let you have him! Try all you want, but you'll never have your way. I'll die a million deaths to keep him from you – to keep him safe from your…your *sickness*!"

Dawn panted, and wiped at the mud smeared across her nose. The beginnings of a bruise darkened her chin and neck.

Scavenger and intruder eyed each other in a prickly standoff. Landfill stared through bleary eyes at Dawn's rigid form, and heard the grind and gnash of Babagoo's teeth. The passing seconds felt stretched enough to snap.

Dawn made her move. In one swift motion, she swung her black device up and aimed it at them both. Babagoo howled at its muted flash, and threw Landfill aside to run at Dawn when she leaped for the tunnel.

"No no no!" Both of his hands were on the device before she could duck into the hole. "Won't! Let! You! *Akkk!*"

Dawn had hurled her head upwards, and the crunch of her forehead against his nose sent him reeling. He clutched at his face and stumbled back to the tunnel, but Dawn was gone.

With his head clamped in his palms, Landfill watched Babagoo attempt to climb foot-first into the hole. The scavenger grunted and writhed, and roared when he got jammed in the tunnel's muddy mouth. He glared at Landfill and roared again, the skin crimson around his bristling beard. "Well don't just sit there snivelling! Get me out!"

With lips quivering, Landfill dashed forward to take Babagoo's hands and drag him from the hole.

As soon as he was out, Babagoo turned and pointed at the tunnel. His entire body shook with rage. "What is *this*? What happened here?"

Landfill was kneading his hands. "I found her…the Outsider…when I was checking the wall. Was trapping her in the cabin so you could—"

"LIES!"

Landfill blubbered while Babagoo shook him. "It didn't look like *trapping* to me. And you've seen her before! Why else would you be asking all those idiotic questions about Outsiders? Good job I checked on you. So tell me the truth, you treacherous little scat. *What's going on?*"

Landfill's head lurched when Babagoo shook him again. He looked at the hole, pushed his palms against his eyes. His cheeks were red-raw with tears.

Babagoo glared at him before turning his gaze to the tunnel. "Wait… Wait a minute… Caught you lurking here a couple of days ago, didn't I, when you were supposed to be tending vejbles." His eyes simmered in their sockets. "And there was that time in summer, when you got all slippery and said you were kicking the cabin. Has this been going on since then?"

"No! I promise it hasn't!"

"That fibbing look! Don't even *attempt* to feed me more tripe! Was this hole…" His lips contorted and he leaned in close. "Was it anything to do with you?"

Landfill tried to speak, but choked on his tears.

"*Was it?*"

"It was Longwhite's idea, not mine!"

"Longwhite? The Outsider?"

"No." Landfill squirmed in Babagoo's grip. "Longwhite lives under the Rippletop. Was all his idea, I swear!"

Babagoo twisted his neck to eye the warehouse's walls.

"Longwhite… What does Longwhite look like? Is it another Outsider?"

"Been here a long time. You don't know about him. He's…thin. Long and white. Sharp teeth."

"A snake?" Babagoo's tongue flashed across his lips. "Is that what he is? Always a serpent in paradise…"

Landfill gave the scavenger a puzzled look, and gasped when Babagoo snatched his hand and dragged him away from the tunnel.

"We'll deal with this *Longwhite* later," he rumbled. "And we'll deal with you too. But right now we need to act. It's not safe here any more."

Landfill struggled to keep from stumbling as Babagoo hauled him past the cabins, the Rippletop, the barking dogs at Muttbrough. "She was different!" he wailed. "Not like the one in the Pit. She was…softer!"

"Of *course* she was different! The Outsider in the Pit failed so they tried a different ploy, and this time it worked! Masks and mischief, Landfill! You've seen first-hand how they try to hurt you!"

Landfill yelped when Babagoo yanked his arm. "But she had blood! Blood and no rot!"

"Oh she'll have the rot alright. The rot that runs deep is the worst of all. She'll have the hate and hunger in spades. Just wait and see. That scheming Outsider of yours is about to bring destruction to everything we have.

Then you'll see just how 'soft' she is!"

Bursting through the Nook's double door, Babagoo was struck by a violent fit of coughing. He hacked and cursed, and threads of saliva dangled from his lips. The boy reached timidly to pat his back, but received a fiery glare and stayed away.

When the coughing subsided, Babagoo stomped along the hallway and through the metal door. Landfill shuffled meekly behind him, and watched with the cats and goats as Babagoo dashed about the room, grabbing bin bags and cramming them with dross capes, tools, traps, lighters, cans and bottles of oil. "At least make yourself useful!" He nodded towards the water tank in the corner. "Fill up some jerrycans. As many as you can."

The cats began to prickle in their boxes. The goats stopped grazing on rubbish, their slotted pupils trailing Babagoo's movements around the Den. Landfill looked at the water tank and back at Babagoo. "But what's happening? What're we doing?"

The scavenger was knotting a rope around his waist. "Can't stay here. Not now. Outsiders are on the march and it won't be long before they're here. We have to hide and we need supplies. So fill those cans!"

Landfill got to work on the cans and Babagoo said goodbye to his goats. With his eyes damp and red, he pushed his forehead against their noses. He croaked quiet words Landfill couldn't hear over the sloshing water and mewling felines. The scavenger lingered by Kafka, and wrapped both arms around the goat's neck.

The sight intensified Landfill's weeping. His sobbing distracted Babagoo, who released Kafka and scowled at the blubbering boy. "There'll be plenty of time for tears. That's all we'll have left!" He tied the last bag to his waist. "Now let's move. Taken too long as it is."

Babagoo broke away from the goats, took a jerrycan in each hand and headed for the door. Landfill tried to follow, struggling with two heavy cans and dodging the cats that meowed and circled his ankles. Babagoo hesitated at the door, and looked at the floor for a moment before dropping the cans and turning on his boots. With one cheek twitching, he took a rope from his workbench and tied it around Kafka's neck.

"You're coming with me, old bleater." He pulled Kafka along, and couldn't look at the other goats while he addressed them. "I'm sorry, poor lovelies. There's no other way."

Landfill held the door open for Babagoo and Kafka. Lugging two cans with his bony back bent, he followed the scavenger and goat out of the building and across concrete. He realized they were heading for the Burrow, and his voice broke when he shouted out: "What about the other amnals? We can't just leave them."

Babagoo yelled back, over a blustery wind that sent leaves spiralling through the air. "No time and no room! They'll have to fend for themselves!"

Landfill's lips trembled. "But Orwell and Woolf... Vonn—"

"Sure!" barked Babagoo. "If you care so much, choose one to take your place and stay out here. I can probably count more on a mutt than I can on you!"

Landfill dropped his cans on the concrete. Fresh tears surfaced when he looked in Muttbrough's direction and cupped his hands around his mouth. "*Woo—*"

"Not really, you imbecile!" Babagoo and Kafka were at the open cabinet door. "Now get in here before I come down there and save the Outsiders some trouble!"

Landfill scrunched his eyes, gritted his teeth and took up the cans. He heaved them up several carpet rolls and, after slamming the cabinet door behind him, was soon dragging them down the dark steps.

When he reached the bottom of the stairs he dropped to his knees. He couldn't see anything in the thick blackness, but could hear Babagoo's laboured breathing and Kafka's snuffles. He swivelled on the mud and looked back up the way he'd come. He could just make out the pale, rectangular outline of light at the cabinet door's edges.

"Babagoo," he said. "We left water behind. Two more cans in the Den."

A dismal, cracked whisper in the darkness: "Too late. They're coming."

The Outsiders arrived soon after the light had faded from the doorway. Their approach had been signalled by rumbles that began while some light was still visible. The sounds were faint to begin with – just suggestions of splutters and groans, borne by the wind across some unknown distance. But by the time the light had died, they'd become roars that reverberated through every part of the Burrow.

The roars didn't sound like those of Hunger's Eye. They were punctuated by loud chugs and spurts of angry hissing. The dense chorus suggested a rabid pack of huge, ravenous animals.

The noise settled briefly, then exploded into cacophony. Heavy sounds of pounding came from somewhere at the edge of Hinterland, and Landfill's eyes welled at the faint barking of dogs. Each thump pealed like thunder, causing the Burrow to shudder so that dirt fell upon the heads of the boy, scavenger and goat. On and on the thumps went, louder than a storm cracking open the sky, until a deafening crash was followed by sounds of tortured steel, cracking masonry, a thousand tearing roots. A long, resounding squeal forced Landfill to push his palms against his ears, and the Burrow shook once more to the twisted clatter of metal upon stone.

The roaring picked up again, then thinned out upon spreading in all directions across Hinterland. Landfill heard angry shouts, stomping boots, snarls and barks from dogs he didn't recognize. Whenever these alien sounds neared the Burrow, Landfill saw blue lights flashing repeatedly through the cracks of the cabinet door.

He turned away and could just make out Babagoo and Kafka. Their faces were eerie blue, appearing and disappearing with the flashing light. Landfill wiped his eyes and mouthed an invisible sorry. He held out a hand, reaching for Babagoo's beard, but the scavenger shook his head, his face vanishing as he pulled away.

PART FOUR

THE FLOWER

TWENTY-FIVE

TRAMPLED

Landfill couldn't tell how long they'd been in the Burrow. At first, he'd watched the light come and go at the top of the steps, trying to count the days. But he lost track when exhaustion got the better of him, sending him in and out of a torpid, rhythmless half-sleep.

Barely a word had been exchanged since they'd descended into earth. They listened in strained silence to the sounds from Hinterland – scuffing shoes, rolling wheels, shouts and bickering, metal and masonry slammed and smashed.

Babagoo assembled an oil lamp from a green glass bottle and a rag torn from his overcoat, and positioned it as far back into the Burrow as possible. He always dimmed it with a scrap of cloth when the light at the cabinet door's edges faded, so that the darkness above wouldn't expose the light coming from below..

The first time he lit the lamp, he rummaged through the boxes to the left of the tunnel to the Pit, and took out a few rusty cans of vegetables, along with some dry foods in sealed, battered wrappers. Landfill looked on, noting that Babagoo never touched the locker on its back by the boxes.

The scavenger laid the supplies out next to the lamp, counting carefully and checking the state of the tins. The food was rationed out in small amounts between long intervals and – besides Kafka's farts and snuffles – the loudest sounds in the Burrow came from rumbling bellies. It didn't slip Landfill's attention that Kafka got larger rations than he did, but he decided not to mention it. The water had to be rationed too – just sips and trickles – and Landfill suffered a merciless thirst he could only escape through sleep.

When he first became so hungry that it hurt, he whispered to Babagoo that they should head down the tunnel to the Pit for food.

"Don't be stupid," hissed Babagoo. "They'll be scouring the Pit too."

"What about this?" Landfill crossed the Burrow and tried the locker next to the boxes, but its door wouldn't open. "There grubbins in here?"

Babagoo's eyeballs were green in lamplight. "That locker's none of your business. If you ever touch it again,

236

I'll cut off your fingers and force them down your throat. That should stop your growling gut."

It was the only exchange they'd had over several days.

Whenever the rectangular line of light disappeared, the three of them curled up on the gore-crusted blankets by the steps. Coldness from the dank, clay-like floor penetrated the blankets, and the Burrow reeked of wet earth, sour goat, old sweat, urine and dung. Babagoo slept with Kafka at his back, and Landfill tried his best to sleep close to the scavenger, who no longer offered him his overcoat. Whenever Babagoo started to sweat and tremble, Landfill worked quickly to soothe him, and had to press his hand to his mouth to muffle the muttering. Sounds of Outsiders were still coming from above.

They listened and listened, and at some point the noises from above finally ceased. But they remained in the Burrow, listening closely in case anything broke the silence. The food was all gone, and by the second day after the noises had stopped, the jerrycans were empty too. Landfill watched keenly when Babagoo finally mounted the steps and peeped through the cracks in the doorway. After a while, he came back down the steps and they donned their capes.

They staggered back, with hands flying to their eyes. Outside the cabinet everything was a severe, searing white, and Landfill couldn't see without the light stabbing his retinas.

While his vision gradually returned, he breathed deeply at the cool, fresh air. A glum shower was falling from inert, grey-black clouds, and he rubbed the water into his face and hair. After opening his mouth to the rain, he dropped his head and gazed at Hinterland.

There was barely an animal in sight – only some ravens cawing at the tips of the Black Fingers. A line of thick fog was suspended above the Gully, and behind that the trees of the Thin Woods looked bare, black and crooked. Their leaves had been blown around Hinterland, and were piled in mushy mounds against walls, overturned drums and toppled pipes.

Landfill looked towards the Pale Loomer. Its towering sides were dark with rain. "The wooflers!" He hadn't spoken for days; the words didn't sound like his own.

Babagoo clapped a hand over the boy's mouth. "Keep your noise down," he muttered. "We're not checking on the wooflers. Not now. There's no point in heading over and collapsing on the way. Before we can do anything, we need food and water."

They slipped down squelching carpet rolls and headed for the Nook. Kafka followed for a few steps, then swerved on his own course to munch dead nettles that had fallen from the perimeter wall.

When Babagoo and Landfill entered the hallway they found lockers torn open and scattered on the tiles. A growl rumbled in Babagoo's throat. They dodged the debris, stepped over the fallen metal door and passed through its doorway.

The Den had been trashed. Ceiling panels either hung from above or littered the floor. The stove had been kicked over and destroyed. The cats were gone, their cardboard boxes pulled down and shredded. Blankets had been ripped from the windows and Babagoo's workbench was overturned. In the far corner lay their disembowelled mattress. The bathtub was gone, with only bloodstains on the carpet to prove it had ever existed.

Babagoo groaned. Landfill noticed a squelch beneath his bare feet, followed Babagoo's eyes and groaned too. The water tank had been split and pushed over.

The boy looked on miserably while Babagoo stomped through the Den, cursing and coughing as he checked the bin bags scattered around the room.

"Ha!" He clutched something inside a bag half-buried beneath flaps of cardboard, and pulled out a can of beans. A sour, demented grin warped his face, and he took his penknife from his coat.

The can proved to be stubborn. With growing unease, Landfill watched Babagoo stab again and again with his shivering blade. His cheeks and beard were twitching, and

Landfill could hear words bubbling beneath clenched teeth. "You won't beat me, little can of beans. You *can't* beat me. *I* am Babagoo – the product of hundreds of thousands of years of evolution and refinement. *You*, on the other hand, are a cruddly can of beans. So no, you won't beat me. You *won't* beat me. You…can't…beat…AARGH!"

Landfill ducked when the can whizzed over his head and bounced off the wall behind him. He gaped at Babagoo, who was now as purple as a vein and clutching his lower stomach.

"Ak!" he gasped, flinching in pain.

Landfill ran to him and rubbed his heaving back. "Sshh. It's okay, Babagoo. We'll get the can open. We'll get it in the end. It's not going anywhere. Let's go to the vejble patch. There'll be food for us there. Can drink on the way. From the Gully. The water'll be fresh from the rain."

Babagoo gradually slowed his breathing. Finally he nodded and, after pocketing the can, followed the boy.

They bowed on hands and knees on the Gully's bank, lapping like beasts at brown water. Then they trudged across the nearest steel bridge and entered the Thin Woods. The ground there had been churned by the prints of too many boots to count. The flowers had all been trampled, their petals pale, ripped and scattered. When they reached the vegetable patch they found it had been torn up. Landfill clawed the earth with his bare hands, but the few vegetables he found were pulpous and dark, cobwebbed in mould.

"It's here," grumbled Babagoo. "The rot."

Landfill looked up at him. Rain hid his tears. "Can we check on the wooflers now, Babagoo?"

Babagoo snorted. "Might as well. Could do with the meat."

Landfill looked at the scavenger's face, trying to work out whether he was joking. It was impossible to tell.

Muttbrough was deserted. The only sound there was the ping of rain as it pounded the metal carts. Beyond the tracks it pummelled the Ivy Stack, causing wilting ivy to tumble and slump. Landfill checked the carts one by one, until something made him cry out. He ducked into the cart, and crawled out backwards with a pup spread limply across his arms. "Orwell," he sniffed.

Babagoo had his eyes on the Stack. "Dead, eh?"

Landfill put his ear to the dog's chest. "Not yet. Very faint, but he's breathing. Don't think he's got long, though." He looked at the other carts and his lips began to crumple. "Where're the wooflers? Where's Woolf? How can they leave little Orwell?"

The scavenger gobbed on the ground and pointed a finger. Landfill followed its course, his eyes running along the Loomer's tracks until they met what used to be a section of perimeter wall. A large steel gate once covered in growth lay on the concrete, its dented bars bright between green tendrils.

Babagoo coughed in the rain. "The wooflers abandoned your little friend because he's a cripple. A hindrance. Too much effort. A waste of space." He looked away, wiped his face with his sleeve. "I know the feeling…"

Landfill's jaw hung loosely open. He shook his head. "They wouldn't leave Orwell."

Babagoo nodded towards the twisted gate. Beyond it the train tracks vanished into a cold, soggy landscape. The earth around the opening had been mashed by scores of giant tyres. "Yes they would," said Babagoo. "Outside is inside now. There's nothing between the two. The hunger has poisoned Hinterland. The amnals are gone."

Landfill held Orwell closer. He blinked in the rain and looked around Hinterland, searching for something, for anything. "How can we fix this, Babagoo? How do we get Hinterland back?"

"Hinterland's gone. Can't be fixed. If we fix anything, the Outsiders'll know we're still here."

"So…so what do we do?"

Babagoo rubbed his flaking lips. "Well, right now, at this particular moment…we eat or we die. Personally, I'm leaning towards the latter."

Landfill looked up at him, trying but failing to meet his eyes. "You still have those beans?"

Babagoo nodded.

"Let's eat them. Can try to feed Orwell too. Then we'll drink again at the Gully, head to the Spit Pit. Maybe some traps'll have fresh gulls. Just one'd be something. Or maybe we can find some grubbins."

The scavenger snorted. He looked up and allowed the rain to fall on his face. After a while he began to nod. "Okay. But before the Pit we need to deal with something."

"Something?"

The scavenger kept his face to the sky. "This... Longwhite of yours."

Landfill stared, swallowed and nodded.

With a slightly steadier hand, Babagoo got into the tin of beans. They tipped them from the can into their mouths. Landfill tried to offer some to Orwell, but the pup didn't stir.

When Babagoo was done, he belched and wiped a sleeve across his lips. "Now take me to Longwhite."

Landfill nodded glumly and started to move towards the Rippletop. A quiver in the air caught his eye. Something dark was soaring through the spray, and he heard a shrill cry that almost raised a smile. "Winterson!"

He freed a hand from Orwell to wave at the kestrel, but stopped when he saw something orange and bloody hanging from her beak. It was the squirrel, Joyce.

"Stop blubbering," grunted Babagoo. "Can't afford to linger. This place has turned against us now. Just like everything else."

They were soon deep in the Rippletop's belly. Landfill heard the thin scuttle of insects when he stepped from the ladder to the floor.

The scavenger hopped off just after him. He whispered roughly: "Can't see a thing. Where is he?"

Darkness was dispersed by Landfill's lighter. He pointed reluctantly at the low aperture in the far wall. Babagoo squinted an eye at the black crevice and sucked his top lip.

Landfill, not moving from the ladder, watched the scavenger shuffle towards the hole. Upon reaching it, he crouched with his shins on the ground and slowly, silently, carefully slid his arm into blackness.

"Ak!" Babagoo jolted upwards and slammed his head on a pipe. "Oh you little – *argh!*" He threw himself back from the hole, and Landfill saw Longwhite coiled around the scavenger's arm. The boy made to move his foot, but Babagoo's fury had him faltering by the ladder.

Longwhite shrieked and squealed and Babagoo fell back against the floor. His roar was so loud that it sent pale spiders toppling from the ceiling. He rolled and started slamming his arm against the ground, but Longwhite wouldn't let go.

Tears gathered against the hand Landfill held over his mouth. He could see Longwhite's bristling white fur, his blazing red eyes – the needle-like fangs buried deep in Babagoo's palm.

Babagoo roared again. "*A stinking ferret, eh?*" He clambered to his feet, lurched and smashed his arm against the brick wall. His eyes were locked on Longwhite's while he threw his free hand into his coat and yanked out his penknife.

Landfill stumbled forward, his hand shooting out. "Please—"

"A whispering weasel!" bellowed Babagoo. "A serpent in furs!" With just the one hand he managed to flip out the knife's blade.

"No!" cried Landfill. "Longwhite—"

There was a loud chink. The squealing stopped abruptly and Landfill was on his knees. "No," he moaned. "No…"

"Had to be done," growled the scavenger.

Longwhite's tail fluttered momentarily, then fell still. Babagoo kept his arm pushed against the bricks. Eventually, he eased the fangs from his hand and let go of the knife's handle. He sucked angrily at his palm and spat blood to the floor. He turned to Landfill. "That's that, then. Now to the Gully and Pit. And on the way, I want you to tell me everything – *every little thing* – that happened with that Outsider and that hole."

Landfill just stared in reply, his face pinched and wet in the lighter's flame. A look from Babagoo forced him to nod, and he pocketed the lighter before dragging himself to the ladder.

TWENTY-SIX

MARKED

After they'd been to the Spit Pit, Landfill and Babagoo hid with Kafka in the Burrow. They sat in the glow of the oil lamp, huddled around a small grill improvised from a cracked colander. Their eyes watered from the greasy gull-smoke that filled the Burrow. It made them choke and cough, but also hid the stench of mounting dung. They stared at the grill, licking their lips to sounds of popping fat.

When the meat was ready, Landfill tried to feed a lump of breast to Orwell, who was lying limply in his arms and had barely moved since being found. A tired grin creased the boy's face when Orwell sniffed and shifted himself to dig in. Satisfied, Landfill began to gobble his own portion of the scalding meat.

Babagoo gobbled too, before muttering: "Not so fussy about gull now, are you, boy?"

Landfill didn't respond. He sucked at a bone, and when not a fleck of flesh remained he frowned at the scavenger. "You won't look at me."

Babagoo fingered a dribble of fat on his lower lip and pushed it into his mouth. He shrugged and studied his food.

Landfill shuffled a little closer. "*Please*, Babagoo. You've barely gandered me since we started hiding."

Babagoo took a deep breath and slowly raised his eyes to the boy. "There. I'm looking. Happy now?" His mouth curled into a sneer. "I'm looking at the ungrateful little skulk who singlehandedly destroyed *everything* I built to protect him."

Landfill had to turn his head away.

"Oh," spat the scavenger. "So now who's not looking at who?"

Through the tears that pricked his eyes, Landfill gazed at Longwhite's head, which seemed to float in the gloom like a ragged ghost. It had been torn off and nailed to the mud above the blankets. Its eyes were as dry and dull as brown beads.

Babagoo fingered the bite on his palm before nodding towards the floating head. "There it is, boy. A pale reminder of everything you did wrong. A white warning about listening to anyone but me. Rule three – Babagoo's always right. Rule four – believe only Babagoo! And believe me when I tell you that vile ferret never said a word to you. None of the amnals do!" He jabbed a finger into his temple. "It's all *you*, so don't even try to shift the blame!"

He began to shake his head. "No no – the *ferret* didn't tell you to dig a hole. The *ferret* didn't tell you to talk to an Outsider. And the *ferret* certainly didn't tell you to keep the Outsider secret from me! It was all *you*, Landfill! All that, up there, all that rot and ruin" – he jerked a hand towards the stairs – "was YOU."

Babagoo's hands began to clench. "You were well and truly *played*, boy. That venomous Outsider had you eating from its hand! It was *this close* to luring you out of Hinterland! From having you spill your fickle beans on me!" Emerald light crinkled along his beard. "You've seen it now, in the Pit, in that cabin – in the carnage up those stairs. The Outsiders are as cunning as they are hateful. They have method to their madness and madness to their method."

Landfill bowed his head and said nothing.

They sat in silence until the light faded from the top of the steps. Babagoo moved quickly to throw the cloth over the lamp, draping the Burrow in the dullest green glow. "We should slumber. Need our strength for the Pit tomorrow."

After the four of them had settled on the blankets, Babagoo crossed his arms and kept his coat for himself.

Landfill lay on his side, with his forehead against Babagoo's back and Orwell snuggled against his belly.

The Burrow was soon filled with Orwell's sleepy whimpering and the snores of the scavenger and goat. As exhausted as he was, Landfill couldn't sleep. He felt haunted by the pale head that hovered in the darkness above him. When he managed to peel his eyes from that floating phantom, he spotted something twinkling with the rise and fall of Babagoo's chest. It was the scavenger's key. Its rope was tangled beneath Babagoo's beard, and the key was hanging just above the blankets.

Landfill stretched out a shaking hand and reached slowly for the key. Upon contact, Babagoo's fist grabbed hold of his fingers. Landfill's gaze flitted to the scavenger's face, and he saw a wide, green, glassy eye. But Babagoo was still snoring, so Landfill hushed and stroked his arm. The eye closed and the hand dropped away.

Landfill rolled away to squint at the locker across the Burrow. He reached into his pocket and felt his own key there, but shook his head. After that he rolled back again, pulled Orwell close and cried himself to sleep.

Daylight was fading by the time they hit the Pit the next day. The sky had been swallowed by seething clouds, which raced across the sky with disorientating haste. Decked in their dross capes, scavenger and boy trekked through the filth.

Landfill turned his head to Babagoo. "You could have stayed in the Burrow."

"I've already told you – I'm *fine*."

"You've been stuck on the blanket all day. Not looking too hunkadory. I could have come for gulls alone."

The scavenger cackled bitterly. "What? So you can find more of your precious Outsiders and finish the job?"

Landfill's wrist went to his mouth.

Babagoo snorted. "If you think I'm going to let you out of my sight, boy, you've got another thing coming."

They'd almost reached the traps when Landfill spotted something through a miasma of flies. "Look at that."

Babagoo didn't look. He kept lumbering through the grime with his head bent low, pausing only to hiss and suck the wound on his palm. "Unless it's a new Hinterland, I'm not interested. Let's get to those traps."

Rubbish tumbled as Landfill freed the object from a bin bag bursting with dull plastic cubes. "But look. It's got a face. It's a bit like us. A little copy of us."

Babagoo revolved on the spot. His features tautened before softening sadly.

"Is it a little Outsider?" asked the boy. "A dead one?"

Babagoo sagged and sighed. "It's called a doll. And it's not dead. It was never alive."

"A doll?" One of the doll's eye sockets was dark and empty. When Landfill turned the grubby toy in his hands, its remaining eye winked mechanically at Babagoo, who began to back away.

"Put it down, Landfill."

"Hm?"

The scavenger's voice coarsened. "Put. It. Down. Before I use it to crack your skull."

Nodding meekly, Landfill dropped the doll. He looked up at Babagoo, whose eyeballs started to jut as if trying to escape his face. The scavenger stood frozen, as silent and still as a dumped bag of rags.

Landfill shuddered at the sight. "What's wrong?"

"Your hands."

The boy looked down, saw black smears on his fingers and palms. "Just dirt. From the doll."

"No." Babagoo shook his head. The flaps of his hat flailed in a sudden gale. "No no no. You've been marked."

"Marked?"

"The shadows. They've marked you." The scavenger had been moving away, but now took a cautious step back towards the boy. Landfill could barely hear his whisper over the crying gulls. "It's *you* they want. Not me. I see it now. They've…they've always wanted you."

"But…" Landfill's breaths quickened. His eyes searched the dunes. He felt acutely aware of the darkness lurking in every chink and crevice, pooling beneath every ridge and rim.

Babagoo gripped his hand. "We have to get back to the Burrow! Not safe here. They're coming for you!"

They pushed against the wind as they went. Dusk was falling when they reached the glade. Babagoo squinted ahead before dropping abruptly to his knees. Landfill grabbed his elbows and tried in vain to lift him to his feet. "Nearly there, Babagoo. Keep moving."

Babagoo's mouth opened and closed, releasing nothing more than stuttered wheezes. With his eyes agape, he stretched out his arm. "Moving?" he gasped. "Moving… where?"

Landfill followed Babagoo's trembling finger. Where there once was a fridge sat a huge, dark drift of rubbish. Landfill could just make out the outlines of car tyres, bicycle parts, the arm of a sofa.

He looked up at Babagoo. "The wind! Must have blown the rubbish down from the fridge."

The scavenger shook his head. "Not wind. Shadow work."

Landfill had already sprinted to the mound. He tossed smaller debris aside and heaved hopelessly at scrap. "The door's still under there! Just need to get this stuff off! Dig our way in!"

"No, boy. It's too dark for untangling all that. Even the sky's sided with the shadows."

"No, Babagoo, no."

"Can't you see, lad? One wrong tug and that'll come down on you like death. We're stranded."

Landfill took a step back, and lapped the back of his wrist while studying the heap. His lips puckered with the rise of his gaze along the mound's arc. When he reached the peak, he clapped his hands together. "Not stranded at all. We don't need the tunnel. The night'll help us. Can cover us while we climb the hill."

Babagoo arched his neck to follow Landfill's ascending gaze. Gradually his features hardened, and he ruffled the boy's hair. "Wise goblin. Where there's a hill there's a way. Get moving. You're not safe till we're in the Burrow."

TWENTY-SEVEN

STARLIGHT

Landfill had no idea how far up the hill they were. The darkness made it impossible to tell. They had to use the feel of the slope for direction. Babagoo wheezed and Landfill panted, his tongue hanging out like a dog's. The wind had eased off, but unseen shrubbery scratched his feet and pulled at his jeans, forcing him to yank his legs as he slogged his way up the hill.

Babagoo trailed behind, dragging his coat and bags through gorse. "You can see why I built that tunnel, can't you!" He broke into coughs and caught his breath. "Not just to close up Hinterland. It's this wretched hill! It was misery then and it's misery now. Hold…"

The instant Landfill heard Babagoo slump behind him, he pivoted and stumbled down the slope. "Babagoo! Are you—"

"*Fine.* I'm fine. Hunkadory! Just need a breather." The scavenger rolled onto his back, unbuttoned his coat and mopped his beard with its hem. "Boiling brownberries! Hotter than muttler breath tonight. I'm stewing in my clothes."

"Hot?" Landfill sat against the slope by Babagoo's side. "It's cold, Babagoo. Really cold."

The scavenger didn't respond. They gazed in silence at the darkness below. Landfill could see a few luminous specks along what he assumed was the Spit Pit's edge. Just beyond the Pit hovered the large grid of yellow and orange lights – presumably the tract of buildings he'd seen while high up in the Pit.

He pointed in its direction. "What's that?"

Babagoo grunted. "Where Outsiders gather. Best not to even look at it."

"What about that?" Landfill's finger rose to the deeper distance, and settled on a faraway glow that radiated like a weak, rising sun. Dots of light drifted around the darkness, many of them forming a line that headed in its direction.

"That? That's history."

"What's…history?"

"The past. A long time in the past."

"Oh." Landfill squinted at the light. His breathing began to quieten. "Is that because it's so far away?"

"Eh?"

"Like the stars. I remember once… Once, you said looking at stars is like looking at the past. Because they're so far away. Is it the same for that glow?"

Babagoo wiped a sleeve across his forehead. "Might be on to something there." He puffed some air through his nose. "Quite the philosopher, aren't you, lad?"

"Don't know. What's that?"

"Someone who thinks too much."

Landfill considered this before nodding earnestly. "Then I'm a fillofficer."

Babagoo chortled and spat into some nearby bracken. "A fillofficer if ever I knew one."

The boy tapped his lips. "So if the past is like light from stars" – he nodded towards the distant glow – "does that mean it always reaches you in the end?"

Babagoo stifled a whimper. Landfill reached out into darkness, felt warm wetness against his fingertips. "Babagoo. I thought you said you'd run out of tears."

A shuddering breath. "Seems…seems some wells have no bottoms, my boy."

After hauling himself up, the scavenger staggered a little, and Landfill caught him just before he fell.

"Need to keep moving," panted Babagoo. "No time for dawdledallying. Shadows don't rest."

With time, they finally dragged themselves across

Hinterland's fallen gate. Upon reaching the Burrow they staggered down its steps with Babagoo propped against Landfill's shoulders. After Landfill had eased Orwell aside, the scavenger fell to the blankets like a pile of old clothes. He was joined immediately by Kafka, who bleated gruffly and lapped at his hand. Even in the dim green light, Landfill could see the wound from Longwhite festering there, swollen and greasy with pus.

Babagoo was moving stiffly, straining with his arms and fumbling at his overcoat. After Landfill helped to remove it the scavenger groaned and held it up in quaking hands. It took the boy some moments to realize he was offering it to him. With tears in his eyes, he accepted the acrid bundle, pulled the pup to his stomach and laid down close behind Babagoo. After trying to spread the coat so that it covered all three of them, he pushed his nose into its sour fabric, inhaled deeply and fell instantly asleep.

Landfill woke up cold and damp. The only warmth he could feel came from Orwell, who was snoring peacefully in the crook of his belly.

The boy shivered and rolled over to find Babagoo sat nearby, with the black goat by his side. The scavenger was gazing at some dominoes, which had been placed on their ends in a straight line along the locker's top.

Orwell stirred and whined when Landfill sat up. "Is it morning?"

Babagoo nodded.

Landfill pointed at the dominoes. "You want to play?"

Babagoo kept his eyes on the lengthening line. "No games. No play. That's all long gone. The doll that marked your hands was an omen."

"Oh…" Landfill frowned. "What's an omen?"

Babagoo didn't look up. He took one of two dominoes left in his hand and added it to the end of the line, positioning it a little further from its neighbour, so that there was a larger gap between the two than the regular space between the others.

He repeated the boy's question. "What's an omen?" A noise left his throat that could have been a laugh, were it not so brittle and broken. "An omen means that no matter what you do" – with a tap of the finger, he marked the domino that was slightly separate from the line – "no matter how you repent, no matter how much you suffer, no matter how you *try* to make amends…" He filled the gap between the marked domino and the rest with the final domino. "No matter what, there's no escaping what's owed to you."

With a sigh, he nudged the domino at the opposite end of the line. Scavenger, boy, goat and dog watched while domino after domino toppled, until the one Babagoo had marked hit the locker's top.

Landfill hugged himself. "Don't understand, Babagoo."

After pushing his knuckles into his eyes, Babagoo raised his face to the roots that dangled above him. "It's so unfair, Landfill! You're nothing to do with this. Yet you've been marked. It's you the shadows want. They're getting to me through you!" Tears were trickling steadily into his beard.

Landfill shuffled on his knees to Babagoo and put the overcoat around his shoulders. "Does that mean you're safe?"

"I don't know. I don't care! But I know they want you. They want you because I don't deserve you." Babagoo ground his teeth. "But you're nothing to do with this. Not you, Landfill – my sweet, sweet wallflower. You don't deserve this. You're above it. You're above everything. And yet…" He tremored when he felt the boy's forehead against the side of his hat. "It's all my fault, Landfill. I brought this upon you. I'm so, so sorry."

Landfill shifted to face the scavenger, pressed his palms against his cheeks. "Listen, Babagoo. Look at me. *Look* at me."

The scavenger sniffed, and opened his eyes. They looked so red against the clammy paleness of his skin. Landfill could feel the heat blazing in Babagoo's cheeks.

"Now listen," said Landfill. "The shadows haven't got me. I'm still here. We need to stop moping and we need to get food. We didn't eat yesterday and neither did Orwell.

Not even Kafka – he won't touch the plants up there now the rot's got in. We need to go to the Spit Pit for food."

Babagoo's gaze fell. "There's no getting to the Pit, my lad. Can't use the tunnel; the fridge is buried, and we can't work at it from the inside. Have to work at it from the other side. In daylight. But that means going down the hill in daytime. We'd be exposed. I used to have a grass cape to get down, but even—"

"Then we go down when night comes and wait for daylight! But we need food today – need to find something. Something in Hinterland. In the Den… There might be something we missed. Or the vejble patch. Maybe the vejbles are better."

The scavenger was shaking his head. "Pointless. We're done. The shadows have us scuppered."

"We have to try, Babagoo! That's all there is. Try or die." Landfill got to his feet.

"Stay here, my boy. Starving's far prettier than what the shadows'll do."

"*No.*" Landfill crouched to push his forehead against Babagoo's. "No, Babagoo. Not fair. I made this mess, but you can't choose for Kafka and Orwell. Stay here and starve if you want, but you can't tell the amnals to do that too." He pulled away. "I'm going to check Hinterland. If you won't even *try* to feed your bleater, I will."

Babagoo raised his eyes to the boy, and studied his face

in the growing light from the stairway. His mouth curled into something like a smile. "As stubborn a miracle as ever," he grumbled. "Such a wilful little sc—" He gasped and clutched his stomach.

"You're burning with the fire-flush. Stay here and rest. I'll go alone. I'll be careful."

Babagoo moved to get up, but the boy pushed him back down. "*Rest*, Babagoo. I'll be back with whatever I can find."

TWENTY-EIGHT

BOTH WAYS

Several hours later, Landfill left the Thin Woods. He pouted and kicked at a flap of black moss. The trees behind him were bare, their leaves wind-torn and gathered in a slimy pulp around buildings and chutes. The flowers and weeds that once peppered Hinterland were trampled and translucent, and the vegetation clinging to pipes and chimneys was turning grey, releasing its hold and joining the mulch. Much of the perimeter wall's foliage was on the ground, topped by glass teeth that had dropped from crumbling bricks.

Landfill's head twitched when he heard what sounded like approaching thunder. Looking quickly about, he loped towards the Ivy Stack and took cover beneath its conveyor. Panels rattled above him with the scream of the Eye overhead, and when the roaring died away Landfill noticed movement by the Black Fingers.

Keeping to the cover of barrels and debris, he crept to the perimeter wall and moved westwards until he reached the two silos adjacent to the tall black chimneys. He pulled at pipes and steel frames to mount one of the silos as quietly as he could. His stomach churned with dread while he gained height, and when he peeked over the silo's curve he gasped at the sight of Babagoo.

The scavenger was on the flat roof of the building that formed the base of the Black Fingers. Shuffling back and forth, he arched his neck to study each chimney and mutter beneath his breath. He held a hammer and chisel, which he used to remove a brick from a chimney before adding it to a row of other bricks at the roof's edge.

Landfill clambered to the top of the silo. "Babagoo! Should be resting!"

The scavenger showed no sign of hearing. His eyes scanned the closest of the four chimneys, and he removed another brick before adding it to the others.

Landfill moved across the silo for a closer look. He eyed the hollows in the Fingers where bricks had been removed. "What're you doing?"

Babagoo scratched beneath an ear flap. "You were right, my boy. The shadows don't have you yet, and moping'll achieve less than nothing. You find any grubbins?"

Landfill's stomach gurgled at the word. "Nothing. Not even by Kafka's standards." He looked at Kafka, who was sniffing black weeds by the Gully and turning his nose up at them. "What are you doing? Tell me."

Babagoo frowned at his row of bricks. "Dominoes. That's what I'm doing."

"What do you mean? You said no more games."

A curt laugh. "This is no game." The scavenger pointed at the nearby perimeter wall, in the direction of the Spit Pit. "There's shadow trouble down there, lad. Shadow trouble to curdle your blood and blister your bones. They're gathering – getting ready to come for you. But I won't make it easy. We can be ready for 'em."

"Don't understand, Babagoo."

"We need to have *something*, Landfill. Something in our favour. Dominoes fall both ways, my boy. If you can't have walls you need weapons."

Landfill gave up. "Whatever you're doing, you shouldn't be doing it. You need to rest and fight the fire-flush."

Babagoo raised a trembling finger and hobbled across the roof to the chimney that was furthest from the perimeter wall. "Almost done. Just one more thing."

He examined the brickwork at the east side of the chimney's foot, ran his fingers over its surface and leaned to study the other three chimneys. Then he took up a shovel, aimed it so its tip faced the chimney, and rammed it in. Next, he crouched to grasp a branch which had a sledgehammer's head fashioned onto its end. Grunting with every swing, he thumped the shovel's handle with the makeshift hammer. As soon as the bulk of the shovel's head had disappeared into the chimney, the improvised sledgehammer fell, and Babagoo collapsed.

Landfill leaped from the silo to the Black Fingers' base. "Babagoo!" He rolled the scavenger onto his back and propped his head on his arm.

Babagoo blinked weakly at him. Tears gathered in the red rims of his eyes. "Won't let you down, my lad. Promise I won't. You're—" He grunted and his hand flew to his stomach. "You're the only good thing left. Only thing to live for. To fight…for."

"You need water and rest. Shouldn't have strained yourself." Landfill helped him to sit up. "Can you make it to the Gully? We'll get you watered, then you can rest in the Burrow."

Babagoo nodded, and Landfill heaved him up.

That night in the Burrow, Babagoo lay with his head propped against the black goat. Landfill held a damp rag to his brow, and hushed when the scavenger's head began to loll.

Babagoo stirred slightly, returning from the cusp of sleep. "Medicine," he breathed.

Landfill put his ear to flaking lips.

"Medsin? What's medsin?"

There was an eerie, almost tranquil calm to the scavenger's tone. "Will make me better. Fix this." He raised a palm to show his fierce, weeping wound.

Landfill flinched at the sight. "I'm so sorry, Babagoo. Sorry Longwhite did that."

Babagoo shook his head, his voice a crooning croak. "Oh no no no. Longwhite gave what I've long had coming."

"Where do we get medsin?"

"Chemist. There's bottles and paper. Powders and packets. Will make me better. Need to get better. Can't fail my wallflower."

"But where's kemist?"

Babagoo hummed to himself, smacked his lips. "Beyond the Pit. Where Outsiders gather. We'll go. After rest. Need to slumber…"

Landfill gave the scavenger a gentle shake. "No slumbering. Not yet. How can we go to where the Outsiders gather? They'll catch us."

"Perhaps." Babagoo's head rolled from left to right. "Perhaps not. They think we're gone. Won't be sniffing. We'll blend in. Can blend when there's many."

"Blend?"

"Keep our heads high. Meet the eyes. Be cruel. Show scorn, not fear. They smell fear. If you're weak they'll know. They'll smell it and feed like crows. Believe me. I know."

Landfill swallowed and nodded. "Okay. Medsin. Kemist. No fear."

"And money."

"Munnie?"

"Coloured paper. Swap for medicine. Need to be wary, though. Money's the trickster. Dangerous. Angers the hunger. Stokes the madness."

"Where do we find munnie?"

"I have some."

"Where?"

Babagoo shook his head.

"Tell me, Babagoo!" Landfill searched the Burrow's gloom. The green glint of a metallic edge caught his eye. "Wait… The locker. Is it in there? Is that why it's locked? To keep the dangerous munnie in?"

Landfill jolted when Babagoo sat up and clutched his arm. The scavenger glared at him, his eyes suddenly wide and lucid. "Leave the locker, *boy*. Leave it be."

"Okay, okay. Shush now. Shush." Babagoo's head fell forward, and Landfill eased him back against Kafka. "Rest now, okay? We'll work it out. Get medsin. Make you better."

Soon after the scavenger fell asleep, he began to shiver and grind his teeth. Landfill soothed him until the gibbering became snores, then got to his feet and peeked up the stairway. A dim blue rectangle of light sat at its top; morning was on the way.

He turned and stared at the locker before taking some cautious steps towards it. A quiet yap from the blankets made him falter; he frowned at the panting husky and pressed a finger to his lips. "Need to get medsin, Orwell. And to get medsin I need munnie. Don't know if Babagoo –" his voice became a croak – "if he'll be able."

Landfill reached the locker, took his key from his jeans and slipped it into the keyhole. Each click from its teeth made him wince, and he kept his eyes on Babagoo while easing it in. Then he tried to twist it, but it wouldn't move. Sighing quietly, Landfill turned to face the scavenger. With his wrist tapping his lips, he studied Babagoo's neck, glanced at the key in his hand and nodded to himself.

Crouching low, he moved slowly towards the scavenger and squatted beside him. Watching his face closely, he held his key between the thumb and forefinger of his right hand and raised it to Babagoo's neck. Then he gradually lifted his left hand and – with his own key trembling in his right – plucked the string on Babagoo's neck, so that its key slipped out from beneath his jumper.

Babagoo's hand shot out towards the string, and Landfill deftly pushed his own key into its path. He felt Babagoo grip the decoy key, and looked up at the scavenger's wide, shuddering eye. He hushed him and – keeping the decoy in Babagoo's hand – eased the string away and gnawed through its threads. He pocketed the scavenger's key as soon as it was free, then stroked Babagoo's cheek until the eye closed and the hand fell away.

Landfill remained squatted, watching Babagoo closely and listening until the snoring deepened. With a gulp and a nod, he crept away and returned to the locker. Holding his breath, he slid the key in, and had to cover his mouth when it turned with a click.

The locker door whined when Landfill lifted it slowly open, forcing him to keep watch on Babagoo as it rose. Its contents sat in darkness before him, and he reached in to feel something silky but firm. He took it out and held it towards the lamp. It was a rectangular block with small patterns etched into its front, side and back. One side was indented and silky to touch, and brought to mind the magazine he'd found at the Pit. He opened the block up, and a dusty smell rose from the thin paper pages that flapped from one side to another.

Landfill put the block down and felt around the locker before extracting several similar blocks, all of various sizes and with differing patterns on their fronts and backs. He piled them up on the mud and reached into the darkness again. After brushing something that rustled against his palm, his fingertips touched a small cloth pouch. He held the pouch out towards the lamp and untied its shoelace cord, then reached in to extract a small roll of paper held together by a rubber band. *"Munnie,"* he breathed. He placed the roll carefully on the ground and wiped his hands on his jeans.

There was still some weight in the pouch. He searched its lining and pulled out a small metal ring about the width of a finger, followed by a thin plastic stick with what appeared to be a colourful ball at its end. The ball rattled faintly when Landfill restored the stick and ring to the pouch.

Swallowing drily, Landfill closed the pouch and rested it on the stack of dusty blocks. Then his fingers searched the rustling plastic that lined the locker's base. He felt a knot and pulled it gently up until he was holding a bulky bin bag.

With his heart hammering in his throat, Landfill untied the bag. His heart hammered all the harder as he laboriously pulled out a pair of boots, some coarse baggy trousers, a dirty shirt and yellow vest, some thick plastic goggles.

Landfill was weeping by the time he'd pulled out the white hard hat and stained, bloody bandage. He reached into the bag again. There was one thing left. It was cool and rubbery to the touch, and Landfill blanched when he removed it and faced his attacker from the Pit. The face hung limply between his hands, filthy and flapping, with a ragged gash in its cheek.

Landfill let the mask hang from one hand while using the other to stifle his sobs. He gaped at the insect husks that tumbled from that blank, rubbery face.

A noise from behind, a voice in his ear: "Where're your loyalties, boy?"

TWENTY-NINE

LOYALTY

The mask dropped. Landfill spiralled and fell against boxes.

With a drawn-out groan, Babagoo straightened up and stood over him. "Didn't I always warn you, lad? Curiosity killed the boy."

Landfill scrabbled backwards with a finger aimed at the mask. He tried to find words. "The mask… Those clothes… It was *you* in the Pit. You who…tried to kill me!"

Babagoo sneered. "Not kill you, you cretin. Just frighten you. You went too high, remember? Reckoned you might flout some rules, so I went ready that day – ready to teach you a lesson. Was for your own good! You weren't respecting your fear."

Landfill stared aghast. "I thought I was going to die! All the jabber about Outsiders and masks… You wore one!

You tricked me! You... You *hurt* me!"

He jolted when Babagoo slammed the locker with his boot. "And I'll hurt you again if that's what's best for you. I told you to stay away from my locker. Said I'd cut off your fingers and feed them to you if I caught you touching it." He put his hand into a plaid pocket and pulled out his penknife. "So come along now. Open wide and give me those prying little hands."

Landfill's eyes moved to the glimmering blade. "Please, Babagoo. I..." He shot a glance at the locker. "I did it for you! Was gandering for munnie, to get medsin, to—"

"Twaddle and tripe! You were disobeying, plain and simple. You weren't heeding like a good boy should." Babagoo swayed a little, then steadied himself to shake his blade at Landfill's forehead. "Isn't that the least you can do? Is that too much to ask, after *everything* I've done for you? Why the hell can't you just *listen* and do what you're told? Is it really so hard? Is it—"

He was distracted by shrill sounds of yapping. Both of them looked towards the blankets, where Orwell was barking and trying to drag his rear legs across the mud.

Landfill was shaking, but when his gaze returned to Babagoo he swallowed and tightened his lips. "Listen to what, Babagoo? To your fibbery? To lies about an eye in the sky that'll snatch me away but never really does? To lies about swellings and all the little amnals coming from

Outside? Or how about stories of me coming from a seed – of how I'm the only thing that *doesn't have a mother*?"

His expression quivered before hardening into a scowl. "What other stories have there been? How many fibs? Has *anything* you've said been true? Or is it all fear and gibberish? Is all that rot and hate and trickery out there actually in here?" His finger pointed back and forth between them while he snarled and clacked his teeth.

Babagoo clacked back and pulled away, then raised an eyebrow and leaned back in. "And there it is again – the little brat's faltering loyalty. Whose side are you on, boy? Are you one of *them* now? Are you an Outsider?" His free arm shot out towards the black goat, who was shuffling across the mud towards them. "Stay put, Kafka! The brat can't be trusted."

He coughed and winced before flashing a fevered grin at the boy. "You really want to know about your precious *mother*?"

Landfill's eyes shimmered with tears. His hands flexed stiffly into claws, and all the while Orwell yapped on.

"Pah!" Babagoo gobbed at the boy's feet. "You've got a mother alright, but she's not interested in you. I found you in the Spit Pit, just like I always said. Not as a seed, but as a tiny pile of limbs on the brink of death. Found you in a suitcase, thrown out with all the other rubbish that wasn't wanted. That's what *landfill* means to them, boy! Unwanted trash to be discarded and forgotten. That's all you were to your mother."

"No!" Landfill shifted down onto his haunches. "You're lying again! Mothers care! I saw Woolf – how she was with Orwell."

"Oh yes? Then where's she now?" Babagoo searched the Burrow with exaggerated jerks of the head. "Woolf dumped her little runt, just as your mother did you."

Landfill's breaths felt too vast for his chest. Each exhalation shook his entire body. His lips moved, but no words came.

"Was nicer to come from a seed, eh?" The scavenger spat into mud. "Don't you get it? Sure, I've bent some truths. But nothing I've said doesn't stem from fact. Truth and lies are more tangled up than you'd ever believe. Most of the time they're indistinguishable! Truth is an impossibility – a patchwork that falls apart as soon as you touch it. The closest thing you'll get to truth is with me. There's no truth Outside, my lad. There's only the lies they choose to believe."

He huffed and wiped his lips. "You have no idea how hard I've worked to build somewhere safe for you, Landfill. I've worked myself to the bone for you. And yes, there've been some prices to pay." He shrugged bitterly. "A few fibs and fancies are the least of it. The things I've had to do!"

A questioning look began to weaken Landfill's expression.

Babagoo huffed. "Do you think all the fluffy amnals from the swelling had the privilege of sharing this sanctuary with you?" He shook his head. "You've seen it yourself – half of them ended up in the Pit as food for the flies. And those Hinterland amnals I was seeing to, with all their whining and the scars between their legs... Same as the littluns left to the Pit. It's a little thing called *population control.*"

Babagoo leaned in closer and stared into Landfill's eyes. "Hinterland could only sustain so much life, boy. If territory starts to shrink, life turns against life. That's why I did what I did! That's why I did what *had* to be done! Paradise isn't free, Landfill. There's always someone who pays a price.

"Like your precious gulls – they paid it too. Can you comprehend what Hinterland would've been like if we didn't feed the amnals? It'd be like inviting Outside in! They'd turn fang and claw against each other and in no time the hunger would have ravaged the perfect Eden I built for you. For *you.*"

Babagoo's knife quivered by the nub of Landfill's nose. "Don't look so surprised! Wipe that miserable look off your face. You see now how much I've done for you? How much I've toiled? I've twisted *nature* with my own bare hands! All for you! *Everything* for you! And are you grateful? Do you appreciate it? Do you listen when I set a few rules and try to keep you safe from what's out there? Or do you rebel? Do you ignore my warnings and spit in my face? Do you slink and scheme with Outsiders and destroy everything I've spent years building for you?"

Orwell's yapping became shriller and shriller. Landfill drew his face slowly back from Babagoo's blade. "All those amnals in the Pit," he began. "All those tiny, dead amnals… How could you do it? One of them could have been Orwell…"

Babagoo snorted through flaring nostrils. "A few abandoned amnals. A daily handful of gulls. A small price compared to what you pay Outside. Dead mowlers and muttlings are sunbeams compared to the horrors out there."

Landfill's hand was edging subtly towards his jeans. "But it wasn't just them who paid a price."

A tilt of the head. "Eh?"

The boy's hand was in his pocket. "I paid too."

Babagoo sneered. "With what?"

"With blindness."

Babagoo leaned back and winked both eyes as if struggling to focus. He cackled abruptly. "Blindness isn't a price, my lad. It's a privilege."

He cackled again, and Landfill swiped his glass blade

through the air. There was a spark when it caught the scavenger's knife. Babagoo reeled a little, whisked his hand back and raised an eyebrow at the boy. "There you go again! Where does it stop, you wretched little skulk?"

He inhaled sharply and looked at his hand. Landfill looked too, and his mouth dropped when he saw the red slit in Babagoo's finger.

Babagoo glared at the boy and put the finger to his lips. "So. My wallflower's grown thorns, eh?" He scrunched up his face and raised his knife. "Try that again, lad. Try it again, so I can knock that toy out of your hand and bury this blade in your head."

Landfill shuffled backwards and got to his feet. He held his blade up to Babagoo's, trying his best to stop its trembling. Babagoo leered at the shaking glass. Something caught between a grimace and a grin was warping his face.

He lurched suddenly forward, and Landfill jumped to the left. While Babagoo staggered and coughed, Landfill grabbed the lamp from the ground and blew out its flame. Propelling himself through sudden darkness, he swung the lamp through black air and felt a thump as the lamp shattered.

Something slumped to the ground.

There was silence. Even Orwell's barking had stopped.

Landfill took the lighter from his jeans and sparked its wheel. Babagoo was lying still with his face against the ground. Kafka snuffled at the glass splinters covering his hat and neck.

"Babagoo… Are you…?" The boy's words were broken by sobs. He crouched and put a hand to the scavenger's back, saw blood trickling from beneath an ear flap. A small yip drew his attention away, and he nodded at the pup. "Breathing. But only just." His voice began to break. "He's bleeding. I…" He thrust a hand into his hair. "Had no choice!"

Orwell yapped again, and Landfill got to his feet. "You're right. Medsin. He said it can make him better." He looked at the stairway. "Need to get down the hill. Before daylight. Go where Outsiders gather. You and Kafka look after Babagoo. I'll be back soon as I can."

Landfill seized the roll of coloured paper and sprinted up the steps. He kicked the cabinet door open to find indigo skies tinged red. After sucking in some cold air, he leaped down carpet rolls and ran.

PART FIVE

THE PLUCK

THIRTY

THE SCENT OF FEAR

The sun had begun its ascent by the time Landfill made it down the hill. He skirted the dunes of waste, trekking through mud and gorse along the Pit's northern side. Occasional movements along the Pit's rim – sunlight catching on hard hats and luminous vests – sent him ducking and quaking behind thickets.

With his heart hammering, Landfill left the Spit Pit behind and climbed over a low stone wall. He found himself on a strip of asphalt that stretched in a shallow curve to the left and right. Heading right, the strip cut into a wide wedge of trees; going left it headed towards squat buildings and tall wooden poles connected by cables.

An attempt to get his bearings provoked a giddy rush of dizziness. Landfill gripped the wall with white-knuckled fingers, trying to focus his eyes on the poles' cables. He couldn't tell whether they were swaying with the shifting ground. A trembling ran through his soles and a loud blare sent him scrabbling back over the wall. He covered his ears when something rushed by, fluttering his fringe with its own whipping wind.

Panting heavily, Landfill followed the sound and saw two rolling machines – each like a giant, limbless metal bug – racing away along the asphalt strip. The ground began to settle beneath him while he watched them disappear. With eyes clouding, he turned towards the Pit and gazed longingly at Hinterland's four black chimneys. After taking some steps back the way he'd come, he clenched his fists, turned back around and headed left along the asphalt strip.

The strip was soon bordered by the rows of brick buildings he'd seen from high up in the Pit. They stretched out in long lines, broken only by the strips that crossed them further ahead. Rolling machines of various colours – brighter and shinier than any trinket he'd polished in Hinterland – were roaring by more regularly now. Landfill held his breath every time they passed, but appeared to be safe on the cracked, raised slabs that lined the asphalt strip.

He was struck by the lack of foliage or decay on the bricks and concrete. There was a cold, grimy starkness to every surface; corners and edges were naked and sharp. He stiffened when he clocked an Outsider coming towards him, just ahead on the slabs. Its black jacket had white stripes running like tracks down its arms, and was open to reveal a T-shirted stomach the shape and size of a bag of gulls.

Landfill stared at the Outsider, bewildered by the bluish clouds of smoke that erupted occasionally from its nose. It drew nearer and Landfill noticed it was sucking at a thin metal tube. He muttered his mantra – "*Blend. Blend. Blend.*" – scowled and tried to still his shaking limbs. When the Outsider was close enough to touch, Landfill strained to hold his head high, and reached for the glass blade in his pocket. Its tip pricked his thumb, and his senses sharpened to the point that he could see every pore on the Outsider's ruddy face.

But the Outsider didn't notice him. Its attention was fixed on a small plastic rectangle cradled in its hand, which emitted a small, shifting light that had Landfill enthralled, until he was startled by a puff of fragrant smoke.

The blade stayed in the boy's pocket. He watched the Outsider walk away, wiped his clammy hands on his jeans and continued along the slabs.

He was among more Outsiders now – Outsiders of shapes and colours as varied as they were baffling. There were soon so many Outsiders that Landfill struggled to keep a wary eye on each of them. Like him, they walked along the slabs flanking the strip. Some of them looked blankly ahead as they strolled, while others gazed absently at the rectangles in their hands. But Landfill noticed that one – young looking and in a hooded top – was watching him from the other side of the strip. Its plastic rectangle was pressed against its ear, and it was nodding and appeared to be talking to itself.

Goosebumps erupted all over Landfill's body; the young Outsider wasn't alone in watching him. Other Outsiders were slowing down to stare at him – to ogle his dirty face, crusty jumper and bare, muddy feet. He did his best to keep walking and stare rigidly back, and the Outsiders often looked away. But some continued to stare, parting their lips to reveal teeth so uniform that Landfill couldn't help running his tongue along his gums.

These staring Outsiders usually stepped aside when Landfill passed, as if trying to maintain their distance. But others kept their eyes locked on his. Some even changed their course to trail him for one or two steps before stopping on the spot. Landfill fondled the glass in his pocket, continued to mouth his mantra and picked up his pace.

He scanned buildings, doorways and windows, searching for signs of bottles or paper, powders or packets. He sniffed keenly at the air, which smelled all at once of more things than were imaginable. There were clashing scents of rain, of soot, of sulphur, mildew and urine – of hot grease, cold dirt and remoistened faeces; of damp weeds and chemical sweetness and something caustic he couldn't identify. His nostrils twitched frantically and his eyes continued to roam. Every muscle was sore in his limbs, taut against the urge to turn around – to drop to all fours and bound away.

Sometimes, between the yawns of thunder from rolling machines, Landfill heard other noises: plastic cacophonies that poured from open windows in narrow brick buildings. He lapped at his wrist and screwed up his face, trying to make sense of the jumbled barrage. As he passed a window he peered through to glimpse several Outsiders gathered around a huge rectangle of light, which hovered and flashed against a smooth yellowish wall. The Outsiders laughed and the rectangle laughed back. Landfill rubbed wildly at the back of his neck – at the hairs so keen and erect that they felt like pins in his skin.

He was trying to look through the next window along when something touched his arm, causing him to yelp and spin. Groping clumsily for his blade, he found himself face-to-face with a bulky Outsider. It was sat on a wheeled machine reminiscent of those on the strip, but much smaller, with four tiny grey wheels and no roof.

"Are you alright, young man?" it squawked.

Landfill gaped at its crease-ridden face. Its hair was

bunned up in bluish rolls, and grey-yellow teeth chattered beneath a faint moustache of fluff.

Landfill swallowed deeply, spoke through rigid lips. "Kemist. Where is it? I have munnie." He took the roll out from his pocket, tearing off the rubber band so that coloured sheets flapped in his hand.

The Outsider's rheumy eyes were agape. "Put that away!" It pushed his hand down and guided the wad back into his pocket. "You want to get robbed?"

The Outsider twisted in its seat to peer around, and Landfill noticed that other Outsiders – some of which he'd passed earlier – were gathering behind the wheeled machine. They seemed to consult their rectangles and mutter to each other in hushed tones.

"...*coke works...*"

"...*said there was a boy...*"

"...*never found him...*"

"You need to take more care," continued the blue-haired Outsider. "Where are your parents? Are you lost?"

One of the muttering Outsiders met Landfill's gaze. The moment it stepped forward, Landfill submitted to his instincts and ran. He felt sick as the slabs raced by beneath his feet, and someone shouted behind him. He ran and ran, dodging the Outsiders that were too distracted to move aside, or weaving widely around those that trailed him with their eyes. His lungs were raw, and his ribcage felt sore with the pounding of his heart. Watery, acidic bile flooded his mouth and trickled down his chin.

And then, after skidding around a corner, he saw her. He cried out, triumphant and terrified: "*Dawn!*"

THIRTY-ONE

EXISTENCE

Dawn turned her head. Her lips parted. "Landfill?"

Landfill had lost all control of his limbs. The legs attached to his hips pumped on their own accord, driving him towards her. The arms on his torso swivelled in their sockets, threw themselves around her waist. He took cover behind her back, and pushed his watering eyes into the grey fabric of her top. "Daawwwnn…" he moaned, then peered around her side to see a pack of Outsiders closing in.

Dawn thrust a palm out towards them. "Back off, will you? Can't you see he's terrified?"

The Outsiders slowed to a shuffle. One of them, with a hard, rectangular case in its hand and some sort of black ribbon dangling from its neck, pointed at the boy. "That's him, isn't it? From up the hill? It must be."

Landfill gawked at the speaker's smooth, hairless head. When it moved closer, Dawn held up a finger. "Please. Just give him some space."

"But—"

"I'll deal with it, okay? I know him. You can see he knows me, can't you?"

The Outsider hesitated.

"Good," said Dawn. "So leave him with me, okay? You just doddle on to the office or wherever it is you're heading."

The Outsider reddened before muttering and falling back. Murmurs were exchanged within the pack, and after shrugs and lingering stares, they finally turned and scattered.

Dawn eased Landfill's arms from her waist so she could swivel to face him. Her smile sent a familiar flutter through his stomach. "Landfill! It's really you! I got a call from a friend who said he might have seen you up the road. I didn't believe him but thought I'd look around, just in case. And here you are!" She put her hands on his arms. "I was so worried – you know, after what happened with that man..." Her smile faltered while her pupils searched the slabs and asphalt. "Are you safe? He's not here, is he?"

The mention of Babagoo had Landfill pulling away. His heartbeat settled into a steadier rhythm, and his limbs felt once more like his own. "No."

She looked eastwards, in the direction of Hinterland. "Is he still at the coke works? If he is, we need to tell the police."

"Pulleess?"

"Yeah. So they can get him and find out who he is, what he's been doing. It'll help them to help you."

Landfill took another step back. His expression shifted with growing wariness. "No pulleess. He's not there."

"Then where is he?"

"He's gone."

Dawn tilted her head, her expression mirroring Landfill's. "You said that before. Is he *really* gone?"

"Where's kemist?"

Landfill's question had the desired effect. Dawn was thrown. "Kemist?"

"Need medsin."

"Oh… You mean medicine? Are you hurt?"

Landfill shook his head. "Need to find medsin." He took a step back towards her, then reached out before hesitating. "Can you help me?"

Dawn fidgeted with the golden chain on her neck, and spent some moments searching the boy's face. "I can help you," she finally said. "I'll help you by taking you to the police – to the authorities."

"No pulleess! No othrites! *Medsin.* Need to get medsin and go back."

"You can't be serious, Landfill. You're safer here. Let me take you to people who can help you."

"If you won't show me where kemist is…I'll find it myself!"

Landfill was turning away when he felt Dawn clutch his shoulder. His heart kicked and he lowered himself, bracing to flee, until a sigh stopped his feet.

"I'll take you," said Dawn. "Just stay with me, okay?" She released his shoulder and shrugged. "There's a chemist not far from here. I'll show you the way."

Landfill followed a few steps behind as Dawn moved briskly along the slabs. She turned abruptly. "Why are you hanging back like that? And what's that look for? I'm helping you, aren't I?"

Landfill eyed her darkly. The edge of his lip curled to reveal a sliver of teeth. "Why'd you do it?"

"Do what?"

"You destroyed everything." The boy's voice began to break, but he maintained his steely expression. "You tore Hinterland down and drove away the amnals."

He tipped his head eastwards and Dawn's eyes flashed with comprehension. "You mean the coke works? *I* didn't do that."

"You sent Outsiders."

"Things got out of hand up there, Landfill. The police headed up when I showed them the negative of you and that man, but then word got round and before the police knew it they had a mob on their hands. From what I heard, things got heated. Stuff got trashed." She snorted bitterly. "Some people are just looking for an excuse to smash stuff up, you know?"

Landfill scowled. "Hate and madness."

Dawn shook her head. "It wasn't like that, Landfill. It's not so straightforward. Those people only got worked up when word spread that I'd been hurt. They were looking out for me. In fact, they were looking out for *you*. When the rumours spread about a man keeping a boy up there... Well, that's when it *really* kicked off."

She closed her eyes and massaged her forehead. "I mean, yeah – maybe they shouldn't have gone so overboard. They should have let the police do their job. But sometimes it's a fine line, you know – between anger and caring. Can you understand that?"

Landfill's lips tautened. He felt his head begin to bow, for he understood more than he liked to admit.

"Are you okay, Landfill? You're sure you're not hurt?"

The boy nodded and felt Dawn's hand on his elbow.

"Landfill. Listen. I'm really sorry the coke works got trashed. But it's for the best, believe me. And there's something I need to say.

"I'm sorry I left you that day. After that man attacked me it was fight or flee, you know? I ran for help, and only realized as I got into town that I shouldn't have left you with him. I felt *terrible*. I still do. But by then, the best thing I could do was stick to the plan – get to the police so they could deal with that guy and help you."

Landfill looked up to notice the scar that lined Dawn's temple, deep and dark like the rim of a mask. His throat began to expand, and he swallowed the salty lump that was swelling there. "I'm sorry too."

"Hmm?" Dawn followed his gaze and touched her scar. "Oh. You mean this."

Landfill frowned at the mud crusting on his feet. "I'm sorry I hurt you. Didn't know what was happening. I… I don't know *anything*. I'm so…jumbled up."

Dawn's nostrils flared momentarily. She closed her eyes and sighed. "I'm over it, Landfill. As over it as I can be. I know it wasn't your fault. It was that man. That's who really did this."

She squeezed Landfill's hand. He felt the warmth of her fingers through the sweat covering his own. "Come on," she said. "Let's get you to that chemist."

They made some headway, until something ahead made Landfill pause. There was an Outsider that looked different to the others. While most of the Outsiders wore clothes that were clean and intact, this one was limping on torn shoes and wore a filthy, baggy coat with a missing sleeve. The rims of its eyes were dirty and red, and long clumps of hair hung against cheeks that were dark with scabs and stubble.

Two Outsiders with orange skin, long hair and metal hoops in their ears were heading towards the one-sleeved Outsider. They tottered on silver shoes with tall, pronged heels that bewildered Landfill more than anything he'd seen.

Landfill watched the scruffy Outsider hobble meekly towards the orange-faced pair. Its palms were clasped together in a gesture of pleading. Landfill was too far away to hear its words, but when the Outsider spoke he saw teeth as brown and crooked as Babagoo's.

Dawn tugged the boy's hand. "Come on, Landfill. We're nearly there."

Landfill pointed at the Outsider. After calling out to the orange pair now walking away, it approached other Outsiders with its palms still pressed together.

"Can you see that one?" asked Landfill. "With the missing sleeve? The one a bit like…like…" He couldn't help casting a glance towards Hinterland.

Dawn watched the limping figure. "Sure I can."

"Can the other Outsiders see it?"

"Why wouldn't they?"

"But if they can see it…" He rubbed his eyes. "If they can see it, why aren't they looking at it? I think it wants help. Why aren't they helping?"

Dawn exhaled slowly. "It's complicated."

Landfill looked confused. "But it doesn't make sense."

He turned his damp eyes to Dawn, who was examining him sadly.

She bit her lip. "I'll explain at the chemist, okay? So let's keep moving." She squeezed his trembling hand, tugged him gently and they continued on their way.

The one-sleeved Outsider mumbled when they passed: "Spare change for food?"

Dawn didn't respond. She kept her eyes firmly ahead. Only Landfill returned that pitiful gaze, and the scruffy Outsider jolted on its feet, as if surprised to discover it actually existed.

THIRTY-TWO

THE HUNGER

They turned a corner and started along another strip lined by red-brick rows. Upon passing a ceilinged, vertical pane of glass that jutted from the slabs, Landfill stopped again. He was contemplating an overflowing metal box sat next to the glass pane. "What's that?"

"A bin. Now keep moving." Dawn pointed at a wide building just ahead, with a shiny blue façade covered in white squares and symbols. "The chemist is just over…"

Her words fell away when Landfill started digging through the rubbish piled on the bin. "Landfill?"

Dawn moved towards him, but hesitated when she got close. He was throwing empty packaging to one side and piling food scraps on the other. While Landfill rummaged, he shoved bits of rubbish – orange peel and pale lumps of burger meat – into his face. In the corner of his eye, he noticed a nearby Outsider with wires dangling from its ears. It saw him, stopped walking and raised its plastic rectangle in his direction. Other Outsiders stopped to watch too, some of them whispering to themselves or to others.

Dawn groaned and tried again. "Please stop, Landfill. That's kind of gross."

Landfill kept digging. "That Outsider," he began. "With the missing sleeve." He broke off to chew some pale, soggy blocks of potato he'd thrown into his mouth, then gulped and carried on. "Think it wanted food. There's food here – so much good food! We can bring it back! Not complicated at all."

"It is and we can't." Dawn tapped her foot against the ground. "Listen, Landfill. That chemist closes in *one* minute. If you want medicine, we need to go in there right now."

Landfill turned from the bin. He looked back and forth between the building ahead and the corner behind them.

"*I'll* get food to that man," said Dawn. "Clean food. I'll do it straight after we go to the chemist. Okay?"

Landfill tilted his head. "You swear?"

Dawn put a hand to her chest. "I swear. Now let's go, you little weirdo."

A glass door slammed behind Landfill as they entered the building, and his hand shot out for Dawn's once more.

His pupils darted in every direction, taking in the scuffed, rubbery floor; the rectangular sheets of paper stuck to the walls; the dusty, glass-fronted cube suspended in an upper corner. Some Outsiders were sitting on plastic chairs to one side of the room, and there was a wide rectangular hole in one of the walls, behind which sat two Outsiders in clean white shirts with black patches on their shoulders.

Dawn squeezed his hand and pointed at the plastic chairs. "Take a seat, okay? I'll get your medicine for you."

Landfill frowned at the chairs. "Take one? Where to?"

"It means sit down."

Landfill winced and scratched his head. "Oh."

Dawn watched him cross the floor, and waited until he was sat on a chair before turning to talk quietly to one of the Outsiders behind the hole in the wall.

Landfill massaged the blade in his pocket. He cast a suspicious eye over the Outsiders sitting around him, and clocked that one of them – with long dark hair and a string of shiny beads around its neck – was watching him.

It leaned over and smiled. "Are you okay, little man? You look like you could do with a square meal. Are you hungry? I might have something in here, if you're lucky." It started to dig through the little black bag on its lap. "I'm sure I packed an apple this morning."

Landfill drew away and narrowed his eyes. "Not hungry. Just ate. Grubbins in the…bin out there." He tipped his head towards the door and showed his palms, which were slimy with burger grease and flecks of potato.

"Oh." The Outsider's smile faltered before stiffening awkwardly. One of its eyes twitched. "Well isn't that nice."

While it cleared its throat and moved to another seat, another Outsider shuffled onto the chair beside Landfill and cackled. "Proper street food, right?" It laughed again and pointed at the boy's feet. "You here to report some missing shoes?"

The Outsider grinned and Landfill was startled by a mouthful of metal teeth. He looked towards Dawn, who was still talking to the Outsider behind the hole. The Outsider she was speaking to glanced quickly at him before nodding at her words.

Landfill licked the dryness from his lips. He forced himself to meet the eyes of the metal-mouthed Outsider. "Medsin."

"Eh?"

"Here for medsin." The boy looked around. "Where's medsin in here?"

The Outsider leaned back and crossed its arms. "You mean *medicine*? You won't get it here, bud. Not in a police station. Just a taste of your own, yeah?" That wide mouth clucked and sparkled.

Landfill tensed. *"Pulleess?"* He searched the room again. "This is pulleess? Not kemist?"

"Course it is, yeah? What's up, bud? Gone as white as a sheet!"

Landfill was already on his feet and sprinting for the glass door. He heard Dawn call out, and dropped to all fours the moment he hit concrete. Other voices were calling too, and he heard the thick clopping of boots behind him.

Landfill loped as quickly as he could back the way he'd come. There were sounds of slamming metal, rubbery screeches and revving roars. Rolling machines skidded aside and another machine raced by – a wailing blur of white metal and flashing blue. It screeched to a stop and released two white-shirted Outsiders, who stepped out and blocked the path ahead. Landfill skidded on his heels, and before he could even pivot was gripped by a white-shirted Outsider who'd pursued him from behind.

"No!" cried Landfill. "Let me go! Got to get back!" He caught a glimpse of Dawn, who was hovering behind his captor with tears in her eyes and a hand to her mouth. "Fibbing trickster!" he screamed.

"Please!" shouted Dawn. "It's for your own good, Landfill! I had to make you safe!"

Landfill's head thrashed towards the Pit. "You sound just like *him!*" He growled and looked around, his gaze skimming the faces of Outsiders that had stopped to stare. Some stretched on their toes and craned their necks, while others aimed plastic rectangles at his face.

"Lies everywhere!" wailed the boy. "Fibbery and mischief! That's what's over the wall – just like Babagoo said! You're all mad and you're all blind!"

"No," pleaded Dawn. "You'll see, Landfill! Give us a chance to let you see!"

"Don't want to see! Just want medsin! Someone give me medsin! I have munnie!" Landfill wrenched his arm free of the Outsider's grip, thrust his hand into his jeans and waved the papery wad in the air. Murmurs and gasps ran through the swelling crowd.

Landfill was taken by surprise when a hand slipped out to snatch at the wad. He barked and yanked back his arm, and the paper flew up into the air. There were loud cries, and Landfill was released while coloured slips fluttered above his head. The crowd heaved beneath them, forcing the white-shirted Outsiders to spread out in an attempt to fight the surge.

Landfill crouched and scrabbled between scuffling feet. Outsiders all around him were screaming and yelling as they fought over papery sheets, pulling and pushing and barging with shoulders.

Landfill looked on with an expression trapped between awe and horror. Howls of pain and rage rang in his ears. He saw fists thumping, elbows jabbing – hands flailing for sheets scattered across slabs or twisting in the wind.

A hand clamped his wrist and snapped him out of his

daze. It was attached to a burly Outsider with blond fuzz for hair and a grimace that became a smirk beneath its flat, crooked nose. Landfill snarled and bit into the hand, and the Outsider bellowed but refused to let go. Landfill saw the knuckled ball of its fist coming at him, and was cowering when he heard a familiar voice – "*No!*" – and saw the fist knocked aside by someone else's forearm.

The Outsider scrunched its face, released Landfill's hand and turned angrily to Dawn. Dawn returned its scowl before showing Landfill a sorry, wretched look of defeat. Her expression gripped him tighter than the hand that had held his wrist, until another Outsider dived for a nearby paper slip and cuffed his head.

With a yelp, Landfill tore himself from Dawn's gaze and continued to weasel his way through the tumult. With scrapping and savagery behind him, he bolted across some slabs and around the corner.

THIRTY-THREE

THE SLIP

After tearing through gorse, Landfill had to stop. He dropped to his knees and panted in the bracken. When he saw the four Black Fingers pointing sunwards, he wiped his face with his jumper's hem and ran for the hill.

His run was more of a limp by the time he passed the ducts lining the Gully. His cheeks were crimson and a fiery ache consumed his thighs. His chest strained and burned like a stove about to explode.

He could see the Nook up ahead. Kafka wasn't far from the metal cabinet, stood beside a crumpled mound of rags. The mound moved, and when Landfill realized it was Babagoo, all agony was forgotten.

The scavenger shifted to his knees at the sound of slapping feet, and froze when he saw the boy running towards him. He leaned stiffly back when Landfill drew nearer. Something that was either fear or wonder filled his eyes.

"You're…" wheezed Landfill. "You're okay." He kneeled in dead moss, gasping, with his hands pressed to his thighs.

Babagoo gaped at him. His jaw hung limply open. He reached out for the boy before stopping himself. "Landfill…" he croaked. Spidery tear trails shone along the mud that caked his cheeks. "Me and Kafka… We searched all over. Where were you?"

Landfill's eyes watered and he put his palms to his face. "I'm sorry, Babagoo. Went for medsin. But I couldn't get it. Down where Outsiders gather, it's…it's…"

"You went to the town? You tried to get medicine for me?" Babagoo reached out again, but his fingers stopped before they could touch Landfill's cheek. "But after… everything I did…"

The flaps of his hat lifted while he grimaced and shook his head. "Why'd you come back to me?"

Landfill stared at his hands. "I hurt you."

That sad, frightened look of awe was still on Babagoo's face. "But, my lad," he began. "You had every right. You know what I did. I lied about where you came from. I hid you away. I…I'm as bad as them. I have the hunger. I tried to fix…" He rubbed his own arms and shuddered. "I *used* you. Everything I did – I said it was for you, but it wasn't. It was for me. For my own hunger. For my own madness.

I don't deserve you, Landfill. You shouldn't be here."

The boy sniffed and gulped. He clutched the fingers hovering by his face and pressed them to his cheek. The scavenger seemed to gasp at the heat there. "I *should* be here," said Landfill. "With you."

Babagoo stared at the boy. Fresh tears ran into his beard. "But your mother. Maybe you can find her. You wanted so badly to—"

"My mother dumped me. I believe you now. I've seen what they're like Outside. They lie and they hurt and they don't make sense. The rot's everywhere. It's in the air – in what they do."

Babagoo moved his fingers against the heat of Landfill's cheek. His word was a whisper. "Wallflower…"

Landfill tightened his grip on the scavenger's fingers. "You *do* deserve me, Babagoo. You saved my life when someone else threw it away."

Babagoo winced and shook his head. "No, my boy. That day, just before I found you in the Pit, I'd dug myself a grave in the rubbish." He wiped a plaid sleeve across his nose. "Long ago, I turned away from people – from good people who cared for me and wanted to help. And in the end they gave up and turned away too. It was too late to go back, and I was tired and done for and digging a hole to die in. But then I found you, Landfill, and I thought that maybe I'd been given a chance to—" Babagoo choked on his words, coughed red spit into moss. "I left that grave empty, Landfill. I didn't save your life that day. You saved mine."

Landfill's jaw trembled. "Then we're even." A glint of fallen glass distracted him, and he turned his gaze to the wall. "The Outsiders. They know we're still here."

Babagoo's eyes followed Landfill's. He scrambled to his feet and pulled the boy up. "Then they'll be coming. We have to go."

"Where?"

"Somewhere new. Somewhere you can start again. But you won't get the chance if we're caught. And they'll be close now. No doubt about it."

"Can we give them the slip?"

"Maybe. If we stall 'em." The scavenger's eyes narrowed. "How?"

Babagoo turned his head northwards. He eyed the Black Fingers. "Dominoes."

They ran for the four towering chimneys. While Babagoo lumbered and splashed through the Gully, Landfill scampered across the pipes overhead. They were soon moving through the Thin Woods, crossing wet mulch and fallen branches. Kafka trailed behind, bobbing his gnarly head as he trotted.

Landfill stopped and twisted to check on Babagoo. The scavenger's beard was sopping with sweat, and he clutched his lower stomach as if something was gnawing into it. His arm shot out towards the building that formed the base of the Black Fingers. "Get onto that roof and climb one of the chimneys! See if they're coming!"

Landfill scaled the building's wall and was soon some way up the westernmost Finger. The gaps from Babagoo's work on the bricks helped him to ascend quickly. When he was high enough he looked out over the perimeter wall. The shrub-covered hill rolled away beneath him, and beyond that he saw the Spit Pit. Gorse, grass and bracken stretched out to each side, and just west of the Pit he saw the tract of buildings he'd so recently fled.

A gruff call from the ground. *"Are they coming?"*

Landfill surveyed the landscape. He saw small blue flashes. Several rolling machines were racing along the bracken to the right of the Pit. A gust blew by, and he heard an alien, monotonous wailing on the wind.

He leaned out from the chimney to yell. "Rolling machines with blue lights! Coming round the side of the Pit, heading this way!"

Babagoo yelled back. "Police! Probably off-road! We don't have long! What about the Pit? Is anyone there?"

Landfill looked over the wall. His eyes searched the Pit. Outsiders were moving across the dunes and buffs, some on foot and some in the yellow machines with spiked wheels. He saw more Outsiders on their tracks, pouring out from the area of buildings and heading for the landfill site.

He leaned to call back. "Yes! Outsiders are crossing the Pit!"

"Good! Then go to the chimney with the shovel in its side! Pull the shovel down as hard as you can!"

Landfill climbed back down to the flat roof and ran past three chimney bases, towards the Finger furthest from the perimeter wall.

"Pull down the shovel! The Finger needs to fall!"

Grabbing the shovel's handle with both hands, Landfill pulled down as hard as he could. He ended up hanging from the handle, hunched up with his feet kicking the air. "Nothing's happening!" he cried.

"The hammer! Use the hammer!"

Landfill searched the roof and spotted the branch with the sledgehammer's head at its end. It wasn't far from his feet, and he threw himself forward to drag it back to the chimney. It took some effort to raise it high, and he let it drop so that it slammed the shovel's handle. "Nothing!" he shrieked.

"Keep at it! Keep at it!"

Landfill heaved the hammer up and let it fall. He tried again, and then again, but still nothing happened. He was struggling to raise the hammer yet again when he heard scuffing sounds nearby, and the hammer dropped with a thud. He saw Babagoo – with red eyes bulging and blood oozing from his nostrils – trying to pull himself onto the roof.

The boy took Babagoo's hand and hauled him over the edge. Babagoo lugged himself on hands and knees to the hammer. "They won't get my boyling," he growled. "You'll have your time for giving them the slip, lad!"

He got up and began to slam the shovel, gritting his teeth and roaring with every swing. Landfill noticed a pattering sound that followed each wallop. Chips of mortar were falling from the chimney's other side, tumbling from brickwork lining the cavities made previously by Babagoo.

The scavenger kept at it. His face was glistening purple-red, and veins stood out like cables around his neck. He slammed and slammed with the hammer, and threw it down when a thump caused a cracking sound to travel up the chimney.

Landfill looked up to follow the sound. Large chips of rubble had begun to tumble down the Finger's west side. He kept his gaze on the Finger's tip, and thought he could see it lean, just very slightly. The movement was barely visible, but it was enough. Momentum began to build, and Landfill hopped back when chunks of masonry fell and smashed against the rooftop.

The chimney continued to lean, slowly at first but gathering speed. Red, dusty clouds began to pop from its side, and Landfill's chin dropped when the Finger toppled westwards and smashed into the next Finger along. The second chimney groaned, and rubble exploded around its missing brickwork. The second chimney toppled too, and crashed into the third. Landfill covered his ears, but it was impossible to block out the deafening groans.

The third chimney fell into the fourth and final Finger, which smashed through the perimeter wall and toppled onto the hill, followed closely by the chimney that had taken it down and the upper half of another. Landfill scrabbled through the dust cloud and over high piles of red rubble. He gripped the edge of a cracked, curving slope of masonry, and stared through the destroyed section of wall to see the chimneys thundering down the hill.

The rolling, hulking structures left huge swathes of torn earth behind them. Landfill could feel the rubble trembling beneath his feet. Down below, the Fingers plunged into the edge of the Spit Pit. Landfill thought he could see ripples moving outwards from the impact.

The Fingers lay motionless, and for a moment all seemed still. Then the shifting began. Rubbish started to quiver along the ridges of colossal dunes. Even from so far away, Landfill could hear the hiss and tumble as crests began to crumble. Down slid the dross, down slumped the junk; down and down until it piled onto the Outsiders below.

Landfill heard distant yells, and saw that the rolling machines with the blue lights had stopped by the verge of the Pit. White-shirted Outsiders left the machines to run across the grass towards the flailing figures.

Landfill began to hop and shout. "Babagoo! It worked! We did it! It worked!" A smile almost touched his lips, but faded when he turned to find he was alone. He scrambled down the rubble and peered over the roof's edge. Babagoo was lying on the ground, coated in dust and rubble, with Kafka bleating wretchedly by his side.

Landfill whimpered and clambered down the wall. He sank to his knees and touched the scavenger's forehead. "Babagoo?"

Babagoo's eyes stared up at the paling sky. His mouth was wide open, but it didn't move. He was as still and silent as the moss that made his bed.

The boy croaked again. "Babagoo…" He grabbed his arms to shake him gently, and flinched when Babagoo's head lolled to one side.

Landfill's lips trembled briefly. Water pooled at the rims of his eyes and he burst into tears. His forehead fell upon the scavenger's, and he blubbered while pushing away debris to find Babagoo's hand. Clasping it tightly between his palms, he emitted a moan that was almost a howl, pulled the limp fingers to his hair, and put his own hand into the scavenger's beard.

Landfill kneeled like that for a while, sobbing silently, until a brush from Kafka's nose roused him. He raised his head and cocked his ear. It was that sound again – the wailing he'd heard from the rolling machines on course to Hinterland.

Landfill sat up. "More Outsiders. They're coming." He jumped up and looked back and forth between the wall and the scavenger. After squeezing his eyes shut, he moved to the black goat and pulled at its neck. "Come on, Kafka! No choice – got to give them the slip!"

He pulled and pulled but Kafka wouldn't budge. He just gazed at the fallen scavenger with those blank, horizontal pupils.

"Plleeeaaasse!" wailed Landfill, but the goat was as set as stone.

Wiping the snot and tears from his face, Landfill backed away, revolved and ran for the cabinet. After staggering down the Burrow's stairway, he grabbed Orwell from the blankets, ran back up the steps and sprinted for the toppled gate.

Landfill ran as far north through the bracken as he could. Hinterland was far behind when he clocked movement at the shallower side of the hill's brink. As soon as he saw blue lights he dived into a hollow tucked behind some ferns.

He gripped Orwell to his chest and kept his eyes on Hinterland. Outsiders were leaving their rolling machines and running through the gap by the fallen gate. More came up the hill, trampling through grass and waving their arms at each other. Pickaxes, tools and hatchets flashed in sunlight.

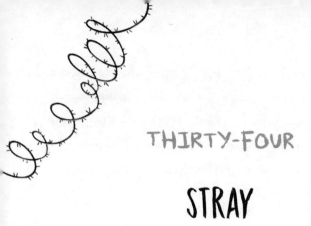

THIRTY-FOUR

STRAY

It was dark by the time the Outsiders finally departed. Kafka had left earlier in the afternoon. Landfill saw him following a long black bag, which was being carried from inside Hinterland to the back of a large rolling machine. The two Outsiders lugging the bag tried to shoo Kafka away, but the old goat bucked his horns and kicked at the grass. The Outsiders seemed to exchange some words, and Landfill thought he saw a shrug before they loaded the bag into the machine and allowed Kafka to climb in after it. The machine then trundled down the hill's gentler edge, followed over the course of the day by other machines and Outsiders on foot. The Outsiders with tools and axes never made it into Hinterland. From what Landfill could tell, the white-shirted Outsiders wouldn't let them in.

Landfill had watched through ferns with Orwell on

his lap. When dusk fell it became harder to see what was happening so far away, but many Outsiders had already left and headed downhill. There were no more rolling machines waiting by the wall, and Landfill watched for a long time without finding any sign or movement.

"Think they're gone." The boy took the pup in his arms. Keeping low, he moved across dark terrain until they reached the hill's edge.

Landfill stared down into darkness. He saw the firefly specks that lined the edges of the Pit, and the gridded lights from the tract of buildings. Beyond that was the glimmering line that stretched out westwards, on its way to the fiery glow on the horizon.

Orwell yipped and panted in Landfill's arms.

Landfill looked down at him. "Where now?"

He glanced over his shoulder. The dark outline of the perimeter wall was barely visible. "Nothing for us here now. It's all…dead. Baba—" The word snagged in his throat, and he wiped his nose against Orwell before trying again.

He whispered hoarsely. "Babagoo said we have to find somewhere new." He turned his head towards the gridded lights. "We need somewhere safe from the rot. Far from Outsiders."

Orwell barked again.

Landfill looked at him through tears silver with starlight. "I know. You're hungry. I am too." He nodded towards the darkness beyond the Pit. "There's an asphalt strip down there. If you go left it takes you to where Outsiders gather. But if you go right there's trees – like the Thin Woods, but bigger. We can go there. Maybe there's vejbles. Like at our patch. Could be gulls too."

A quiet yap.

Landfill ran his knuckles through the fur on Orwell's neck. "We have to try. Need food to get our strength up. Then we need to find somewhere. Will you help me?"

The husky's lapping tongue tickled his fingers.

Landfill's voice broke. "Good. Don't think...I can do this alone."

He wept as quietly as he could while descending the hill.

Daybreak found Landfill bargaining with a fox. With Orwell held tight against his soggy jumper, he climbed down from a fallen log and took a cautious step towards the animal. The fox bristled and snarled, its snout sticky with the blackbird clenched between its teeth.

"Please, foxler," pleaded the boy. "Share your bird with Orwell. He won't eat the berries here, but you will, won't you? I'll help you find some – get the ones you can't reach. Hunkadory?"

The fox growled when Landfill ventured closer. It shook the bird in its jaws, speckling fallen leaves with red.

"*Please,*" whispered Landfill.

The fox snarled and scarpered, leaving boy and pup alone. Landfill groaned and took a seat on the log. He looked forlornly at Orwell, who returned his gaze with dull blue eyes. A grey drizzle fell between the leaves left on the trees, its patter broken by the distant hum of rolling machines.

Landfill looked in the asphalt strip's direction. "Have to get moving. Don't know where, but we need proper food. And somewhere warm." He shivered and rubbed the rain from the husky's coat. "Can follow the strip away from where Outsiders gather. Maybe we'll find somewhere that'll look after us. Like the Pit, but far from the rot. Maybe there's somewhere like that." He sighed and lapped his wrist. "Maybe."

They'd made some progress northwards when Landfill noticed a rolling machine that had stopped by the woods' edge. He studied the metal carapace glinting between tree trunks, and began to move in for a closer look.

He whispered to Orwell: "Might be grubbins. But keep close to cover. Rule ten – never stray too…" His eyes welled up and he wiped them with a damp sleeve. "Never stray."

The machine's front was open like a giant metal mouth. An Outsider in a beige coat was glaring into the opening. Its long brown hair was wet and matted against its neck, and it had bits of metal in its ears that sparkled when it shook its head. The Outsider shifted its gaze to the rectangle in its hand, rolled its eyes and shoved it into a pocket.

Landfill was skulking behind a low-hanging branch when he heard a shrill whine from within the machine. The Outsider's glare fell away, and it walked quickly to the machine's side to open a door and pull something out.

Landfill gaped at the creature lifted from the machine. It wasn't unlike the doll he'd seen in the Pit: small and stumpy enough to be held in the larger Outsider's arms, with a head that was round and pink and topped by a mess of brown fluff. It clenched its eyes while squalling through a wet, gummy mouth.

The large Outsider bobbed and stroked the creature and returned to the front of the machine. It waved frantically at a few rolling machines as they raced by. And after some time it stopped, kicked the machine's wheel and climbed inside with its creature.

Landfill spied no sign of food, and was about to move on when he heard the grinding of wheels. Another machine had come to a stop just in front of the first one. Its side door opened and a dull, rhythmic noise filled the air. Landfill crept forward a little, turning his ear towards the sound. "Meeyoo…" he whispered, trying to recall the word. "Meeyoozic…"

The sounds stopped just before a tall, short-haired Outsider exited the machine's side door and leaned into the first machine to speak. It then returned to its own machine, took something from inside and opened the machine's front, so that both machines faced each other with metal mouths open.

The boy watched the tall Outsider faff and fidget, and before long both machines' mouths were connected by red and black cables. The tall Outsider climbed back into its own machine, which suddenly began to tremble and purr, and gestured at the other Outsider with its thumb. The other machine spluttered momentarily, then began to purr and tremble too. A happy whoop pierced the rain's glum spatter.

Cables were removed and metal mouths shut, and both Outsiders were soon stood by the trees. They grinned and jabbered in the rain. The long-haired Outsider held its tiny creature, kissed its head and pointed at its machine. The tall Outsider nodded, shrugged and smiled, and laughed while pinching the little creature's cheek. Sounds of gurgly babbling blended with scraps of laughter and – though his heart ached even more than his limbs – Landfill was surprised to find himself on the cusp of a smile. His lips moved to form Dawn's words: "*Big little things…*"

Metal doors slammed, and the two machines rolled off in opposite directions.

After leaning out to check no other machines were coming, Landfill left the cover of trees and stood at the edge of the asphalt strip. He looked to the right, to where the first machine had gone, following the strip with his eyes until it disappeared around a bend. Then he looked to the left, following the course of the second machine, towards where Outsiders gather.

A faint cawing caught his ear, and he looked up to see a flock of crows crossing the sky. Landfill watched them disappear behind the treetops, then buried his nose in the nape of Orwell's neck. He breathed in deeply.

When he spoke his voice was muffled by fur: "Maybe."

After looking once more to the left and right, he put his wrist to his mouth, turned left and took a step along the asphalt.

DISCUSSION QUESTIONS
BEWARE OF SPOILERS

- Where and when did you think the book was set when you started reading? What did you think had happened to bring Babagoo and Landfill there? How did you feel when you found out more? Why do you think Darren, the author, left so many things for you to work out by yourself?

- Discuss your first impressions of Hinterland. What makes it different from our world? Would you like to live there? Explain your answers.

- Hinterland is filled with animals. Do you have a favourite? Who is it, and why?

- Do you think Landfill does anything wrong in the story? Give reasons for your answer.

- What did you think about Babagoo when you first met him? Did your opinion of him change as the story developed? What do you think his life was like before he came to Hinterland? Does the book give you any clues about his past?

- Discuss Babagoo and Landfill's relationship. Explore the different ways they relate to each other; father/son, teacher/student, bully/bullied. Do they always treat each other in the same way? Do their feelings about each other appear consistent?

- There are lots of made-up and unusual words in this book. Pick your favourite(s) and think about why you like them. Try making up your own words.

- What did you think Longwhite was at first? Do you think he talks to Landfill? Why do you think Landfill wants to keep him a secret? How do you feel about what happens to Longwhite at the end?

- How old do you think Landfill is? Give reasons for your answer. What does he do that makes him appear young? What does he do that feels grown-up? How has his life been different from yours? What do you think his life will be like after the book ends?

- *Scavengers* is filled with unexpected discoveries and surprises, both for the characters and the reader. Think back to the moments that surprised you the most. Why did these have such an impact? Did it change the way you read the book or viewed any of the characters?

- There are lots of disgusting moments in the book. Why do you think the author chose to include so many of these? Go back to some you remember and look at the way Darren describes them. What kinds of words does he use, and what effect do they have?

- What were your first impressions of Dawn? Think about her relationship with Landfill. Why do you think she makes the choices she does? Do you agree or disagree with them?

- Landfill has a strong reaction to music in the book. Imagine experiencing things you enjoy for the first time now. What would that feel like? Imagine what it would be like to hear music, watch a film, sit in a moving car or use a smartphone, having never known they existed.

- Look again at the scenes Outside. Can you work out all the things that Landfill is seeing for the first time? Does seeing these things from Landfill's perspective change the way you look at them now? If so, how and why?

- Turn to page 215 and look at Dawn's dialogue. Discuss the idea of "big little things". What "big little things" are important in your life?

- Go back to the very last scene in the book. What is happening? Why do you think Darren, the author, chose to end the book with this moment?

INTRODUCING HINTERLAND'S ANIMAL AUTHORS

The wild animals that live in Hinterland play a key role throughout *Scavengers*. Babagoo gave them all their names, save for Longwhite, who was given his name by Landfill. Each creature in Hinterland is named after a famous author. Here's an introduction to some of those writers.

ATWOOD THE CAT, NAMED AFTER MARGARET ATWOOD (BORN 1939)

Multi-award-winning Canadian writer whose work includes eight books for children. Her picture book, *Wandering Wenda and Widow Wallop's Wunderground Washery* even inspired an animated TV series called *Wandering Wenda* which focuses on wordplay.

CARTER THE FOX, NAMED AFTER ANGELA CARTER (1940–1992)

English novelist, short-story writer and journalist, whose work draws on myth, folklore and fairy tales. Often her work contains elements of magic realism, depicting our world, but with surprising touches of the magical or supernatural.

HESSE THE TURTLE, NAMED AFTER HERMAN HESSE (1877–1962)

German-born poet, novelist, and painter. His best-known

works include *Steppenwolf* and *Siddhartha*, and explore an individual's search for truth and self-knowledge. In 1946, he received the Nobel Prize for Literature.

JOYCE THE SQUIRREL, NAMED AFTER JAMES JOYCE (1882–1941)

Irish novelist, short-story writer, and poet, best known for *Ulysses*, a 265,000-word book, loosely based on Homer's *Odyssey* and told in a variety of writing styles. The book follows the adventures of one man, Leopold Bloom, in Dublin on 16th June 1904. "Bloomsday" is still celebrated by Joyce fans today.

KAFKA THE GOAT, NAMED AFTER FRANZ KAFKA (1883–1924)

Czech-born Jewish novelist and short-story writer, whose work mixes elements of the real and the fantastic, to explore troubling human emotions. One of his most famous stories, *The Metamorphosis*, is about a man who wakes up to find he has transformed into a giant insect.

MELVILLE THE TURTLE, NAMED AFTER HERMAN MELVILLE (1819–1891)

American novelist, short-story writer and poet. His writing draws on his experience at sea as a sailor, most famously in the epic adventure, *Moby Dick*, the story of Captain Ahab's doomed search for the white whale that bit his leg off at the knee.

ORWELL THE PUP, NAMED AFTER GEORGE ORWELL (1903–1950)

English novelist, essayist, journalist and critic, who wrote about many experiences, including his time during the Spanish Civil War, working in kitchens in Paris and living on London's streets. In his book, *1984*, Orwell created lots of words that we still use today, including Big Brother, Room 101, newspeak and doublethink.

RUSHDIE THE FOX, NAMED AFTER SALMAN RUSHDIE (BORN 1947)

Award-winning British Indian novelist and essayist, who combines magical realism with historical fiction. A lot of his books are set on the Indian subcontinent and focus on the relationships between Eastern and Western civilizations. His fourth book, *The Satanic Verses*, proved so controversial that Rushdie received death threats and was put under police protection.

SWIFT THE PARAKEET, NAMED AFTER JONATHAN SWIFT (1667–1745)

An Anglo-Irish satirist, essayist and poet. Satire is a way of writing where people's foolishness and failings are ridiculed, with the aim of shaming people and organizations into improvement. Though funny, its greater purpose is to draw attention to wider problems in society. One of Swift's most famous works, *A Modest Proposal*, is a deliberately shocking article in which Swift pretends to suggest that poverty could be reduced if poor people started eating their children. He also wrote the famous fantasy satire *Gulliver's Travels*.

VONNEGUT THE ALSATIAN, NAMED AFTER KURT VONNEGUT (1922–2007)

American writer who fought in World War II and was captured by the Germans. He survived the Allied bombing of Dresden by taking refuge in a meat locker in the slaughterhouse where he was imprisoned. His sixth book, *Slaughterhouse-Five*, expressed his powerful anti-war opinions. Published in 1969 during the Vietnam War, it became a huge bestseller and was even made into a film.

WOOLF THE HUSKY, NAMED AFTER VIRGINIA WOOLF (1882–1941)

Influential author who pioneered the use of stream of consciousness, a way of telling a story that attempts to reflect the way multiple thoughts, feelings and memories can pass through our minds, all at the same time. Her book *Mrs Dalloway* focuses on one day in a woman's life but travels forwards and backwards in time and in and out of different characters' minds to tell a much bigger story.

WINTERSON THE KESTREL, NAMED AFTER JEANETTE WINTERSON (BORN 1959)

Award-winning English author, who shot to fame on publication of her first book, *Oranges Are Not the Only Fruit*. This semi-autobiographical novel tells the story of a teenage girl rebelling against conventional values.

ACKNOWLEDGEMENTS

I'd like to thank the following people for their support and general greatness.

Wanda, my ever-patient wife and sounding board, for her endless love and faith, and for being beside me for all the dips and bumps.

Oskar and Charlie for the laughs and wonder.

Mum and Dad for the books, motorway heroics and everything else.

My kick-ass agent, Laura Susijn, for toasties and tenacity.

My super-savvy editors, Stephanie King and Sarah Stewart, and all at Usborne HQ for adopting Landfill and giving him such a wonderful home.

Tom Clohosy Cole for the awesome art, and for bearing with me.

Kirsty Fox and James Alexander for critiques and cake.

Tilda Johnson for her eagle eye.

Dan Layton, Phil Formby and Bees Make Honey for the Red Stripe, blood, sweat and tears.

Chris Baldwin for frites and positivity.

Christophe Dejous, Richard Dytch, Matt Eris, Jason Holt, Neil Johnson, Graham Langley, Neil Marsden, Gavin McFarlane, Kieran O'Riordan and Mark Spivey for the music.

Diana Pasek-Atkinson for all the reading on the move.

Matt Turpin and all at Nottingham City of Literature for their enthusiasm and great work.

Christina Lee and the University of Nottingham's English Department for teaching me to read between and beyond the lines.

Neil Fulwood, Sophie-Louise Hyde, Chris Killen, Mhairi McFarlane, John McGregor, George Saunders, David Sillitoe, Kim Slater, Jonathan Taylor and Alex Wheatle for their time, kindness and advice.

Samuel J. Halpin, A. M. Howell and Serena Patel for their camaraderie (go Class of '18!).

The Five Leaves Bookshop for shelf after shelf of goodness.

And all of my family and friends for the big little things. Thank you.

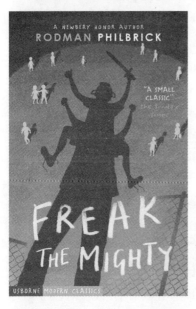

UNLIKELY PAIR
UNFORGETTABLE
FRIENDSHIP

AWARD-WINNER
TEAR-JERKER

HISTORICAL FICTION
RELEVANT NOW

Introducing timeless stories to today's readers

PAGE-TURNER
PRIZE-WINNER

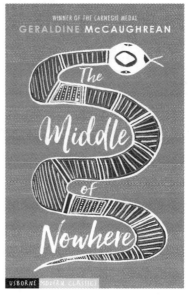

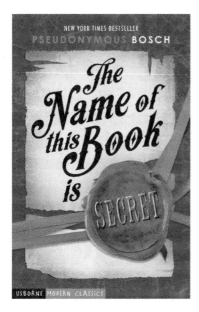

RIB-TICKLER
BEST-SELLER

CULT CLASSIC
TIMELESS ADVENTURE

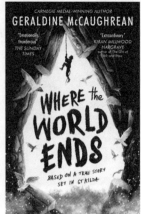

Love this book? Love Usborne fiction

Join us online for the all latest news on Usborne fiction,
plus extracts, interviews and reviews

usborne.com/fiction